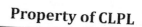

the Memory of Light

FRANCISCO X. STORK

ARTHUR A. LEVINE BOOKS
AN IMPRINT OF SCHOLASTIC INC.

All rights reserved. Published by Arthur A. Levine Books, an imprint of Scholastic Inc.,
Publishers since 1920. SCHOLASTIC and the LANTERN LOGO are trademarks and/or registered
trademarks of Scholastic Inc.

The publisher does not have any control over and does not assume any responsibility for author
or third-party websites or their content.

Library of Congress Cataloging-in-Publication Data

Stork, Francisco X., author.
The memory of light / Francisco X. Stork. — First edition.
pages cm
Summary: When Victoria Cruz wakes up in the psychiatric ward of a Texas hospital after her
failed suicide attempt, she still has no desire to live, but as the weeks pass, and she meets Dr. Desai
and three of the other patients, she begins to reflect on the reasons why she feels like a loser
compared with the rest of her family, and to see a path ahead where she can make a life of her own.
ISBN 978-0-545-47432-0 (hardcover : alk. paper) 1. Mexican Americans — Texas — Juvenile
fiction. 2. Suicide — Juvenile fiction. 3. Depression, Mental — Juvenile fiction. 4. Psychotherapy
patients — Juvenile fiction. 5. Friendship — Juvenile fiction. 6. Families — Texas — Juvenile
fiction. [1. Mexican Americans — Fiction. 2. Suicide — Fiction. 3. Depression, Mental — Fiction.
4. Psychotherapy — Fiction. 5. Friendship — Fiction. 6. Family life — Texas — Fiction. 7. Texas —
Fiction.] I. Title.
PZ7.S88442Me 2015
[Fic] — dc23
2014044136

10 9 8 7 6 5 4 3 2 1   16 17 18 19 20
Printed in the U. S. A.   23
First edition, February 2016
Book design by Christopher Stengel

For
Charlotte Annabelle

Nana

I tried to write you in Spanish but my Español no es muy bueno en este momento. *So I try in English. If you're reading this it's because you found it taped to the back of Mamá's painting. Take the painting with you to Mexico and the climbing pink roses will remind you of Mamá and maybe of me too. I know you're sad now as you read this. I wish I could tell you not to be triste but I know you. Think of something happy and funny like the time I finally got you to go in the pool because it was good for your arthritis. Remember how I laughed and you screeched when we went in? How you held on to me for dear life? The Spanish word I never heard you say before when I let go of you.*

Nana I want to tell you this. Please don't think I don't love you or that I don't love Becca or Father or Barbara either. I held off from doing this for a long, long time because I knew how bad you and everyone would feel. But the love I have for all of you doesn't stop the hurt I feel inside. I'm sorry my nana. I love you. It gave Mamá peace to know you would be there to take care of me and Becca. And you did, you took care of me. Like your own daughter. Thank you. Gracias mi nana.

I better go. I'm getting real sleepy and I want to tape this up while I still can.

Love you
Vicky

CHAPTER
ONE

"Victoria."

I open my eyes when I hear my name.

I'm lying down. A white bed. To my left a window. Pale-blue sky. To my right a face. The same lady from last night. Underneath her white coat, I see a shiny green dress.

She told me her name before. In the emergency room when they brought me in. I am in a different room now.

Dr. Desai. I remember.

My head is full of words, floating unconnected, moving in slow motion. Dr. Desai is talking. Sounds without meaning. Some of the words are coming from her and some of them come from someplace in me.

"Victoria," I hear Dr. Desai say again in the distance. "People call you Vicky."

I nod.

Dr. Desai pulls up a chair and sits, but my bed is so high I can see only the top of her gray head. She pushes a button beside the bed to lower it, but nothing happens. She stands and moves back a step or two to give me space.

"How do you feel?"

I can tell she's asking about my body and not my mind. I touch my throat, noticing soreness there for the first time.

"From the stomach pump," Dr. Desai says. "I can give you some lozenges if you like."

I shake my head. I remember waking up, gagging, a rubber tube in my mouth and a woman with dark hair holding my shoulders down. Then I must have passed out again.

I'm wearing a hospital gown. I wonder what happened to my clothes. The skin on my chest is scratched and raw.

"You're at Lakeview Hospital. Your father agreed to let you stay here until tomorrow, but you can decide to be with us longer if you want to," Dr. Desai says.

Want. Decide. The words are like the *cascarones* we used to decorate for Easter when my mother was alive. Eggshells empty of all life, meant to be admired. What I *want* now is the silence I glimpsed last night.

"Do you feel like talking a little?"

"Not really," I whisper hoarsely. I mean that I don't know what there is to say.

Dr. Desai offers me a glass of water and I drink from it. I give her back the glass and she places it carefully on the night-stand next to the bed.

"I'm happy to just be with you without speaking, if you wish."

"Okay."

We are silent for a while, and I don't mind the silence. I think of the times when I would sit by my mother's bed after she became ill. I read to her from her favorite poets, and sometimes she would fall asleep while I read and I would just sit there watching her. I look past Dr. Desai and see an empty bed with magazines on top. I hope whoever sleeps in that bed doesn't talk.

"Do you know who found you?" she asks at last.

"Found me?"

"You would surely have died if you hadn't been found. Another fifteen minutes and you'd be gone."

I guess it was my father and Barbara who found me after they got home. But neither of them ever comes into my room. So how was I "saved"? Who is responsible for prolonging this mess?

Dr. Desai opens a brown file folder. "The paramedic wrote in her report that a Juanita Alvarez called 9-1-1."

"Juanita." Something breaks and burns near my heart. A block of frozen shame dissolves and I am flooded with it.

"Apparently," Dr. Desai says. "You didn't know?"

"I don't remember much. . . . I took the pills. A pain in my chest. My throat. The ambulance." I remember suddenly the scared look on my father's face when he and Barbara came to see me in Intensive Care.

Dr. Desai waits for me to say more.

"Juanita is my nanny. Since I was born."

"She must love you very much."

I look around the room for a place to hide my eyes.

"What happened last night?" Dr. Desai asks.

I bite my lip. Last night. Was it me or someone else who saw my father and Barbara leave, who said good night to Juanita and waited for her to go to sleep? The letter I wrote to her. Did I manage to tape it to the back of the painting?

"Vicky?"

I wait until the pressure in my throat loosens enough for me to breathe. "How can you love someone and still try to kill yourself?"

Dr. Desai does not answer. She hands me the box of tissues, and I stare at it until I realize there are tears streaming down my face. I wipe the tears away.

"Would you like to call Juanita?" She reaches into the pocket of her white doctor's coat and pulls out an old-fashioned cell phone, the kind that flips open.

No. Yes. How can I feel both with equal force? I'm so ashamed, but I want to hear her voice. "She'll want to know why" is all I say to Dr. Desai.

"Do you know why?"

"No."

"Then say you don't know. That it's something you're trying to figure out."

"She's going back to Mexico soon."

"Oh?"

"Her arthritis. She can hardly walk. My father and stepmother thought it better if she was in Mexico. With her family."

There's something like disbelief on Dr. Desai's face. Then she nods with understanding and says, "I'll let you have some privacy." She stands and hands me the phone. She walks out of the room and closes the door gently behind her.

It is after one p.m. That's when Juanita sits down to have her *café con leche* and a slice of white bread with peanut butter. That's all she ever has for lunch. I let the phone ring once, hang up, and dial again. Barbara has told Juanita not to answer the phone because of all the messages she has bumbled, but Juanita and her friend Yolanda have devised this secret code to signal a call for her. The phone rings and rings, and just when I am about to give up, I hear Juanita's voice.

"*Aló.*"

"Nana. It's me."

"*Hijita, hijita.*" Her voice is weak, fragile, tearful. "You okay?"

"I'm okay."

"I so worried about you. You at the hospital? Your father say you come home tomorrow. I want to go with you last night, but the ambulance men say no. I can't believe I hear your voice. *Es un milagro* that you're alive. Thank you, *Diosito.* Thank you, *Virgencita de Guadalupe.*

"You know what happen last night?" she continues. "I in my room asleep and I hear the *gato meow, meow* outside my door. I never heard him meow like that before, like someone pulling his tail or something. So I open the door to see and he's *meow, meow.* I follow him and he run upstairs and on top of the stairs, *meow, meow.* I don't know what, but just then I felt something in heart so heavy. I know something very bad. I climb stairs on hands and knees like a baby. I knock on your door but you don't open, so I think maybe you're not there. But the *gato* is *meow, meow* there by door, going loco. Then I open door and see you in bed with eyes closed, so I think everything okay, you asleep, but the *gato* runs in and jumps on top of you, meowing and pulling your shirt with his nails."

I touch my chest. So that's where the scratches came from. Galileo.

"I saw the empty bottle. I know they sleeping pills from Barbara. I call 9-1-1 right away, then your father on his cell," Juanita continues. "*Es un milagro. Tu ángel de la guarda* made that silly *gato* save you. He climbed tree, went through window, saw you, and climbed down to my room to get me. *Es un milagro.*"

"Galileo?" All that energy and movement are so uncharacteristic of Galileo. He is as serene and lazy and content as only a well-fed eight-year-old neutered tomcat can be. The thought of him meowing or doing anything in a hurry is so strange.

"What happened, *mi niña*? Why you do something so horrible? Something happen in school?"

"No, no."

"Do you miss your mamá? I miss her too. Your mamá wouldn't want you to do this."

"I know," I say, rubbing my eyes with my hands.

"Who hurt you, *mi niña*? Tell me."

"No one, Nana, no one hurt me. It just hurts inside, I don't know why."

"Is it Barbara? Is that what happen?"

"No . . ." I have no answers to these questions, no explanations that make any sense. I feel my head shrinking, tightening with pressure, as if I were taking an exam in a foreign language on a subject I never even knew existed.

"She okay. She tries. She needs learn to smile. So serious

always. But she not bad inside. Your father, he loves you also. They sometimes confused about how to love. But they okay."

It is so painful to hear Juanita's voice. Why? "Nana, I have to go. I wanted to let you know I'm okay."

"I be here, my Vicky. I don't go to Mexico until you come home. I stay here with you if I could always."

"Nana." She hasn't seen my letter, so I need to tell her. "This thing I did. Taking the pills. It doesn't mean I don't love you."

"I know that, my *niña*, I know. I no never have doubts. Don't worry. I be here waiting for you. Don't forget the *gato*. *Diosito* didn't want you to die."

"I have to go now, Nana."

"Don't cry, my little baby. Everything okay. You see."

The call ends. I lie there for I don't know how long, my hand on the telephone, as if I'm afraid to let go of the voice that flowed through it. It is possible, I realize, to have people in your life who love you and who you love, and to still want to kill yourself. It's almost as if part of the reason you're doing it is for them, because you are not worthy of their love, and you want to stop being a burden to them, contaminating their lives with your moodiness and grumpiness and miserableness. I feel Juanita's love now. I even feel Galileo's love. And it makes me feel so much worse.

There's a gentle touch on my shoulder, and I let go of the phone and look up to see Dr. Desai.

"My cat," I say.

She sits down in the chair, her hands folded.

"He meowed outside Juanita's room and took her to my room."

Dr. Desai doesn't look one bit surprised, as if in her experience, saving lives is standard cat behavior. "I'm glad your cat saved you," she says. "Are you?"

"No." The word rises up on its own, a lone air bubble from some drowning breath. It surprises me to see it there, floating on the surface between Dr. Desai and me.

She nods as if she appreciates the honest answer. "Vicky, I'm going to recommend that you stay here for a couple of weeks, if it's okay with you. I think it would be helpful for you to be in a different environment for a while. You can come to our daily group therapy meeting. There are three other young people currently attending, and it would be good for you to be with others . . . like yourself, in many ways. You and I would also meet regularly, and a few hours of your day would be spent helping around the hospital. I believe this combination of talking, listening, doing something useful, and being around other young people who are learning to live will give you some tools you can use when you return to your previous circumstances."

"Tools?" I imagine a hammer and a chisel, my life inside a boulder I need to crack.

"A greater understanding of who you are and what you need to do to be at peace with your life." She pauses. "At the very least, a time for the thoughts of killing yourself to quiet down."

I look up at her quickly.

"Do you have anything you want to say to me or ask me?" she says.

I want to tell her that she's right, that I'm going to try again. Sooner or later, the days, hours, minutes, and seconds of my life will slowly choke me until I feel like the only way to breathe is to die. All the group therapy meetings or private sessions full of talking or comfortable silences are not going to stop me. She shouldn't feel bad when that happens. I want to tell her this because I like her. I want to spare her whatever it is she feels when she fails.

But I don't tell her any of this. I don't even know if I could find the words, because the sentences that struggle to come together inside my head get gobbled up by the silence that I'm yearning for, the one I know is always near.

She continues, "Just think about whether you would like to stay here. You can let me know tomorrow morning."

Two weeks, two days, two minutes, it's all the same. Lakeview or home, here, there — does it really matter?

Sooner or later, I will kill myself.

CHAPTER TWO

I'm lying in bed, looking out at a sky that has turned a darker blue, when I sense someone breathing behind me. I turn over.

"Hi, I'm Mona. Your roommate," the girl says, and when she grins, I see a gap where one of her front teeth is missing. She's bony with wild uncombed black hair streaked with faded pink. "My real name's Domonique Salas but everyone calls me Mona."

"Hi. I'm Vicky," I say in a way that I hope will discourage her from talking.

"You don't have any stuff?" she asks as she comes over to my bed. Her whole body twitches and squirms like an electric wire wriggling on a street after a storm.

She's not going to go away, so I sit up. She fluffs my pillow and fixes it behind me. "Thanks," I mutter. Then, to fill the awkward silence: "No stuff. I'm only here one night."

Mona looks shocked. "One night? That's nuts. I don't care what your home life is like, you can't go back to the same place you did the deed after one night."

The deed, I repeat to myself. I glance quickly at Mona's wrists and see the scars there. Some are new, some old.

Mona walks over and opens one of two doors in the room. She fishes around inside and comes out with a pair of jeans, a V-neck men's T-shirt, and a black sweater. "Here you go," she says, bringing them back to me. "They have this little room in the hospital full of clothes people leave behind. You're gonna need the sweater because it gets freezing here at night and all we got is this blanket, which is nothing more than a glorified sheet." She points to her bed and grins again.

"Thank you." I place the items at the foot of the bed and slide down onto the floor. The bed comes up to my chest.

"The jigamajig that lowers it is broken," Mona explains. "The girl that was here before used one of the chairs to climb up and down. I could've taken that bed when she left, but I don't like being near the window."

I put on the clothes she gave me. My head still hurts. I notice that the pain increases every time I talk. "Do you mind if I open the blinds all the way?" I say. The "blinds" are these grayish cardboardlike slabs that twist open when you crank a lever.

"Not one bit. But once you get them open, you won't be able to close them. Jeannette, that was the name of the girl that was here, she had to get someone from maintenance to come with pliers to close them. She couldn't stand the light first thing in the morning. Me, personally, I like the light. Heck, I'm usually awake a couple of hours before the sun comes up. When I can't sleep, I turn on that light over my bed and read. I tried to get a lamp put next to my bed when Jeannette complained, but they wouldn't give me one. They don't like things with cords here on the mental ward."

The mental ward. That's where I am. I open the blinds. At home, I always kept the window in my room open so that Galileo could come into the house after a night of gallivanting. He climbed up the mesquite tree and leaped into my room from the nearest branch. The few times I fell asleep and forgot to open the window, he meowed desperately until I woke up.

"They moved Jeannette to the other side on account of she upgraded. This side of the mental ward is the low-grade side — us mentals who aren't an immediate danger to themselves or others. Of course, we can get like Jeannette at any moment. That's why the windows don't open and there's no mirrors anywhere and two to a room and a nurse checking in every half hour. One night I woke up to these grunts, and when I looked under the bed, there was Jeannette, butt-naked, chewing her finger off. She upgraded."

I close my eyes. I feel like I stepped off the moon and am dropping through space, and I grab on to the side of the bed. When I open my eyes, Mona's there beside me. She holds on to my arm as if to keep me from falling.

"It's gonna feel weird for a while. Like you're not really here."

"Yeah," I say. *That's right. I'm not really here. I died last night and this is just a dream.* That's a good way to put up with life while you have to. It's just a dream.

"Take a snooze. I have to work a couple of hours at the beauty shop, but I'll come get you for dinner. You coming to the GTH tomorrow?"

"GTH?"

"Group Therapy Healing, or as I call it, Gripe to Heal. Who knew complaining could make you sane?" She grins at me. "There's three of us, E.M., Gabriel, and yours truly. E.M. is here because a judge sent him for beating the daylights out of one too many people, last one being his own father. And Gabriel? God only knows what ails him. But that's the group, plus Dr. Desai. We just talk about stuff."

"Oh," I say, grabbing my head. Dr. Desai mentioned group therapy earlier, but it is not only actual talking that hurts. The very thought of listening and being polite, of having to say "please" and "thank you" to others, makes me cringe.

"I know what you mean," Mona says. She pats my arm a few times. "But you got to force yourself to talk even if it's hard. Don't worry about what you say. For some reason that I've never been able to figure out, talking helps, even if it's nonsense."

"What's there to say?"

"There's all kinds of talking going on in your head. Just let some of that junk come out, who cares what it is. Look at me. If it's in my head, it's out my mouth."

"I noticed," I say.

Mona laughs. "That's good. So there's a little humor in you. You were trying to be funny, weren't you?"

I shrug. I'm not sure I was.

"You think my watching TV will bother you?" she asks. "I like to watch reruns of old sitcoms at night before I go to sleep. There's this guy in the cafeteria who says he can get me some of those remote control earphones. You watch much TV?"

"Some. When I can."

I can tell by her face that she understands what I mean — that there are times when nothing works to numb the pain, not even mindless TV. "Nice thing about sitcoms — you can watch them while you're mental."

"Mmm," I say. Maybe sitcoms are like the poems I liked to read when things got really bad. Even when my brain stopped working and words were hieroglyphics, the images and rhythms kept me company.

"You cut your own hair, didn't you?"

"Yes."

Mona's look is serious, professional. She tilts my head left and right. "I could maybe even it out a little if you want me to. I'm a cosmetologist. You wouldn't know it by the way I look right now." She pulls a strand of her hair and examines it. "Yuck."

"Who cares?" I say. "We're mental."

We look at each other for a moment, and then she grins at me again. I have a feeling that our backgrounds are very different. My family is wealthy and hers is probably not. I've lived a life of ease and comfort and she hasn't. But right now we have at least one thing in common: We are both here at Lakeview, failures at the thing called living.

THREE

Later that day, Mona and I go to the fifth-floor dining room. She tells me that unlike other floors of the hospital, patients in the psych ward do not get trays of food delivered to their individual rooms. Instead, we all eat in a common dining room, including patients from the upgraded side of the floor. After we pick up our trays of food, Mona heads straight for a table where a young guy is sitting. I follow her. The pain in my head has diminished and I'm not anxious about the talking that's bound to come. Listening to Mona's chatter has somehow made me feel strangely (and gratefully) numb.

"Hey, you," Mona says to the guy as we sit down. He has a rocklike head that was shaved not too long ago but is now growing black, bristly hairs. Tattooed, massive muscles bulge out of his T-shirt.

"Hey," he responds, his eyes on me.

"E.M., meet Vicky," Mona says.

He nods without smiling. I nod back, also without smiling. I think he expects me to be scared of him, and maybe I should be. But I'm not. How nice not to care what someone thinks of me.

"Where's Gabriel?" Mona asks.

E.M. tilts his head in the direction of the dining room's doors. We all turn to see another young man with an elderly lady in a purple terry-cloth robe hanging on to his arm. He takes her to an empty table and pulls a chair out for her. Then he goes to the tall aluminum rack of trays and brings her one. He removes the lid from her plate and unwraps the cellophane from the plastic glass of fruit punch. Then he picks up another tray, makes his way to our table, and sits. He bows his head for a few moments, then leans back and smiles at each one of us.

"Hi," he says to me. "I'm Gabriel."

"Vicky," I respond. I manage a small smile that mirrors his.

"She's my new roomie," Mona says.

"Welcome," Gabriel says. His eyes are intense in a friendly way, like someone trying to remember where they might have met you before.

"How's your girlfriend doing?" Mona asks him, casting a sideways glance at the lady with the purple robe, who is quietly muttering to herself.

"Gwendolyn," Gabriel says. "Today she finally told me what her name was. I asked her if people called her Gwen, and she said that she prefers Gwendolyn."

"Dude, be civilized. Use your fork and knife," Mona tells E.M., who has picked up the chicken thigh with his hands and is taking big bites out of it. E.M. ignores her.

"I like that name, Gwendolyn," Gabriel says, and smiles at me again.

I look down and stab a single green pea with my fork. I read a poem once by a poet named Gwendolyn Brooks. Something about sweet sleep and the coolness of snug unawareness. I try to remember the exact words but I can't. It is only the poem's feeling that I recall.

"How's your first day going?" Gabriel is still talking to me. I hear his voice as if from a distance.

I try to answer, but my throat closes in on me and I begin to cough. After I peel off the top from a plastic juice container and take a sip, I say, "Okay."

"You're with Dr. Desai?" It's Gabriel again.

"Of course she's with Dr. Desai," Mona says. "Who else would she be with?"

"When I got here, I had some guy could barely speak English," E.M. says with his mouth full.

"That's just temporarily," Mona says. "Eventually all people like us get assigned to Dr. Desai."

"People like us," Gabriel repeats, smiling.

"Kids our age." Mona gives him a look.

"It gets better after the first day," Gabriel says to me.

"Especially the talking about your messed-up life," Mona adds. "That definitely gets easier once you start doing it."

"Like that was ever hard for you," E.M. says.

"Duh, yeah! It's not easy for someone of my perfection to admit slipups." Mona winks at me.

"Slipups." E.M. glances at Mona's wrists. "That's a good one."

Before Mona can respond, Gabriel asks, "How long will you be at Lakeview?"

It takes me a moment to realize Gabriel's speaking to me. I am a little dazed by the speed and tone of the conversation — a gentle but blunt sincerity. "Till tomorrow morning." I push my plate slightly away from me.

"Isn't that crazy?" Mona says. Then to me, "You need more time."

I look around the silent table. I can see in their eyes that they all know why I am at Lakeview.

E.M. speaks first. "Did someone find you or did you call for help?"

"E.M.," Gabriel admonishes softly.

"Don't be such a brute," Mona says to him, less softly.

"Just asking a simple question," E.M. replies.

"What difference does it make?" she asks.

"None," E.M. responds, and leaves it at that.

Gabriel says to me, "The thing you gotta know is that you don't have to answer any questions from any one of us, or even talk if you don't want to."

I clear my throat. "That's what Dr. Desai said to me when I met with her."

"She says that to everyone. But try sitting in front of her for fifty minutes without saying a word." Gabriel struggles to open his milk carton.

"Fifty minutes?"

"If you stayed at Lakeview, you'd meet with Dr. Desai for fifty minutes every day," he explains.

"Fifty minutes go fast," E.M. says. "If you don't feel like saying anything, just close your eyes. That's what I do."

"Really? What does Dr. Desai do?" Gabriel asks.

"I don't know." E.M. shrugs. "My eyes are closed. Some-times when I open my eyes, she has her eyes closed too."

"That's so sweet," Mona says. "You and Dr. Desai taking little catnaps together."

E.M. glares at her.

"You never cease to surprise me." Gabriel is looking at E.M. and shaking his head with something that resembles admiration. "You're not napping when you close your eyes, are you?"

A tiny grin appears and disappears on E.M.'s face. "You gonna eat that?" he says, pointing at Mona's tapioca.

Mona pushes the tiny white bowl toward E.M. "What difference does it make if someone asks for help or not?" she says. E.M.'s eyes are solely on the pudding. "E.M., I'm talking to you."

"What?" E.M. looks up.

"So I changed my mind and called 9-1-1 in the middle of trying to kill myself. What difference does that make? Do you think I was just doing it to get attention or something?"

"Remember your rule?" Gabriel says to Mona. "No heavy-duty stuff at dinnertime."

"It's not heavy-duty. I'm just interested." Mona holds her right arm with her left hand, and I realize she's doing that to keep it from shaking.

"There's no difference," E.M. says calmly. "Whether someone finds you or you change your mind, in both cases you want people to feel sorry for you. You're being cowardly, running away from your problems. That's weak. It takes courage to keep going when life is rough."

Finally, I think. *Truth.*

"That's not always the case," Gabriel says. He waits until E.M. looks at him. "I agree with you that it takes courage to keep going when life is hard. But a person who kills himself can be ill. When you're ill, you can't deal with problems the way healthy people can. Not being able to have courage and hope is the illness." He sounds like some kind of wise old man dressed in a kid's body, but he doesn't seem to be faking it.

E.M. shakes his head. "No matter how bad things get and no matter how sick you are, you still have a choice. You can't tell me you don't. Lots of people have it real bad and they don't give up. That's what courage is, man. Going on when everything's against you."

"How can you possibly not get it?" Gabriel says. There's emotion and conviction in his words but no hostility. "You're talking about an ability to control your thoughts that may not be possible for a person who's mentally ill. Haven't you ever been overcome by a force more powerful than you? When you beat up all those people who made you angry, didn't you lose control then? You're here because you can't control your thoughts."

E.M. is quiet. Then he says, "Sometimes when I beat people, I was in control."

More silence follows. I just witnessed something real, not fake, something personal to everyone here, including me. My head feels strangely clear. Somehow words come out.

"He's right," I say, looking at E.M. "There's always a choice. I could've stopped taking the pills. I didn't want to."

"Do you want to die?"

The directness of E.M.'s question takes my breath away.

"Maybe that's not the right question," Gabriel says kindly. "Maybe the real question is, do you want to live?"

He's right too. They are two different questions: *Do you want to die?* and *Do you want to live?* But in the darkness of my mind, not wanting to live and wanting to die don't seem like two things you can pull apart. They're wrapped up in the *no more* that I feel right now.

Gabriel goes on. "E.M. there wants to live. I want to live. Mona wants to live so she can be with her sister, Lucy. Do you want to live?"

I don't say anything.

"Not wanting to live is an illness. It can be cured," he says with certainty.

"It's a weakness," E.M. responds.

"Emilio, stop," Mona says.

They all look at me again. I clear my throat and try to speak, but the words in my mind have no external sound. I don't want to live. I want to die. It's all the same. I don't want anything. I simply don't want.

I fix my eyes on E.M. because it feels as if he's the one drawing out the words. "I agree with you. Not wanting to live is a weakness. People are poor, hungry, homeless. People in physical pain — they suffer, really suffer, and they don't try to kill themselves. They find strength somewhere, even just a little, to keep them going. I had . . . have, everything. . . ." I picture my room at home, and I can't speak for a moment.

"It's okay," Mona says.

"A family," I manage to continue. "People who care for me. A home. Much more than most. Somewhere in me I probably had the strength to not kill myself. But I was tired of looking for strength. Tired of being strong. That's what I did to make it through . . . each day, go through the motions of being strong. I put on strong every morning. I'm sick of faking strong."

I look down at the table. I have said more about how I feel to these strangers than I have to anyone for as long as I can remember. I should feel disgust, shame, embarrassment, all kinds of familiar things, but I don't.

"Vicky," Mona says, "you can't go back home tomorrow. Can't you stay?"

All eyes are on me, silent. As if my answer matters. As if leaving Lakeview would be a personal rejection of them.

"Dr. Desai wants me to stay two more weeks," I say.

"And?" Mona tilts her head.

I imagine for a moment what my father and Barbara would think of E.M. and Mona and Gabriel. These are definitely not the kind of people they would like me to associate with. But they are more like me than anyone I know, in some way I can't quite put into words. There's something fragile about all of them, like they're holding on to what the world expects of them by some brittle branch that can break at any moment. And none of them seems concerned with hiding it, with pretending that they're something they're not. If I go home tomorrow, I will need to pretend. I don't see any way around it.

Maybe I can stay here and give the pretending a small rest.

"I'll ask my father," I say.

"Yes!" Mona claps her hands. Gabriel nods approvingly.

"If you can survive rooming with Princess Psycho, you can survive anything," E.M. says.

"Yeah," Mona says, not offended one bit. "Stick with us, kid, we'll show you how to survive."

chapter FOUR

My father's first question when he and Barbara come the following morning is "How do you feel?"

I answer him.

The second one is "Why did you do it?"

That one I can't.

"But why, Vicky? I don't understand."

I shrug. Shake my head. We are in a room near the main entrance to the hospital, waiting for Dr. Desai.

"Was it the pressure of school?"

"No."

"Was it the fiasco with the debate team and Cecy?"

"No."

Was it that boy, what's his name? Jaime? Was it the fact that Juanita is going back to Mexico at the end of the month? Was I not getting along with Becca?

No, no, no, no. To all his questions, I answer no.

I was thinking about this last night after dinner, and the truth is, there was no one spark that lit the dry jumble of words in my head into the fire that brought me to the bottle of pills. Why do people kill themselves? Doesn't it always boil down to pain? There is pain in the body or the heart or the soul or the mind or all of the above. Body pain is obvious. Heart pain is the pain that comes from others, when they love you too much or not enough or the wrong way. Soul pain comes from feeling your life is one big waste. Mind pain is what I can't figure out. It's like when you throw body, heart, and soul pain into a blender, then you add a cup of disgust at all that you are, at all that you've become, at all that you will ever be.

So with my father's question, the only answer I have is because it hurt. The words that settled forever in my head, the ones that kept rising endlessly out of nowhere, the words that others spoke, they hurt. All of it hurt, inside and out, everywhere.

But I can't say any of that to my father.

"Well," he sighs, "we all make mistakes sometimes. Let's go home and see if we can figure this out."

I don't know what to say. The thought of going home scares me. I am grateful for the forgiveness I hear in my father's voice, but in my experience, our house is not a good place to figure things out.

"We called Dr. Saenz on the way to the hospital," Barbara says. "He's the best young people's psychiatrist in Austin, and he has agreed to see you even though he's not taking any more patients. His office is in one of our buildings, so he's doing this as a personal favor. He can see you as early as next week. I can pick you up after school and take you."

"School," I say. It starts out as a question, but it comes out almost as a gasp.

"Dr. Saenz recommends a return to your regular routine as soon as possible," Barbara adds.

"When you fall off the horse, the best thing to do is climb right back on," Father agrees. I don't know how many times he's urged me to get back on that imaginary horse. It's what he says every time he reads one of my report cards.

"Dr. Desai thought I should stay here for a while," I murmur.

"Vicky." My father lowers his voice. I get his business face now. "This is a public hospital. They take all kinds of deranged people. You don't belong here. You don't even know who this Dr. Desai is. The doctors who work in these hospitals are foreigners who can't get jobs anywhere else."

"I should stay here," I say softly, fearfully. I don't know why I'm saying this. The words are being forced out by a presence so weak and new I didn't even know it was there.

"Why?" my father asks.

Because I don't want to go home. Because here people believe the words inside your head cause pain. Because there is something real about Mona and E.M. and Gabriel that is like me, that makes me feel like I belong.

Instead, I say: "If I go back now, it will be like before."

My father looks momentarily lost. I can see him wondering whether I have just threatened to try to kill myself again. Barbara looks uncomfortable, like it's hurting her to hold back all that she wants to say.

"Good morning," says Dr. Desai as she comes into the room. My father and Barbara stand and shake her outstretched hand. She sits in the only other available chair, and my father and Barbara sit as well. Both of them look at Dr. Desai as if she's some shady character about to ask them for money.

"Vicky may have already mentioned to you that I recommended she stay here at Lakeview for a couple of weeks," Dr. Desai says. "I think it would be very good for her to stay. The type of thinking that led her to try to end her life is still there, and I'm afraid it will continue if she returns home so soon. Here, we can give her other things to think about and a way to reflect on that type of suicidal thinking." She turns to me. "So, Vicky, would you like to stay here a couple of weeks?"

I nod, avoiding my father's eyes.

"Wonderful." Dr. Desai clasps her hands. She faces my father and Barbara. "And you?"

"Is she on medication?" Barbara asks.

"That's another reason why I would like Vicky to stay. I would like some time to get to know her more before determining whether medication is needed."

"Suicidal thinking?" my father asks me, not quite believing what he heard Dr. Desai say a few moments before. "Is that what you have?"

I look briefly at Dr. Desai. She urges me with her eyes to tell the truth. The best I can do is look steadily at my feet. That's my answer.

"Do you think going back home will make that worse?" I recognize a tinge of anger in Father's voice.

Dr. Desai intervenes. "It's simply a question of giving Vicky a new environment for a short period of time. We want her to be in a place that is different from her usual life so she can see things differently when she returns home."

"And if she wants to come home before the end of the two weeks?" My father's voice is still shaky. He is making an enormous effort to control himself.

"Vicky can go home anytime she wants. She can also call you anytime she wants. But I think it's better if she did not *receive* phone calls or visits."

I remember how she let me talk to Juanita yesterday, and I wonder whether she thinks my father and Barbara are the problem — whether she wants to protect me from them.

"Vicky, is this what you really want?" Barbara asks.

"Yes," I say weakly.

There's a baffled look on my father's face, as if he cannot believe that I'm his flesh and blood. "All right. Two weeks." I hear disappointment and a residue of anger in his voice.

Then he stands and we all follow suit. He comes over and hugs me. He holds me gingerly, as if I were expensive crystal, the kind that breaks if you look at it the wrong way, and I can tell I've hurt him.

Outside, after we watch Father and Barbara walk out the front entrance, Dr. Desai says: "There's one more thing." She waits until I look at her. "If you're going to stay, I ask that you do not try to kill yourself while you are here. I need to hear you say that you promise."

"While I'm here?"

"While you're here."

"And afterward?"

"Afterward will be afterward. For now, I want a promise that you will not try to hurt yourself."

"Okay," I say.

"Okay?"

"I won't try to kill myself . . . while I'm here."

Words, I remind myself. *They are just words.*

CHAPTER
FIVE

My first few days at Lakeview pass more quickly than I expect. I thought staying at the hospital would be boring with nothing to do. But boredom only happens when you have some place you'd rather be. Time slows down here, but that's all right. It's as if the world and my brain can finally move at the same speed. The mental playlist with such hits as "I'm a Monumental Failure" and "I'm Lazy" and "I'm Bad and Worthless" and let's not forget the very popular "I Don't Belong Anywhere in This Here Universe" keeps on playing, but the tempo is different, slower. And slower thoughts, I discover, mean not less pain, but a different, more solid and real kind of pain. There is more time for me to remember actual examples of my failures and worthlessness and not belonging anywhere, and this makes the thoughts more substantial and less ghostlike. It's more painful than before, but somehow more endurable, if that makes any sense.

Not that my days are spent sitting around thinking. I listen to Mona, who stops talking only long enough to sleep a few hours at night or to watch one of her shows, which totally absorb her. I eat all my meals with E.M., Gabriel, and Mona in the fifth-floor dining room. And I have my daily sessions with Dr. Desai and the GTH — Group Therapy Healing. We meet in a small room with a row of windows on one end and six chairs in a circle.

The GTH is like a person with different moods. Some days it is lively and funny and other days it is gloomy and dark. At first I thought it was Mona who infected the GTH with how she feels on a particular day, but after a few sessions, I think the tone is set by Gabriel. I still have no idea why he's here, but sometimes there's a quiet about him that quickly spreads to all of us. It's almost as if his thoughtfulness reminds us all of the darkness we always carry within. I mostly try to listen and not talk.

"I have something for you all," Dr. Desai says one morning. She reaches for the plastic bag next to her chair, takes out four spiral notebooks, and spreads them out on the wobbly table. "Please, choose one."

Mona reaches in and grabs the purple one. E.M. takes the black. Gabriel waits for me to choose next, but I don't move. He picks blue. I lift the green notebook and drop it on my lap. I remember the dozen or so notebooks just like this in the bottom drawer of my desk at home — my journals, the only place where I don't lie, where I put my pathetic poems. I should have thrown them out before I did the deed.

"What we supposed to write in these?" Mona asks.

"Anything," Dr. Desai says. "Pretend you're writing to someone you enjoy talking to and who enjoys listening to you. A journal-friend. The person can be real or can be imaginary. Write something every day, even if it's just a paragraph. I'd like you to bring your notebooks to our individual sessions. You can share what you write with me, but only if you want. No pressure."

Mona raises her hand. "I think everyone here picked a notebook that fits his or her personality."

"Could you explain?" Dr. Desai asks.

"Well," she says, moving to the edge of her chair, "I picked purple because purple is a royal color. It's also the color for pain, and my life's been one royal pain in the butt."

Gabriel laughs. Dr. Desai tries not to smile, but she does anyway. I think I see E.M.'s eyes soften.

Gabriel lifts up his notebook. "What does blue stand for?"

"Blue stands for mystery. You know, like the blue sky. It looks like that's all there is, but there's a whole scary universe with stars and planets and black holes behind it."

Gabriel's eyes widen, then he says, "It's not all that scary."

Mona ignores him. She's looking at E.M., who is flipping through the blank pages of his notebook. "Black is for the darkness in your heart," Mona tells him. She could be joking or she could be serious, I can't tell.

"That sounds a little like a judgment," Dr. Desai says, "which we've promised not to do here."

"It don't bother me," E.M. says. He smiles at Mona and she almost, but not quite, smiles back at him.

"What about green?" Gabriel asks, looking at me.

"Enough personality assessments," Dr. Desai says before Mona can speak again. "I want to spend some time today talking about our fathers."

I can tell by the dead silence of the group that no one is excited about the topic. None of us want to go first. Finally, Dr. Desai asks Gabriel to start.

Gabriel speaks quickly but distractedly, his thoughts and words on different tracks. I've noticed that he has different speeds that switch from one moment to another. "I don't know my father, so I'll talk about my grandfather. My grandfather is seventy-four and still works as a gardener — Romero Landscape. That's what he's done all his life, since he came from Mexico. He's been married to my grandmother since he was eighteen. She has some kind of mental illness. She forgets things. She sees things. But it's not Alzheimer's. Some kind of senile schizophrenia, maybe." He looks at Dr. Desai for confirmation. She nods, and he continues, "My grandfather loves her. It makes him happy to take care of her. He works twelve hours a day so he can pay to have someone stay with her. His life is for her, and for my mother when she was alive, and now for me."

He breathes deeply and then continues. "My mother and me, we always lived near my grandparents. When she died, it broke my grandfather's heart, literally. A month later, he had a heart attack. I quit school to help him out. We have forty yards. We mow four lawns a day, five when we can. We work Saturdays and sometimes on Sundays to catch up. That's pretty much it."

Dr. Desai asks E.M. to talk next, but E.M. flatly refuses. "I got no real father" is all he says.

Mona says, "Okay, I'll go," and takes off. "I'm like Gabriel, I never knew my father. That only leaves Jerry, my stepfather, to tell you about. He's the definition of Mr. Jekyll and Dr. Hyde, or is it the other way around? He's a flipper. One moment he's hugging us all and buying us giant teddy bears, and the next moment he's yelling because we woke him up at night. The only good thing he's ever done is get my mother pregnant, and the one good thing in our miserable lives was Lucy.

"I've already told you how I took care of Lucy since day one. But I couldn't be with her every single second. We were getting welfare, but that wasn't enough. Someone had to work in our sorry family and that was me. So one day the social worker shows up and they take Lucy. I cry and beg, but it's no use. Then, just before she goes, the social worker, this fat lady, she says, 'I want to show you something.' She shows me these purple marks on Lucy's arms. 'Those are finger marks from someone shaking her,' she says. That's when I realized what Jerry had been doing. I had to leave her alone with them sometimes, even though they were addicts and all that. But how could it be that I never saw those marks?"

We are all silent while Mona sobs quietly. There is not supposed to be any pressure for anyone to speak in the GTH. But we have gone around the circle now, and I feel like I owe it to the group to tell them about my parents.

I hesitate. Then I look up and see Dr. Desai nod. It is the smallest nod, just a tiny movement of her head, but it's as if she knows exactly what I'm thinking and she's encouraging me to go ahead and let the words come out. Yes, my circumstances are very different from the others'; yes, I am privileged in comparison to the rest. Yet here I am at Lakeview, in the psychiatric ward, after I tried to kill myself. No matter how good my living situation is, something isn't clicking. I inhale deeply and begin to speak.

"My father is in the real estate and construction business. He's been in real estate and construction all his life. My grandfather owned a brick-making factory here in Austin, and when he died, my father inherited it and grew his business from there. He takes buildings that aren't in great shape, fixes them, and slowly fills them with people who can pay more rent. The money he makes, he invests in bigger buildings and so on. He has a knack for finding out what part of the city well-off people will want to live in, and he goes in there and buys property that is not worth much. He does it with houses too. He buys the homes of people who can't pay their mortgages, fixes them, and sells them. He makes deals. All day long, that's what he does. He makes deals."

I glance quickly around the room. E.M. is looking at me as if everything I said proved that what he thought about me has been right on. Mona is biting her nails, or what is left of them, but she is paying attention, waiting for me to continue. Gabriel looks sad — I don't think I've ever seen that sadness on him before. Dr. Desai has a worried look on her face.

I might as well go on now. It's the most I've ever spoken at a GTH and I feel an energy pushing me to continue.

"My father married Barbara about six months after my mother died. She was my father's assistant before he married her. Barbara is pretty, real pretty. She works out every day. She was married to a lawyer, but they divorced sometime after she started working for my father. She's smart also. My father never went to college, but Barbara has a degree in business." I pause for a moment. "I don't know how I ended up talking about Barbara. When I think of my father, I think of her, I guess."

"What's she like? Is she nice?" Mona asks.

I shrug. "Barbara? She's nice in her own way. My sister, Becca, gets along great with her, but she makes me nervous. She's always thinking of the next thing she has to do." Then I say impulsively, "She doesn't sleep. The sleeping pills I took were prescribed for her. My father takes them too."

The group is silent. I can hear Dr. Desai's labored breathing next to me. E.M. clears his throat. "I know your father's company," he says. "They bought a whole bunch of buildings over on the east side and kicked the poor people out. Then the rich people moved in."

"Yup, that sounds like my father's company," I say.

"What about your mom?" Mona asks.

"My mom?" I swallow. My stomach muscles tense.

"Only if you want," Dr. Desai says.

"I remember my mother as quiet, maybe a little shy," I say, my eyes on the floor. "I thought she was beautiful, with her short black hair. Let's see. She helped me with my homework because I've always needed help. I used to ask her to read to me from whatever book she was reading. She liked to read poetry in Spanish. Her favorite was love poetry from famous Latin and Spanish poets, some modern, some very old. What else? She loved to play Scrabble. We played it all the time." I glance at Dr. Desai, who smiles at me. "She got breast cancer when I was eight. It went away and then it came back, and the second time it was in her brain. She died when I was ten. The last three months she was mostly in bed. She wouldn't eat that much either. Juanita, that's my nanny, would bring her dinner up to her room. I would read to her."

"Go on," Dr. Desai gently urges me.

"That was six years ago," I say.

"You still miss her," Mona says. "You're still sad for her." I notice that she stopped biting her nails while I was speaking.

"I don't feel sad," I say. "I don't feel anything. I hardly ever think of her. How could I feel sad after so many years?"

I look at Dr. Desai, but E.M. speaks before she can say anything. "You don't feel sad, you just feel sorry for yourself."

"You're a jerk," Mona tells him.

"Because I tell it like it is? If that makes me a jerk, then it does. Me feeling sorry for her is not gonna do her any good."

"You're about as sensitive as a worm," Mona continues. "Besides, what do you know about feeling sad? Psychopaths don't feel sad."

"Psycho what? Psycho pat? Is that what I am? That doesn't sound too bad."

"Psycho-*path*! Not psycho-*pat*!" Mona corrects him. "Idiot."

"Okay," says Dr. Desai, "let's do this without calling each other names. Gabriel, would you like to say something?"

Gabriel shifts in his chair. He speaks slowly now, with choppy pauses, as if he's just climbed a hundred steps. "About six months. After my mother died. I noticed. I was no longer feeling sad. Missing her. Like I used to. I didn't feel anything. But that was worse than feeling sad. When I was sad, I felt my mother. Next to me. Helping me. When I stopped feeling sad. She was gone. I was all alone."

His eyes redden and then moisten. I wish I could feel whatever it is that he is feeling. I remember how I tried to picture my mother's face when I took the sleeping pills. I closed my eyes and waited as I sank deeper and deeper into the silent darkness, but her image never came.

"People mourn in different ways," Mona says. "You could still be mourning your mother after six years while others mourn for just a few months. I mean, hey, look at your dad. Six months after your mother dies, he marries somebody else. I bet you a hundred dollars that your stepmother is younger than your father."

"She's ten years younger," I say.

"Told you!" There's a triumphant look on Mona's face. "Pardon me for asking, but do you think he was having an affair with her — before your mother died, I mean?"

"I don't think so," I say quickly, almost defensively. Then I stop to think. But no — the one thing I know about my father is that once he gives his word, he sticks to it. "If you knew my father, you'd know he's not the type to do that."

Mona makes the kind of face you make at someone who's being extremely naïve.

"Okay, we're going astray again," Dr. Desai says. "Gabriel, I'm interested in the distinctions you made between different kinds of sadness. You said you felt different six months after your mother died. Can you talk more about that?"

E.M. jumps in. "It's the same thing I said. First you feel

sad, and then you either get on with your life or you stay stuck feeling sorry for yourself. You know, 'Why did this happen to me?' and all that crap. That's what I was trying to say. People don't kill themselves because they're sad, they kill themselves because they feel sorry for themselves."

"Have you ever tried to kill yourself? What makes you such an expert on suicide?" Mona snaps.

"I've thought about it. Everyone thinks about it sometimes, but only the weak do it," E.M. responds.

"Let's let Gabriel speak," Dr. Desai says.

Gabriel closes his eyes for a few moments and then opens them. He talks more to himself than to us. "Sometimes I wonder why Jesus said blessed are those who mourn. Why? What's so blessed about mourning? Mourning is painful. I thought about it. And it came to me. When you mourn . . . you feel alive. When you mourn . . . it means you care. But when you can't mourn? You're dead inside." He stops suddenly, and then adds, blinking, embarrassed, "Sorry. Forgot the question."

Dr. Desai smiles. "Let me see. I think you were trying to distinguish between the sadness you felt after your mother died and how you felt six months later."

"But why was I trying to do that?"

Dr. Desai looks at him. "Are you okay?"

"Yes," Gabriel says quickly. "I lost track. Of what we were talking about."

Mona pushes herself to the edge of her chair like a student eager to recite the correct answer. "What you were trying to say is that it's normal to feel sad for a while after your mom dies, but it's not normal to feel numb and empty like you did six months after your mom died, or like Vicky feels now, which is not normal sadness but clinical depression. There. Any questions?" She wags her head left and right, beaming.

"That's what I said," says E.M.

"That is so NOT what you said!" Mona snaps.

"Mmm," Dr. Desai comments. "Vicky, you want to add anything?"

Depression. It's not like it's the first time I've ever heard the word. It's only that right then and there it becomes more than a word. Suddenly, it is something I can feel and touch and taste. I can even picture it. It's a heavy, thick fog, yellow and pale purple, the color of a bruise, that fills up a room with no windows, no air, no light.

"I'm depressed?" I say.

"Welcome to the club," Mona says.

CHAPTER SIX

Margie, one of the fifth-floor nurses, lets me use the computer in an empty doctor's office, so I am able to do some research. Depression can be a normal reaction to a life event, like my mother's death, or it can be a symptom of another physical illness, or even a side effect of drugs. But sometimes depression is in itself the illness — an illness like any other illness, like the flu or the mumps. The only difference is that instead of affecting the lungs or skin, depression affects the mind. It interferes with certain chemicals responsible for transmitting messages from one part of the brain to another.

As I read this, I imagine a whole bunch of little minerlike elves who live and work inside the dark tunnels of my brain. They wear flashlight hats of different colors and push clanging carts full of words on steel rails from one corner of my mind to another. They are happy workers, these elves, except when the yellow-purple fog of depression comes in. It's so thick and viscous that the wheels of the carts gum up and the elves can't breathe. So they struggle, struggle, huff and puff, as they try to push the carts with the messages. And of course, after a while the elves get tired and grumpy and sore and frustrated, and they start dumping messages of gloom and doom in the cart, which for some reason are easier to lug. I say this because for a week or so before the deed, the little elves had no trouble delivering carloads full of *Kill yourself.*

In my next private session with Dr. Desai, I tell her about my research and the brain elves.

"Fog can be a good way of looking at it," Dr. Desai says, smiling. "And how do you feel about these brain elves?"

"I kind of feel sorry for them," I say. "They have it pretty rough."

"Yes," she agrees.

"I don't know," I say. "Thinking about the brain elves is nice, but they just deliver the messages. I'm the one who acts on them."

"What do you mean?"

"I decided to act on the message to end it all." A message that the brain elves are still delivering, although less frequently. I don't tell this to Dr. Desai, but I have a feeling she knows.

"Tell me about that," she says. "When did you first decide to yield to their message?"

Dr. Desai, I've noticed, likes specifics. She always brings the topic of conversation back to me, my life, to a particular place or a time or a person. I'm not sure I like it. It's much easier to talk in general terms about, say, the symptoms of depression, or about chemical transmitters that are like tiny elves, than to talk about how depression feels in me, what it makes me do or not do, like or not like.

"I can't say exactly when I decided. The week before the deed is when the idea . . . solidified. Like a vapor of possibility that turned to water and then to ice. But I think suicide has been on my mind for a long, long time." I shake my head. "Sometimes it was like the hum of an air conditioner, you know? Always there but noticeable only when I paid attention. And other times it just appeared out of nowhere, like my cat jumping on my lap."

Dr. Desai smiles. "That's a nice comparison."

I go on. "About nine months ago, I took five sleeping pills from Barbara's medicine cabinet. Then I took five more every month when she had her prescription refilled. I knew she didn't keep track. I didn't actually know that I was going to try suicide."

"Then why take the pills? What was going on in your mind when you took them?"

"I don't know. Having the pills around was comforting. The idea that I could end the pain was my only hope." I think for a second. "It felt like a door that I could open when things got so bad that it didn't matter what the door opened to. The other side has to be better, right?"

Dr. Desai does not answer. She doesn't agree with me, or maybe it is one of those unanswerable questions. Instead, she says, "You said you decided a week before. What was that decision like, or that thought? Did something bring the thought to the surface?"

"There was just . . . pain, disgust, hatred. More than before. More than I could bear."

"Be specific," Dr. Desai insists. "Who do you hate? Who disgusts you?"

"Me," I answer. "Vicky. Victoria. I make me sick."

"Tell me one thing you did that disgusts you."

I'm glad she doesn't argue with me or list all the good

things I have going for me. "It's not about what I did." I stop, thinking. It's more about who I am than what I do or don't do. It's like a bad odor coming from me that only I can smell and is always there.

"But there must be something that you did that disgusts you." Dr. Desai is persistent, pushy. She wants words, as if words matter.

I say the first thing that comes to mind. "When I started at Reynard, the school I go to, my father wanted me to join the debate team. He and my sister had both done debate when they were in high school and they were both really good at it. Debate helps you see both sides of an issue. It makes you quick on your feet. It teaches you all kinds of ways to be strong and tough and a fighter. All that." I stop. The thick, yellowish fog has entered my head and slowly begins to fill it.

"Go on," Dr. Desai prods me. "It's important that you push through."

"So I joined debate when I started at Reynard. That's where I met Cecy. We were paired as debate partners. Cecy was my only friend at Reynard. We didn't do things together outside of school, and we weren't close, but we were debate friends. Cecy loved debate. We were given topics like 'Should the United States deport children who cross its borders illegally?' and in the tournaments, we would argue both sides pro and con. Yeah."

The fog has turned from vapor to an oily liquid, and now it is becoming a tarlike substance that makes my head feel stuffed up, my arms and legs heavy.

"Did you enjoy debate?" Dr. Desai asks.

"Enjoy?" That's a foreign word. Meaningless.

"Did you like researching an issue, speaking in public, arguing the pros and cons?"

"I tried. I tried. So much pretending."

"Pretending?"

"When I got up to speak, I had to sound convinced of the truth of what I was saying, like I believed it with all my heart. I had to pretend I was confident and upbeat."

Dr. Desai waits for me to continue.

"We never won. When we looked at the judge's comments, they said I wasn't convincing. 'Pep.' They liked to use that word. 'Not enough pep.' Or 'oomph' — 'not enough oomph.' I was supposed to attack the other team's weaknesses. One judge said I lacked the necessary viciousness."

"And you felt bad that you couldn't muster the necessary viciousness? Is that your example of something disgusting about yourself?"

"Yes. No. What I wanted to say, the example was . . . It happened a couple of weeks before. . . ." I try to concentrate, to remember. "Cecy and I were in a tournament, and when it was my turn to speak, in the middle of my argument, I stopped. Everything seemed so stupid. So silly. I was arguing that marriage should be only between a man and a woman. My mind felt so heavy. It froze. I couldn't generate any more words or pep or oomph. I looked at Cecy, and then I walked out of the room."

Dr. Desai nods. "And the disgusting thing about yourself was?"

"I left Cecy without a partner. I didn't care. I didn't give a damn. I quit."

"And Cecy was mad at you? You were no longer friends?"

"No more friends with Cecy." I see Cecy coming over to the table in the Reynard cafeteria where I sat alone that first day of school, sitting down, saying hello, making a face at her Mexican pizza.

"Did you ever talk to her afterward?"

"Afterward?" I return to the present and Dr. Desai.

"After you walked out of that tournament?"

"She wouldn't talk to me at school. I sent her an email, explaining as best I could."

"And what did you say?"

"That I couldn't do it anymore, that I never liked debate. I couldn't pretend anymore."

"And your father? What did he say when you told him?"

"He . . ." The last time I thought about my father's words was the night I took the pills. "He wasn't angry." I swallow. My mouth is dry. I get an image of an empty riverbed, cracked and hard. "I expected him to be angry. Quitting is not allowed in our family. But he only shrugged and said, 'You can't ask a mule to be a racehorse.'"

"And how did that make you feel?"

I'm silent.

"What kind of little message did the brain elves deliver when your father spoke those words?"

"That I was a loser. Useless," I say.

The word *loser* suddenly takes me back to our last Christmas vacation. My expression must change, because Dr. Desai asks, "What are you seeing?"

I blink. "Just then I saw Father, Barbara, Becca, and me sitting in this fancy restaurant at Padre Island. We have a condo there. This was last Christmas."

"And the four of you are talking about . . ."

"My future. Or non-future. They were throwing out the names of colleges I might get into if I worked my butt off spring semester and the next two years. The Ivy Leagues were out of the question — I would never be able to overcome my C's and D's. The only hope was that I might sneak into the University of Texas, where Father has some connections."

"Ah! And what did you say?"

"I don't remember saying anything. Then Barbara asked me what I wanted to be, you know, when I grew up."

"And?"

"I couldn't think of anything. And everyone was stumped about what I would be good at. They listed what I *wasn't* good at. I wasn't good with people. I wasn't good with numbers. I wasn't good on my feet."

"You couldn't think of anything you were good at?"

I chuckle, remembering. "I told them that maybe I could work at a Holiday Inn as a maid."

"And what was the reaction of your family?"

"They kind of looked at me like they didn't know how I could possibly be related to them. Then Father asked Becca which law firms she was going to apply to for summer jobs."

We are silent. The loneliness I felt at that dinner table surrounded by my family is the same loneliness I feel now.

"The thing is," I say, quickly, before the tears come, "I was serious. I had secretly been helping Juanita with the housework since her leg had gotten worse, and I enjoyed it. There was something about making the beds and getting them just perfect, vacuuming the carpets, doing laundry, and washing dishes that made me feel good."

Dr. Desai reflects. "You think differently than your family. How did that happen?"

"How did what happen?" I ask.

"You and the rest of your family value different things. I'm just curious how that came about. They value high achievement, success, status. You don't seem to care too much about those things."

I think for a few moments. "Sometimes I think that the reason I'm not ambitious and I don't care about what my family cares about is that I'm lazy and . . . not all that smart."

Dr. Desai gives me one of those *Get serious* looks.

"Really. It's not like I have big philosophical reasons against status and success. I've tried to care about grades and Ivy League schools, but I just don't have the drive that my sister has, or the brains."

"Mmm." The way she says this, I know she's not buying what I'm offering. "Maybe you're more like your mother. Did she have this drive?"

"She loved gardening and doing things at home. But she was ambitious in her own way. She took Spanish literature courses at night so she could understand the poets she loved better. She belonged to a studio of women painters who helped each other. She was, I don't know, content, but also interested in learning new things." *Unlike me*, I want to say. *I'm neither content nor interested.*

Dr. Desai moves forward in her chair. "Content but interested," she repeats. "Like your father?"

"No. Different."

"How?"

There's a restlessness about my father, a hunger for him and others to be better, to succeed in whatever it is they do. I don't know how to describe it. "Different," I say. I don't want to blame my father or Barbara or my sister for how messed up I am. It's just too convenient to blame your family. It seems cowardly.

"Go ahead, tell me." Her jaw is firm and her eyes are fixed on me. She's not going to let go.

I exhale. "I don't fault my father for wanting me to get good grades or be somebody. All he wants is for me to try. To do my best."

"And you don't do that?"

"It's like part of me wants to try and another part can't. I sit there in geometry class and I understand maybe ten percent of what the teacher is saying. I could ask my brain what one plus one is and it wouldn't know the answer. Or I'm at home trying to write a paper on macroeconomics, and I end up staring at the screen for an hour, my brain blank." I rub my head and feel the uneven tufts of hair sticking out.

"You get up, you go to school every day," Dr. Desai says. "You sit in classes even if you don't understand everything. You come home and stare at the computer. You participated in debate for years. Isn't that trying? I don't understand."

"Is that enough?"

"Sometimes." She sits back in her chair.

"It always feels as if I can be doing more, and the only reason I don't is because I don't want to, because I really, really don't like what I have to do. I don't like anything or anybody. It's all a big not-like."

"But you kept at it, doing things you didn't like, being with people you didn't like. How did you manage to do that?"

How did I manage to do that? "I pretend," I finally say. That word again.

Dr. Desai breaks into a big smile. "You say that as if pretending were a big sin. We all do that kind of pretending to survive, Vicky. Some pretending is necessary and even good. We can tolerate all the pretending we need to do if we have some . . . islands of honesty in our lives. Places where we don't lie to others. Most of all, places where we don't lie to ourselves."

I'm quiet, wondering if I ever lied to myself. Maybe I lied to myself about Jaime for a little while. I tried to convince myself that I liked him, that there must be something wrong with me for not seeing what so many other girls at Reynard saw and longed for.

"That pretending, as you call it, is nothing more than effort. It's simply doing what you need to do even when you don't like it. But it can be a very difficult kind of effort." She leans forward again. "This dislike you have for everything — that's not your fault, that's not something you're responsible for. The dislike comes from looking through these dirty glass goggles of depression that distort everything and everyone you see. You kept on going for the longest time, pretending you were seeing clearly when all was blurry and gray and ugly."

That's how it is every single day. Blurry and gray and ugly.

"There is beauty and goodness out there and in you, no matter what the brain elves might tell you," she says. "Depression not only makes it hard for the brain elves to deliver messages. Sometimes it makes them put the wrong messages in the cart."

And then something in my head opens, a small window.

chapter SEVEN

Dr. Desai requires that we use two to three hours of each day for some kind of service to the hospital. Mona helps in the hospital's beauty salon, doing manicures and dye jobs. E.M. works with the construction workers who are building a new Alzheimer's wing. Gabriel mows and weed-whacks the grassy areas surrounding the hospital grounds.

Of all the choices for work that Dr. Desai offered me, the laundry room seemed like the one that would require the least interaction with people, the least talking. And I was right. Stuffing soiled linens into giant washing machines and dryers and then folding them into perfect squares is not as bad as it sounds. In fact, those three hours make up my favorite part of the day. The Mexican girls who work in the laundry room never hurry but never stop moving. Every once in a while I can hear them hum some unknown song. They are friendly, but they keep their distance. I have the impression that they know I tried to kill myself and they're afraid to pry, as if their questions might tip a fragile scale the wrong way.

The hardest part of the work is memorizing the precise moves needed to fold a sheet with a partner, a process that reminds me of a minutely choreographed dance. Once the girls patiently teach me the art of folding, I can do the laundry work almost as carefully and efficiently as they can. There are times, as I fold the sheets and pillowcases, when my mental playlist is nearly inaudible, the self-accusing songs drowned out by sensations: the salty smell of starch, the warm softness of cotton cloth.

Today, as I'm folding sheets, I'm thinking about what happened after that family dinner in South Padre Island, when Becca and I were back in our room with the lights out.

"Do you ever think about Mamá?" I asked her.

It took so long for her to respond that I thought she hadn't heard me or was ignoring me. "Now and then," she finally said. "Why do you ask?"

"Remember when you wanted to be a veterinarian? You and Mamá used to talk about it constantly, and Mamá would get you books about dogs and horses and all kinds of animals. You used to tell Mamá about them, and she would quiz you about the different animals, and you'd know the answers right off."

Becca, who had been facing away from me, turned and lay on her back, staring at the ceiling. "How old was I? Six? Every kid wants to be a veterinarian at that age."

"No, you were eleven. You wanted to be a veterinarian up to when Mamá got sick. I know because that's when she took you to the shelter to get Galileo," I said.

"Oh, yeah."

"And then after we had him for about a month, you started to get mad at me because Galileo would come sleep in my bed every night. That was in our old house when we shared a room.

You thought I waited until you fell asleep and then moved him, remember? Then you found out he was doing it on his own and you gave up on him."

"That cat never liked me."

"That's not true. He liked you. You stopped liking him."

There was a little silence. I kept talking, I didn't know why. "About a month after we got Galileo, Mamá started her chemotherapy. That's when you stopped wanting to be a veterinarian."

"What exactly is your point?" She sounded annoyed.

"No point," I said. "This whole talk about careers and all got me thinking about how you and Mamá used to dream together about having a veterinary clinic, where Mamá would be the receptionist. I was just wondering if you remembered that."

"I've moved on. That was childish stuff. I don't dwell on the past. Why are you bringing all this up?"

I took a deep breath. "It makes me sad that you gave up on your dream. You gave up on Galileo." I paused. "You gave up on Mamá."

"That's not true!"

"She needed you so much that year."

"Shut up! You have no right to talk to me about giving up. Look at you. You gave up on yourself, just like Mamá did when she decided to stop the chemo and let herself die. At least I didn't do that. Damn it, Vicky! Don't you ever talk to me about Mother! Just because I'm not obsessed with her death like you doesn't mean I didn't love her. I moved on. Life goes on. I didn't abandon her when she was sick. She didn't want me to see her suffer. She was *glad* I didn't have to witness that. She wanted me to have good memories of her. Look at what being with her every day and watching her turn into a cadaver did to you. You're a mess. You're stuck back there by her bedside watching her die." She jumped out of bed and stood over me. "Leave me the heck alone, okay?" Then she went out of the room.

That night and every other night we were there, Becca slept on the pullout sofa in the office. A few days later, she left for Harvard without saying good-bye. I called her every week the first month after she left, but she never answered my calls or called me back. I'm not sure exactly why I kept calling. The last time I tried was the night I did the deed.

Maybe it is time to try again.

Patients are not allowed cell phones in the psychiatric ward, but Mona got one from her connection in the cafeteria, this guy named Rudy. I borrow it that night. The phone rings and rings. Finally, just before it goes to voice mail, Becca picks up.

"Hello?" She sounds suspicious.

"It's me. Vicky."

"Vicky! I almost didn't answer. I didn't recognize the number."

"It's my friend's phone." I look at Mona. "Well, not her phone exactly. A phone she borrowed."

On her bed, Mona lowers her *People* magazine and smiles at me. She seems glad I called her "friend." She's fiddling with an iPod — another piece of contraband from Rudy, no doubt.

She sticks the earbuds in her ears, slides down the bed, and closes her eyes. Her right foot begins to twitch in rhythm to something fast.

"So." There is a dramatic pause on Becca's end of the line. "How are you, really?"

"I'm okay. I wanted to call you so you wouldn't worry."

"I was going to fly down as soon as I heard, but Miguel said the hospital had a rule about no visitors allowed."

She cuts off suddenly, and I hear muffled voices. Becca's talking to someone with her hand over the speaker.

"I just called to tell you I was okay. I should probably go," I say when the line clears.

"No, I'm just in the middle of a study group in someone's apartment. Hold on. Let me go to the kitchen." There's another little pause, then she says, "Okay, now I can talk. So, Vicky, what happened? Did something make you do that?"

I close my eyes. Every conversation I have with everyone who knows about my suicide attempt will be like this. People will want to know why, and they will ask, whether out loud or in their minds. "No. Nothing specific happened. I'm still trying to figure it all out."

"There's all kinds of theories out there. Leslie said some boy broke up with you and that's why you did it."

"Leslie?" She's a friend of Becca's from high school.

"Cecy told Joan. Joan told Martha. Martha told Leslie. Leslie called me."

"Oh, God." It shouldn't bother me that people know. What do I care, after all? But it does.

"So the whole world knows. Big deal. Can you tell me what happened? What boy is Cecy talking about?"

"His name is Jaime. He's a senior at Reynard. But it wasn't about him."

"But there was something with him?"

"No. He liked me. I mean, he said he liked me, but he wasn't for me. I told him I didn't like him."

"Was he nice?"

"Yes, he was nice."

"Oh." The way Becca says this, I know she's wondering how I could reject any nice guy who showed an interest in me. It's not as if I've had many boyfriends. In fact, it's not as if I *ever* had any boyfriends.

"It's complicated," I say. "Or maybe it isn't that complicated. But it wasn't because of Jaime. It wasn't anything. It was everything. I don't know."

"Listen, Vicky," Becca says, "I know it's stressful to live with Miguel and Barbara. They like to push, but they mean well. There were lots of times when I felt like slacking off and they pushed me, and I'm glad they did. That's just the way they are. Miguel wants you to do your best and be your best — that's how he was brought up. That's how he shows that he cares. He doesn't understand what you did at all."

"I know."

"I'm sorry we lost touch." There's silence on the line. I hear Becca breathe. Maybe she's thinking about all my calls she didn't answer. Then, "No one told me anything. I didn't even know you had quit debate, for God's sake."

"I couldn't do debate anymore. I couldn't."

Another silence. It feels like Becca is trying to keep herself from telling me how irresponsible I was. It's not as if I don't know that.

"I wish someone had told me you were having problems," she says again. "We're sisters, aren't we?"

"Yes."

"Were you mad at me?"

The question surprises me. "No, why would I be mad at you?"

"You know, last Christmas at Padre Island."

"No, I was never mad at you," I say.

"I thought you were mad because I haven't talked to you since then. It's been almost two months. I was really upset for a long time about what you said. Then I got busy. This place is wicked hectic."

"I know. Becca, you're not responsible. It wasn't your fault."

"I meant to call you on your birthday but . . . I'm sorry. Did you get the T-shirt I sent you?"

"Yes. I like it. I wear it all the time."

"Are you mad at me because Barbara and I are close?" The small stutter in her voice tells me that it was a hard question for her to ask.

"No. I'm glad you two get along. I'm happy for you." But my words come out sounding bitter. I don't want to sound that way. Am I bitter? About what? That she and Barbara are good friends? Becca likes Barbara and Barbara likes her. Barbara's approval is not something I've lost sleep about. If I'm not bitter, why do I sound like it?

"She's not that bad, Vicky. You should give her half a chance. She tries."

"I know," I say.

"This has really affected her. It's thrown her for a loop."

I don't want to talk about how the deed affected other people. "I'm sorry," I say. "I better go. I want to make sure the phone still has some power left so Mona can make a call she needs to make. I don't think she has the charger."

"Who's Mona?"

"My roommate."

"Is it horrible there? Barbara said the place reminded her of *One Flew Over the Cuckoo's Nest*. She said the psychiatrist did not fill her with a lot of confidence."

"Barbara's already so full of it, it's hard to fill her up with anything else." It feels good to say that.

Becca laughs, and then she says, a serious tone in her voice, "Vicky, I'm sorry about what I said to you at Padre Island. Some of the things you said about me abandoning Mamá must have hit home. I was hurt."

"I know. I said hurtful things too." Did I mean all the things I said to Becca? Do I still believe they're true? I see my mother's face, so thin the skin barely covered her bones, and you could see what she would look like after she was dead and buried. Can I blame Becca for being scared, for staying away?

Yes. I'm surprised to find that quiet, simple *yes* inside of me.

Becca is saying, "I'm sorry about not returning your calls and for not calling you on your birthday and just sending you that stupid T-shirt. I'm sorry for not being there for you as a sister. Can we try again?"

"Becca, it really wasn't your fault. Don't worry."

"Okay. You're going to be okay?"

"Yes."

"Okay. You buck up, cowboy. Like Miguel says, when the going gets tough, the tough get going. Okay?"

Becca is so like my father. They think alike, they say the same things. I've always understood why they are so close. But it makes me sad to think that I will never have that closeness with my father . . . or maybe with Becca. "Okay," I say, without conviction.

"Call me anytime, day or night. I'm your big sister, right?"

"Yes, you're my big sister."

"Bye, Vicky."

"Bye."

When the phone is silent, I think about the night of the deed. What if Becca had picked up the phone when I called her? Would it have made a difference?

No, I think. I felt alone then as I feel alone now. A sister needs to be a friend before you feel that you're not alone.

EIGHT

I close the cell phone and hand it to Mona. She has taken her earbuds out and her eyes are open. I don't know how long she was listening to my conversation, but I don't mind.

"Thanks," I say. "That was my sister. I hadn't talked to her since December. I needed to tell her that she wasn't responsible for my . . . the deed."

Mona sat up. "So what she say?"

"She was worried that I might have done it because I was mad at her." I go over to my bed and try to sit, but the bed is so high, I can't do it without jumping up backward.

"And were you?" Mona asks.

"Mad at her? No," I say as I stretch out. I think that's true. I wasn't mad at Becca when I took the pills. Was I?

"Mmm." Mona wrinkles her nose as if she smells something bad.

"What does that mean, 'mmm'?" I imitate the movement she made with her nose.

"Remember how you described your sister in one of the GTHs?"

I shake my head.

"You said that she was super pretty and super smart and super popular. Then you went on to tell us about how she was at Harvard and wanted to be a lawyer and then she was going to come home and work with your dad, who promised he would pay her as much as she would earn in a big law firm."

"I said all that?"

"I remember. And E.M. said it was too bad she wasn't the one who tried to kill herself?"

"Oh, yeah, now I remember." And after E.M. said that, I remember thinking Becca was not sensitive enough to ever try to kill herself. I also remember feeling guilty for thinking that.

"Well, I did detect a little envy in the way you spoke about her."

"That's normal, though, isn't it? When you have a sister who's so good at everything and you're so bad? She's smart. I'm dumb. She's pretty — look at me. She has this incredible willpower. She used to get up at four a.m. to study. Not even for a test, but just for a regular school day!"

"How do you know? Did you share a room with her? And by the way, don't put yourself down. You may be school dumb but you're life smart, like the rest of us here. Even E.M., much as I hate to admit it, he comes up with some things that make you say, 'Wow, this kid's not as stupid as he looks.' And what about Gabriel? Can you imagine the people he's mowing lawns for? They look out the window and all they see is another dumb Mexican pushing a lawn mower. Little do they know what's inside that boy's head. Did I ever tell you my theory about mental illness?"

"Which one? You've told me a few."

"The one about how mental illness makes people smart. It lets us see a part of life that others don't see."

"Yes, you told me."

"Really? Sorry, I repeat myself. Where was I? Oh, yeah, your sister. You were comparing yourself to her and putting yourself down. I've never seen her, so I can't speak to her being prettier than you, but you're pretty. You have those classic Mexican features: clear skin, almond eyes, broad forehead. Your eyebrows are awesome. You don't even need to pluck them."

"A boy said to me once that I was pretty in a quirky sort of way."

"Quirky? What the hell does that mean? It's like this guy I went out with once. He said to me: 'You're not beautiful, but you're attractive.' I looked at him and then waved good-bye with one finger." She waves at me the same way, an insane grin on her face. Then she said, "But getting back to your sister — what does she have that you wished you had?"

"Her energy, for one. She was into a hundred things at school: debate, yearbook, school musical, varsity soccer, school president, Young Republicans. I get tired just thinking about it."

"And naturally she's your father's favorite."

"Of course she is. Why wouldn't she be? What father wouldn't prefer a daughter like her?"

"I think I hear some anger there," Mona teases me.

So I don't care about Barbara's approval, but what about my father's? When he talks about Becca, his eyes light up with pride. When he looks at me, they dim with disappointment. But that's not his fault. It's mine. Isn't it?

"What you thinking?" Mona turns on her side. One of the magazines on the bed falls to the floor.

"Nothing. I was just thinking about your theory, about how mental illness makes people smart. You ever thought about psychiatry as a career?"

She doesn't hear me. She picks up the phone and punches in a number. "Busy. Well, at least he's around."

"Who were you calling?"

"Rudy."

"The guy at the cafeteria who likes you? He gave you that phone, didn't he?"

Mona chuckles. "Yeah, I guess you can say he likes me."

"Do you like *him*?"

"Like? I don't know if I would go that far. He's helping me with something, that's all."

"With what?"

She doesn't answer. She dials again, and this time I hear it ring. "Rudy?" Mona says. "What gives?" She knits her eyebrows and then opens her eyes wide. "No way!"

I jump down from the bed, grab clean underwear from the dresser Mona and I share, and then go into the bathroom to take a long shower. When I come out, Mona has stopped talking. She's standing by my bed, uncharacteristically looking out the window.

"Is everything all right?" I ask.

"Yeah," she answers absently.

I go and stand beside her. The parking lot lights flicker on even though there is still at least an hour left of daylight. "You don't have to tell me if you don't want to."

"All right. But this has to be our secret, okay? Rudy knows someone who works for some agency who claims he can find out where Lucy is."

"But —"

"Vicky, I got to get her back, I don't care how. If there's anything I can do to get her back, I will do it."

"Anything that you can *legally* do, right?"

She doesn't answer my question. She walks back to her bed and picks up the phone, then opens the top drawer of the dresser and drops the phone in. "Vicky," she says, closing the drawer with her behind, "thank you for thinking I'm smart."

"You're welcome," I say, embarrassed.

"That was nice, when you asked me if I ever thought about going into psychiatry. I know you were joking, but it was still nice."

"I wasn't joking. Not totally."

"When I was diagnosed as bipolar a couple of years ago, I went online and studied everything there was to know about depression, mania, schizophrenia, psychopaths. Oh, and I really dug deep on the grieving process. That's why I said that stuff about your mother at that GTH, remember? I had you diagnosed about ten seconds after I found out your mother died.

"You know how I knew? Because me too. I'm stuck grieving for Lucy, only it's much worse because I lost her on account of people's selfishness, including my own, and not on account of

God taking her like he did your mother. Sometimes I don't understand why I feel the way I do, so powerfully. Why am I still so angry and sad over Lucy? Maybe she's happy where she is. Maybe she's better off. Why can't I let it go?"

We are standing in the middle of our room, Mona with her back to the wall and me facing her. She's looking past me as if I weren't in front of her. She looks the saddest I've ever seen a person look, and what comes to my mind at this moment is that, without Lucy, there is nothing holding her on this earth. I don't know what to do. This is new territory for me. What do friends do when they finish confiding in each other? Do they give each other a hug?

Mona sighs and then heads to the bathroom. I hop up on my bed backward and look out at the parking lot. I think about the Harvard T-shirt that Becca sent me for my birthday. It came in a manila envelope. There was no card inside, only a yellow sticky note with *"Happy Birthday – Love, Becca."*

How strange that I was not disappointed or sad. Is that how depression works? You reach a point where there are no more disappointments or more sadness because every single thing is a disappointment and there's no more room anywhere for sadness? So I was sick. So I am sick. Is that it?

When Mona comes out of the bathroom, she stretches out on her bed and says, "There's one more thing I want to tell you, psychologically speaking, and then I'll shut up."

"Go ahead," I say.

"I'm telling you now because I think it will help you, not now maybe, but someday." She folds her pillow for better head support and then turns on her side to face me. "When Lucy was born and I decided to clean myself up, I went to this NA meeting, you know, Narcotics Anonymous. They have these twelve steps you're supposed to follow. One of them, the one that caused me the most trouble, was about not lying to yourself. The actual words were something like 'Make a complete and fearless moral inventory of yourself,' which I interpreted as 'Don't lie to yourself about how you really feel about things or people or yourself.'"

"You think I'm lying to myself?" A shiver of fear runs through me.

"If you're jealous of your sister or angry at your dad, if you think they're all jerks, so what? You can lie to others if you want — we all have to do that to stay alive — but don't lie to yourself about what you feel. So you're envious of your sister and resentful that your father doesn't look at you the same way. Those things are ugly, but we all have them. It's the uglies. Tell the truth about them is all I'm saying. You follow?"

"Yes," I manage to say. A painful knot grips my stomach. It scares me to think that I may be envious of Becca or angry at my father. Why does this make me afraid? I have no idea.

"But when you're not lying to yourself anymore and you got your inventory of the uglies pretty much complete, you can go on to the next step."

"The next step?"

"Yeah. That your sister and your father may, in fact, be jerks. Or at least act like jerks sometimes. You're not totally responsible for your uglies."

"That's one of the steps in NA?"

"No, that one I made up. Okay, that's it. Therapy's over." She finds the iPod's earbuds, sticks them in her ears, rolls onto her back, and closes her eyes. "Nighty night night," she says.

I lie awake, stunned by the thought that underneath all my sadness, there was anger and resentment and hurt I didn't even know about, the "uglies" Mona named. I see in Becca's face a mixture of fear and disgust when I tell her Mamá wants to see her, like she's afraid of catching Mamá's cancer. Doesn't she think that Mamá notices? I want to grab her and shake her and scream at her, "It's your mother and she needs you! Don't be such a coward!"

Don't lie to yourself, Mona says. Okay, I won't. For the longest time, I've felt like I'm better than my father and my sister. Because I feel things they apparently don't feel, because I see phoniness and self-interest where they see only the rules that everyone must follow to get ahead. How strange that feeling superior to everyone is so like what I imagine E.M. means by feeling sorry for yourself.

But that's not all that is there. I also want to be close to Becca, to have a sister who will understand me and not run away. I want my father to be proud of me like he is of her. I want this alongside all my uglies.

The uglies. It's hard to look at them.

I get up and try to open the window, even though I know it doesn't open.

Here I am, I say to no one in particular. *In all my ugly glory.*

CHAPTER NINE

Over the next two days, I felt again and again what it was like to live in our house. I remember how it felt to come home from school, open the front door, and get hit in the face with a cold, dark loneliness. I remember the leathery, dead smell of the untouched living room furniture, the soul-piercing hum of the air conditioner at three a.m. Living there is like going to a party where you don't know anyone and no one speaks to you and you don't know where to stand or sit. It would have been unbearable for me long before the deed if it weren't for Juanita and the refuge of her room.

We moved into the house a month or so after Father married Barbara, because it was awkward for Barbara to live in the same house where my mother had lived, to sleep in the same bed where my mother had slept. Plus, the new house had the advantage of having a room for "servants" a few steps from the back door of the kitchen, separate from the house, with its own entrance. In the old house, Juanita's room was upstairs next to my bedroom. Barbara didn't think that was appropriate.

My mother liked to paint, and our old house was decorated with paintings of roses she had done over the years. Only four of my mother's paintings survived Barbara's renovations, and those were kept out of the Salvation Army box only because of my stealth. Two of them are in my room and the other two are in Juanita's. I put my letter to Juanita on the back of one because I knew she would take the paintings in my room and save them. The abstract paintings in the living room, bought by Father and Barbara for "investment purposes," remind me of bleeding zebras — black-and-white-striped with dashes of dripping red. They are worse than incomprehensible. Their message is that they don't have to have a message. They leer at you for even trying to find meaning or beauty or, at the very least, some kind of pattern in them.

My house is how I know that sooner or later, I will try to kill myself again. Lakeview is a tiny island from which I see the sharks of suicide circling, waiting. I don't know what brought this gloominess about my future. But there in front of me stands the horrible truth that there is nothing about the life I will return to that I like. I carried on day after day telling myself that my life was not so bad — not so bad at all, when you thought about it. It was even good, in comparison to most lives. But that comparison doesn't help anymore. The truth is that I disliked my life and almost everyone in it. It's a feeling that goes way back, but now I have words for it. I can't lie to myself anymore. It only makes it worse.

Should I tell Dr. Desai about the uglies? Are the ugly truths we discover about ourselves like the messages that the elves of depression wheel to the forefront of my mind? How do you distinguish between an untrue message dictated by depression and a true one that comes from the bottom of your soul? There's no way to tell them apart without someone's help. Are there other truths in there besides the ugly ones? Truths that will help me live?

I think about all of this while waiting for my session with Dr. Desai. She's running a little late. Her desk is full of half-elephant, half-man figurines in different poses. Sometimes the figure is sitting down, his legs crossed like a Buddha, and sometimes he's dancing, his four arms and trunk dangling in the air. He has a good-size belly in all of them. I don't know how I can tell he's a man, but he is. I pick one up and study him.

"Lord Ganesh," a voice says behind me. I think I jump a little. I drop the figure. Gabriel stoops down, picks it up.

"What?" I ask, recovering.

"This little guy is Lord Ganesh." He holds out the elephant-man in the palm of his hand. "He's a Hindu god. More like a manifestation of God. The human part represents the part of God that we are able to see in the world and in others, and the elephant part is the unknowable part of God." He lowers Ganesh gently onto the desk and pats the elephant head with his index finger.

"What are you doing here?"

"Dr. Desai asked me to come to her office at eleven fifteen."

"She told me to be here at eleven."

"Ah," Gabriel says, thinking.

"What?"

"Maybe Dr. Desai wanted us to talk to each other."

I stare at him for a few seconds. "Or maybe she got her schedule mixed up."

"No." He reaches over and picks up another of the elephant-man figurines. "I don't believe in coincidences. Everything happens for a reason." He grins as he studies it for a moment, and then he places it in the exact spot where he found it. He continues grinning at it, forgetting completely that I'm sitting next to him, or so it seems.

"Well," I say, "what did Dr. Desai want us to talk about?"

"I don't know. Maybe we should analyze each other. I'll be Dr. Desai." He sits on the chair next to mine, leans back and crosses his hands over his stomach. "Now, Vicky, what was going through your mind just before I came in and scared you?"

I look at him hard. The way he asks, it seems as if he knows exactly what I was thinking, about how much I hate my father's house and how I'll try to kill myself again. I try to come up with some kind of joke, something funny, but instead I find myself saying, "I was thinking about how this place, Lakeview, how it's a little unreal."

"Mmm." He strokes his chin thoughtfully. "Yes, yes. That's absolutely true. But how does that make you *feel*?"

I laugh despite myself.

"No, really? Is that what you were thinking?" He sits up, stops acting.

"Kind of."

He turns his chair slightly toward me. On the right side of his sneakers, I notice a hole with grass stains around it. "Unreal, as in here it's not like it is out there? Here you're insulated somehow?"

"Yeah."

"Yeah," he says. "It's a little oasis in some ways."

That's the difference between Gabriel and me. He sees Lakeview as an oasis and I see it as an eroding island surrounded by sharks.

"On the other hand," he continues, "there's some harsh, painful realities you face here that you never have to look at out there."

"True," I agree, thinking of the uglies.

"Not to mention the fact that you meet more loony people here than you do out there."

"I'm not sure about that." I don't mean to be funny, but my words make Gabriel laugh.

Dr. Desai has a clock shaped like the Tower of London on one of the shelves behind her desk. It makes a grinding noise every fifteen seconds before the minute hand moves, as if forcing itself to keep time, to inch ahead one more minute even though you can tell the poor old thing has had it. Gabriel and I watch the clock in silence.

"I know what you're worried about," Gabriel says, still looking at the clock.

"I'm not really worried about it." It's true. Worry only comes when you're not sure if something bad will happen or not. When you know it's coming, there's no worry. I know I'm going to go home. I know I'm going to try again. Why worry?

"It could be that things will be different for you after Lakeview."

"No," I say quickly, decisively. "Everything and everyone will be exactly the same."

"But . . . *you* may be different."

"Maybe," I say. I'm already a little different. Calmer, more honest somehow. I catch myself laughing with Mona. But is that enough?

"Hey," Gabriel says suddenly. "Tell me something you like to do."

"Me?"

"Yes, you, Vicky. What do you like to do out there?"

"Out there?"

"Yeah. There must be something you enjoy doing."

That's a hard question. My mind goes totally blank. "I can't think of anything," I say. "That's pretty pathetic, isn't it?"

"No, it's not pathetic."

I focus inwardly for a few moments, searching, searching. "Swim," I finally answer. "I like to swim. We have a pool in our backyard, and I go swimming every afternoon. The pool is heated, so even when it's cold outside, I go in." I stop, wondering whether I sounded as if I was bragging about the heated pool in my backyard.

"What do you like about swimming?" he asks.

"I don't know. I never thought about it. It helps." I can see from his face that he's not satisfied with that. "The water clears my head. It wakes me up. I do a few laps and then I just float there on the surface without moving." *Like a dead person*, I almost say.

"That must be nice," he says. There's no envy or sarcasm in his voice. "I never learned how to swim."

"No?"

"There's a public pool not far from where we lived, my mother and I, before I moved in with my grandparents, but we never went. My mother was afraid of the water, and I think she passed the fear on to me."

"How long ago did you move in with your grandparents?"

"Two years ago."

"And your mother?"

He grabs a figurine of the elephant-man and closes his hand around it. "She died," he says, suddenly serious.

There's a moment of silence. It strikes me that I know more about closemouthed E.M. than I do about Gabriel. I don't even know why he's at Lakeview. Now and then, he shows glimpses that something is not quite right inside his head, but most of the time he seems as normal as anyone. "The other day, when I was delivering linens to the children's ward, I saw you planting rosebushes," I say. "You looked like you were talking to them."

He laughs. "I was wishing them well. Those kinds of roses don't usually like Austin."

"We used to have lots of American Beauties at our old home. They do okay if you water them frequently."

"You know roses?"

"My mother loved them. We used to plant them together. But I'm not an expert like she was. She knew all their names."

"Some of the names are crazy, aren't they? My favorite is Hot Cocoa. The petals actually are the color of hot cocoa."

"Have you ever heard of a rose called Miss Behavin'?" I ask.

"No," he says, laughing. "Have you heard of Rosie O'Donnell?"

"Betty Boop?" I counter.

"Hot Tamale?"

"No. You're making that up. There's no rose named Hot Tamale."

"Honest there is. My grandpa and I planted a yard full of them. That's all the guy wanted, Hot Tamales."

"Heaven Scent was my mother's favorite."

Gabriel's face brightens. "I'm planting Heaven Scents tomorrow. You should come by. You can help. Heaven Scents respond better to a woman's touch. It's kind of traumatic for them, you know, the trip they make from the growers to the nurseries until they're finally in the ground."

"Tomorrow?"

"Yeah. Next to the new Alzheimer's ward, the same place where you saw me before. Come after you finish in the laundry room."

"Okay," I say. "Maybe."

"I know something else you like," he says mysteriously.

"What?"

"You like to write."

"What?"

He keeps his eyes down on the floor as he speaks. "Yesterday, I went to the chapel. I like going there. It's the quietest place in the hospital. I saw you there writing. I sat in the back and looked at you for a while."

First I'm embarrassed, and then I get annoyed. The chapel is my secret hiding place. "I was just writing in that notebook that Dr. Desai gave us. Don't you write in it too? You shouldn't just sit there and look at a person when they don't even know you're there."

"Says the person who was spying on me while I talked to roses."

"I wasn't *spying*. I happened to look out the window. I like looking out windows."

"You were really into the writing. You were lost in it. You've done lots of writing before. I can tell."

"In school. Everybody has."

He smiles a knowing smile, and at that moment I have the strange feeling that he has somehow read every single one of my awful, self-absorbed poems. I look at Dr. Desai's clock. "I have to go meet Mona," I say suddenly, standing up. "I told her I'd meet her at the hospital's beauty shop. She wants to fix my hair."

"I like your hair. It's so . . . Vicky."

"Thanks." *Is that good or bad?* I wonder. "Mona wants to paint it green."

"Like your journal. Now that I think of it, Mona didn't tell us what personality trait green stood for."

"Bitter?" I say. "Envy? Immature? Not ripe? You know, as in green bananas."

"Mmm? No. Have you ever seen a green rose? They exist. They're very, very rare. I saw some once. They were in a garden surrounded by roses of all colors. The greens were hard to see at first, but once you saw them, they were the ones you looked for. So amazing. Green is such a common color. I always took it for granted until I saw that rose. Green stands for life, the kind that's all around us, that we don't notice."

We are quiet for a moment. Green, the color of life. I like that idea.

"Hey," he says suddenly. "My birthday is in three days. I'm trying to get Dr. Desai to let the four of us go to a birthday party at my house. Will you come?"

"I don't know," I say. "I should go find Mona."

Gabriel moves out of the way to let me through. "Vicky," he says.

"Yeah?"

"Swimming and roses and writing. That's three things."

I don't understand.

"To live for," he says.

CHAPTER
TEN

Mona and I walk to the cafeteria for a Coke after she's done with my hair. Somehow I managed to get out with the same color hair I had going in. "Not bad," Mona says of her efforts. "You look like one of those skinny models who starve themselves and wear airy dresses."

We have just gotten our drinks when a man who works in the cafeteria sits next to Mona. "Hey, Rudy," she says. He's one of those thirty-year-old men who tries to look eighteen: greasy ponytail, jeans two sizes too small, gold necklace. I've seen him before in the cafeteria and delivering the food trays to the fifth floor.

"Hello, Mona," Rudy says. "How goes it?"

"Oh, just dandy," Mona answers. "You know Vicky."

"Oh, yeah. I've had the pleasure." Rudy nods and I nod back. I get the feeling he wishes I weren't there. "Listen," he whispers to Mona, "wanna go to the patio and have a smoke?"

"I would, but it be rude to leave my friend here all by herself, wouldn't it?"

Rudy looks at me. "I don't mind," I say.

"She don't mind," Rudy repeats.

"You sure?" Mona asks. "I'll be right back."

"No, I'm sure."

"I can get you a free piece of pie to go with your Coke. We got some nice apple pie," Rudy says, halfway out of his chair.

"Thanks. I'm good," I say.

Mona grabs her Coke and winks at me. It's obvious that Rudy is interested in Mona, but it's hard to believe that she would be interested back. I have spent all of fifteen seconds in his vicinity and I already feel like taking a shower.

I sip my Coke and touch the back of my head. It feels different, smoother. No jagged peaks. I kept my eyes closed while Mona was trimming my hair, and when she was finished and asked me to look in the mirror, I refused. I haven't looked in a mirror for going on three weeks, ever since I cut my hair myself, and I'm not about to start. You would think it would be difficult to avoid looking at yourself in the hundreds of mirrors that are out there, but it isn't. After a while you don't even have to try too hard.

I can see Mona out the back door of the cafeteria. Rudy seems to be asking and pleading for something, and Mona seems to be coyly considering it. Then he says something that catches her full attention. She flicks her cigarette away and crosses her arms.

Gabriel said I was spying on him. Maybe I do like to spy on people, only I don't know if I'd call it spying. I watch people because I want to know what animates them, what makes them take life so seriously. What did Gabriel say? Green stands for life that is all around us, that we don't see.

I slurp the last drops of Coke from my glass. It's so hard to figure Gabriel out. Why is he in Lakeview? What was the name of the little elephant guy? Gilgamesh? How did Gabriel know that? I wish I had told him that I admired how comfortable he is with himself. I wish I could be that way. But I'm split. There's two of me. The person I carry around like a dead carcass inside of me and the one I show to others. This constant effort to be someone else, to pretend to be lively and give people the kind of person they're expecting, is not so bad here at Lakeview.

Thinking about Gabriel reminds me of Jaime, maybe because they're so different. Both my father and Becca mentioned him when they were listing possible reasons for my suicide attempt. It must have been Cecy or maybe Jaime himself who spread that rumor. Now that I've had time to reflect, I think maybe Jaime did influence that final decision, the tipping of *maybe* into *yes*, but not in the way people think.

Early in the fall semester, Mrs. Longoria, our English teacher, paired me with Jaime to discuss our reading assignments. I think it was the first time in my life that other girls have been jealous of me. Jaime was popular with boys because he was the school's star tennis player, and he was popular with girls because of his good looks and friendly personality. His family was also very rich, but that was not unusual at Reynard.

Cecy asked me if it made me nervous to be Jaime's partner, and I had to tell her that I didn't give it a second thought. Then Cecy proceeded to lecture me about how I was thumbing my nose at a gift the Fates had given me, which was dumb, as they had not been too kind to me so far.

"Ask him to your house to study. Meet him in the library. Do something to take advantage of this," she said. "Vicky, listen to me. You gotta go out and open the door to happiness when it knocks. Happiness is knocking, Vicky. You may not have another chance like this."

But I didn't take advantage of the situation like Cecy suggested. I expected Jaime to ignore me like everyone else did. By my sophomore year, I had gathered that the general impression of the student body was that I was allowed to stay in the school only because of my father's money and the memory of Becca, who was class valedictorian. So I had pretty much given up on any kind of friendliness from my Reynard classmates.

One time, Mrs. Longoria had us read "Tintern Abbey" by William Wordsworth. When we finished it, Jaime took his book and pointed to a phrase in the poem. He asked, "Have you ever felt that?"

"Felt what?" I asked.

"You know, a sense sublime."

I had to smile. At that point I would have been happy to feel the simple sense that I was alive. "Have you?"

He smiled back as if he was hoping I would ask. "This is going to sound very weird. But I felt something like that playing tennis."

"Really?" I didn't mean to laugh.

"No, I'm serious. Sometimes when I'm playing against a very good opponent and I'm really into every point, I get into a zone where every shot I hit is perfect, like I'm unbeatable and I kick ass. There's no other way of putting it."

"Mmm."

"You don't believe me."

"No. I find that interesting, actually. I mean, I'm pretty sure that Wordsworth was talking about nature, so, I don't know, I never thought you could feel those kinds of feelings in a tennis match."

"I thought you of all people would understand."

"Me?" I said.

"You think I would share something like this with just anybody?"

"Are you being serious?" I was suddenly nervous. All along I thought he had been playing a joke on me, maybe something one of my jealous classmates had put him up to.

"You write poetry," he said, looking straight at me.

I felt blood rush to my face or drain to my feet, I wasn't sure which. "Yes," I said tentatively, "sometimes."

"You've published poems in *The Quill*." He seemed either impressed or jealous.

"Yeah . . ." *The Quill* was Reynard's literary magazine. It came out twice a year, and it published only a few of the many poems, stories, and essays submitted by students. Getting two poems published my freshman year was my one and only accomplishment at Reynard.

Jaime opened his English book again and took out a folded piece of paper. "I found this on the floor underneath your chair last week. You must have dropped it. I opened it to see what it was. I'm sorry — I didn't mean to read it."

I glanced at the page, and my cheeks burned. I took the piece of paper and put it in my backpack.

"It's okay," he said. "It's not bad. A little on the gloomy side, but not bad."

That night, I received an email from him. The email said:

Hey Vicky, here's a poem I wrote. Let me know if you think this is Quill material. Good talking to you today.

I reached down and rubbed Galileo's neck. I read the poem once and then again, carefully. When I finished, I gently lifted Galileo from my legs and put him on the bed to the side. What could I say about the poem? *This is possibly one of the worst things I've ever read?* But who was I to judge? And maybe Cecy was right. When happiness knocked on your door, you had to accept it. I clicked on my mailbox, found Jaime's email, and clicked REPLY.

Dear Jaime,

Thank you for telling me about how you felt during your tennis game. I'm sorry I made fun of you. I was surprised by your comment. I like poetry. I'm not used to talking about it, but I will try. I liked the poem you sent me. I thought the image of unrequited love as a tennis racket with no strings was certainly unique. With a little tightening up, you could definitely submit it to The Quill.

Bye,
Vicky

The next day, Jaime was outside the building after school. He was sitting on a concrete bench with his backpack by his side.

"Hey, Vicky," he said, standing up when he saw me. "I was waiting for you."

"Me?"

"Yes, you."

"Why?"

"Number one, you didn't come to English class. Number two, I was wondering if I can give you a ride home."

"Me?" I was beginning to wonder whether I could speak in more than monosyllables.

"Come on, I need to talk to you." He grabbed my elbow and turned me away from my bus, in the direction of the parking lot. I was in a daze. By the time I recovered, he was opening the door of a car and I was stepping in. On the grass field next to the parking lot, two players from the girls' soccer team stared at us as if they could not believe their eyes. I waved at them. I meant it as a friendly gesture, but I'm not sure they took it that way.

Jaime got in the car and turned on the ignition. The motor was loud, and I noticed for the first time that I was sitting low to the ground.

"Do you like it?" Jaime asked. He made the motor rev louder.

"It's a sports car," I said. *Brilliant, Vicky.*

"Not just any sports car. A Porsche." He put the car in reverse and drove slowly out of the parking lot. I was aware of the soccer girls' eyes following us. "It's my father's, but I think

I'm going to inherit it for graduation. It'll be a nice car to have at Texas A&M."

I told myself to act normal. I could pretend that being in a car with a boy was something I did all the time, couldn't I? I mean, how hard could it be? But nothing that I said to myself worked. I was getting more and more nervous as we drove. One uncomfortable long block went by before it occurred to me to ask, "Is that where you're going to college?"

"Texas A&M? Yup."

"Isn't that like a science and engineering kind of school?"

"That's what I want to study. Civil engineering."

"You need to take a right at the next street," I told him.

"Do you have time? I want to show you something." He slowed down at my intersection and turned left instead.

"What?"

"You'll see," he said mysteriously.

"Where are we going?" I asked, trying not to sound concerned.

"It's a surprise." He winked. The road we were on was lined with driveways that led to the mega mansions overlooking the Colorado River.

We turned into a gravel parking lot barely big enough for two or three cars. The edge of the lot bordered a hill that was completely covered with trees and prickly foliage. Jaime reached into the small space behind his seat and pulled out a canvas shoulder bag.

"Come on," he said, opening his door.

"Where?" I was scared.

"Trust me," he replied, "you won't regret this."

I stepped out of the car and closed the door as gently as I could. Jaime locked the doors and waited for me. We walked side by side through the parking lot to a path. As we got closer, I could see that the path ascended rapidly up the hill. I hesitated.

"What's the matter?"

"I'm not exactly dressed for hiking," I said. I was wearing a skirt and sandals.

"It's not hiking," he said. "It's an easy path. We'll go slow. I'll help you."

I still did not move. It was one of those moments when you feel that a decision needs to be made. Up to that point I had been carried along, floating in the newness of it all. While we were in the car, I could believe that Jaime was just interested in me for my poetry expertise, but there at the entrance to the trail, I was paralyzed by the thought that maybe he was interested in me the way a boy is interested in a girl. There was no way that Jaime could be interested in me that way. He could have and probably did have any girl he wanted. It was simply an impossibility that he would pick me.

"You all right?"

"Sorry," I said. "Sometimes I think too much."

"Come on," he said, "the view is sublime up there. It'll remind you of Wordsworth."

He waited, but I was frozen in place. Finally, he walked over to me and took hold of my left hand. I felt the warmth travel through my body, and when he tugged my arm gently, as if awakening me, I yielded to him. We moved slowly and carefully up the dirt path, holding hands. Every once in a while he would stop to let me catch my breath, but we didn't speak. I tried to determine whether he was holding my hand like a friend or a brother or maybe a reading partner, but his touch didn't feel like any of those things. There was something urgent and demanding in it, like a question that won't go away until you answer it.

When we got to the top, I let go of his hand and walked by myself to an observation deck. A chest-high stone wall separated observers from the steep embankment. I stood silent and amazed. The dark-green river coiled for miles below us. To the right you could see the Austin skyline with its handful of skyscrapers and the University of Texas clock tower. To the left, hills and houses and open spaces stretched all the way to Oklahoma, it seemed. A small breeze blew a strand of hair over my face and I tucked it behind my ear.

Jaime came and stood next to me. He put his arm around my shoulder and whispered, "'And I have felt a presence that disturbs me with the joy of elevated thoughts, a sense sublime of something far more deeply interfused, whose dwelling is the light of setting suns. . . .'" I recognized the words from "Tintern Abbey." Then he stopped and turned me toward him, and I had one brief moment of panic before he kissed me.

It was my first kiss from a boy ever, and I wish I could say that my legs went rubbery and my heart beat like a wild drum and everything else that is written about kisses. The truth is that in the four or five seconds that the kiss lasted, first I wondered if I was doing it right, and then I wondered if I was easy for letting him kiss me just like that, and then I felt like crying.

I turned away from him and opened my eyes wide so I wouldn't blink. It was a trick I had learned: If you don't blink, the tears don't come. I stared in the direction of Oklahoma until I felt safe, and then turned back to him and said, "What was that for?"

"I wanted to do that ever since Mrs. Longoria put us together."

"Why?" I stared at him.

"Well, actually that's not quite true. I made up my mind to kiss you ever since I read your poem."

"You made up your mind to kiss me?"

"Well, I made up my mind to get to know you . . . and then kiss you. I don't know anyone like you."

"What's so different about me?" I wasn't fishing for a compliment. I wanted to know.

"You're pretty in a quirky kind of way. You think about things. There's a seriousness about you. You don't care about the things that other girls care about. You don't care what people think, you're just you. You're special."

"I'm really not who you think I am," I said.

"Who are you, then?"

I'm someone who's sad all the time. I don't care about school or grades or college. I'm at Reynard as a fluke. I have no ambition. I don't like to do anything. I don't want to do anything with my life. I'm afraid of each day and the nights are even worse.

But I didn't say any of this. Instead, I said, "I don't have the slightest idea."

Jaime thought I was trying to be funny. "Hey," he said, "come here. I want to show you something." He grabbed my hand again and pulled me toward a flat rock big enough for both of us to sit on. He opened his canvas bag and took out a yellow spiral notebook. He cleared his throat, holding the notebook with both hands. "I've been writing poems for a couple of months now. I want you to read them. Let me know what you think. Maybe I can send a couple to *The Quill*."

"Now?" I know it was rude, but I didn't know what else to say. Maybe it was wrong to feel that way, but I felt put-upon, like I was being used somehow.

A flicker of hurt crossed his face. "There's only ten of them," he said.

I turned to the first page and read in silence. The title of the poem was "A Hollow Good Bye." I paused when I got to the end. Then I turned the page and went on to read all of them. Jaime watched me carefully, and I felt like I needed to nod appreciatively now and then and make tiny sounds of admiration.

As I read, I wondered what I was going to say to him. I didn't think I was qualified to make pronouncements on the quality of the poems. I never for one second thought the stuff I wrote was any good. I wrote because writing helped me. When

I wrote, the hollowness inside was filled for a few moments with memories and images, not all of them happy, but at least there was something living in me . . . again, when I wrote. I wrote because writing kept me alive.

When I finished reading the last poem, I went back to the first one and started again. It was hard to concentrate with Jaime sitting next to me expectantly, and this time around I thought I would try to feel the emotion conveyed by the poems. *All poetry that is honestly written is good,* I remember reading someplace. But there was something about Jaime's poetry that didn't seem honest. It was as if he were writing for someone he wanted to impress. He was trying too hard to be seen as a poet. There were images and metaphors where there needn't be any, where he could have said what he felt in a simpler way. But then I also thought that maybe his style was just different from the one I would have chosen to say what he was trying to say. Who was I to judge? He had made an effort to express himself and that was good, and I should not say anything to discourage him.

"These are good," I said.

"Good? Just good?"

"Some of them may need polishing, but I think they're a good start."

Jaime turned to me and looked into my eyes. "Vicky . . ."

I stood up. I did it slowly and I tried very hard not to seem like I was afraid of what he was going to say or of another kiss. "I should be getting home," I said, straightening my skirt.

"Sure," he said, standing up as well. "Here." He offered me the notebook. I shook my head, unsure why he was giving it to me. "Do me a favor. You said they needed polishing. Maybe you could read them over again and make any suggestions that might improve them. Then tell me if there are any you think might be good for *The Quill*. I'd kind of like to submit two."

"Okay," I said. *Is this what you do to be happy?* I wondered. *Say you will do things you don't want to do?*

We walked down the hill, and this time I walked in front so he couldn't hold my hand. When we were in the car, he moved closer to me and I watched Jaime's kiss come as in slow motion. I didn't move my lips or close my eyes as he kissed me. It was like drinking water out of a straw when your mouth is shot full with novocaine. You see the water in the glass go down, so you figure you must be drinking, but you can't feel anything.

"Vicky," he said when he pulled away from me, "I know it may seem like we're going too fast, but I'm real sure about you."

Tears filled my eyes again and I shut them tight to keep them from flowing out, and when I did I saw the image of Mamá right before she died. Her face was so thin and her skin so tight she looked like a skeleton. Of course this memory made the tears flow even more. I don't think Jaime saw them, but he must have tasted them as he moved closer to me and kissed my lips, my cheeks, my eyes. I've often wondered what he thought as he kissed me more and more urgently.

Would I have tried to kill myself a few weeks later if I had lied to him and told him that I liked him too, if I had kissed him back even though I didn't want to? All I had to do was pretend.

He was offering me a hand to climb out of the pit. And after all, was it so bad to be wanted? And was it so terribly bad to be kissed? All I knew was that if I let him kiss me, if I let him believe that I liked him, if I pretended I was happy with him, because of him, I would lose the only precious thing I had left.

"We should go," I said.

"What's the matter with you? Vicky, I really like you. I don't say that too often. In fact, I've only said that to one other person ever." He began to kiss me again.

"Jaime, stop, please."

He stopped. It was the tone of my voice. He pulled away from me.

"Why?"

I wiped my eyes. "I'm sorry. I just don't like you."

He chuckled. "Wow. That's a first."

"It's not you. I don't like anything right now. I don't even like myself. I ran out of like. I'm plumb out of like."

He grinned and shrugged as if to let me know that it was more my loss than his. He started the car, and we drove back slowly and in silence. There was no anger in his face or in the way he drove. He looked straight ahead and I felt immensely sorry for him, for me, and for every living creature.

As we neared my house, I began to feel the strength that comes when you don't care about anything anymore. I was strangely calm. I knew what I wanted to do. Not that night. But soon. Very soon. Happiness had knocked on my door, and I opened it long enough to see that I didn't want what was being offered.

Here in the Lakeview cafeteria, I can see Jaime more clearly. I've been afraid to think about him before. But remembering wasn't as painful as I expected. I'm still glad I did not become the girlfriend of someone I didn't like, but now when I think of him, I feel a tenderness toward him. He's like a spoiled child — not totally at fault for the way he is.

And what about Vicky? I imagine Dr. Desai asking me. *Do you feel a tenderness toward her because, after all, she's not totally at fault for the way she is?*

Let me ponder that one a little longer, I respond.

"Men," says Mona, startling me. "They are so predictable." She pulls out a chair and slouches in it.

"Are they?" I make a mental effort to come back to the present.

She looks over her shoulder at Rudy, who has donned a little blue paper hat and is behind the counter serving meat loaf. "He says he's in love with me. Wants to marry me. He's known me all of three weeks."

"And how do you feel about him?" I ask.

She gives me one of those *Don't ask stupid questions* looks and then says, "Although, he said something today . . ."

"What? Is this about Lucy? You're not planning to do something crazy with Rudy about Lucy?"

She doesn't answer my question. "Vicky, if life offered you a chance to be happy and it involved doing something that was considered wrong by others, but not by you, would you do it?"

"Mona . . ." I want to tell her I'm the last person she should ask about happiness, but she speaks before I can say anything.

"Maybe he does really love me. Crazier things have happened."

"Be careful," I say.

"Yeah, yeah," Mona says. But her mind is somewhere else. Clicking.

CHAPTER ELEVEN

The following evening, I'm sitting next to E.M. and Gabriel in the fifth-floor dining room when Mona comes in waving two cafeteria vouchers. Now and then we can get vouchers to eat on the first floor, where there are more kinds of food to choose from.

"I can't," I say.

"Oh, come on!"

"Stay with us," Gabriel says to Mona.

"But they have chicken pot pies tonight. My favorite. Come on, Vicky. Rudy's working there. I don't want to be alone."

"That guy's bad news," E.M. says. "All he wants is your body."

"You're my father now? For your information, he wants to marry me. And if he's after my body, can you blame the poor guy?" Mona strikes a pose with one hand on her hip and the other behind her head. "How do you know he's bad news? You don't even know him."

"I know," E.M. says.

"Vicky?" Mona pleads.

"Take Gabriel or E.M. They'll help with Rudy."

Mona looks at E.M., considers briefly, and then says to Gabriel, "Will you come with me?"

"Don't you think someone ugly and mean would work better?" Gabriel points at E.M.

"I ain't going," E.M. says, swallowing.

"Yeah, you're right," Gabriel says. "Rudy's tough. I better go. I don't think you can handle him."

"Don't play those psycho tricks on me," E.M. says.

"Go with her," Gabriel tells E.M. "Don't you want to have a little fun? How long has it been since you scared anybody?"

"Yeah?" E.M. says, suddenly intrigued.

"Okay," says Mona. "But you just sit there and don't give me any of your Aztec warrior stuff. No *You're weak*. No nothing. We don't talk or we keep it light, just like we do when we eat here. And don't scare the guy so much that he stays away permanently. It's always good to have an extra guy or two who wants to marry you."

"I guess," he says, pushing his tray away and standing.

"Be back soon," Mona says, fingers wiggling.

When they're out of the room, Gabriel begins to cut his Salisbury steak into little pieces. My mother liked to do the same to her food before she ate it, I remember. "What?" he asks.

"Nothing," I say. "It's hard to cut meat with plastic knives." I stir my mashed potatoes with my fork. When I look up, I follow Gabriel's gaze to Gwendolyn, who's wearing the same lavender terry-cloth bathrobe she wears every day and sitting at the other end of the table. She folds her hands, closes her eyes, and prays. Gabriel stops cutting his meat to watch her. He sighs and then pushes his tray away.

"Not hungry?" I say.

He shakes his head.

"Think the Heaven Scents will make it?" That afternoon, after I finished in the laundry room, I helped Gabriel plant roses.

"I hope so. Sorry about your hands. You should have used my gloves."

I touch the places on my right hand where thorns pricked them. "You know what I've always wondered?"

"What?"

"Why do roses have thorns? Everything in nature's supposed to have a purpose, right? But what purpose do thorns serve? They don't scare away pests or birds or attract bees to pollinate. Do you know?"

"They're not really thorns," Gabriel says, staring at his food. The energy he had earlier today in the rose garden has disappeared. "They're more like sickles — little hooks. My grandpa says that when roses first came into the world, other plants were jealous of their beauty, so they crowded around and smothered them so no one could see them. That's when roses grew these little hooks that would help them climb up above the other plants, because beauty like theirs needed to be seen." He rubs his temples. He seems to be in pain.

"Are you all right?"

"I'm sorry," he says, his voice softer, apologetic. "I'm not having a good day. Sometimes . . . it's like . . . my head is like a radio when you're driving in the middle of nowhere and you're trying to find a station. You hear a few words of a song now and then, and lots of static."

"You never talk about . . . why you're here," I say tentatively.

"It's not easy for me to talk about it. It's hard for people to understand. I feel like I'm burdening them."

"That's what the group meetings are for, aren't they? Mutual burdening."

"You're right." He smiles for the first time that evening. "I'll tell you someday. If you ask me again, I'll tell you. Not today, though. Not here." He glances at Gwendolyn in the purple robe.

"I gave you my whole life," she says to nobody — at least nobody we can see. She speaks loud enough for the whole room to hear. "What about me? It's my turn! Don't I count for anything? What am I? Chopped liver?"

Gabriel sighs again. I try to open the foil on my pudding cup, but my finger is tender from a thorn. He takes the container from my hand and opens it. "Thanks," I say.

"You're very welcome."

I dip my spoon into the runny chocolate pudding. "Mona says that mentals have a kind of intelligence that non-mentals don't have. That the stuff that happens in our heads gives us an ability to see what non-mentals can't or won't."

"I think Mona's onto something there."

"So whatever is happening to you, I'm pretty sure us other mentals would understand."

Gabriel furrows his eyebrows and studies me. "You think you're mental?"

"Not wanting to live is an illness. Isn't that what you said?"

"Sometimes it is. So you believe you're ill?"

"Depression." I say the word out loud. I'm still not used to how it sounds as applied to me. "I don't know. It's something I've been thinking about and talking about with Dr. Desai. It's hard to accept that depression is an illness, that moping around from day to day with no will for so many years is not my fault. It feels like it's my fault. Isn't it your fault when you have all you want and need and much more than ninety-nine percent of the world has, and you still feel miserable?"

Why am I talking so much? It's Gabriel. He's worse than Dr. Desai in the way he listens. It's like you don't want to disappoint that kind of attentiveness. I go on. "So do I believe I have depression? Even if I did, I don't think it absolves me from not wanting to live. Not caring about anything is a weakness. I'm with E.M. there."

"You really, really don't care about anything?"

"If I did, would I have tried to kill myself?"

Gabriel shakes his head. "You're so hard on yourself."

We are both silent. Am I hard on myself? I notice then that I'm not as hard on myself now as I was before Lakeview. The thought of killing myself now comes only at night. It's as if the pointed corners of a square are being slowly rounded off and I'm becoming more of a circle. All the sharing and talking has dulled the sharp edges. Then I say, "We were talking about you, not me."

He takes a deep breath. "Whenever I talk to people about the way that I may be mental, I lose them. You know how many friends I had when I was going to school? Zero."

"Unlike the rest of us, who had tons."

My sarcasm goes unnoticed. Gabriel continues, "But it wasn't just that I had no friends. I couldn't have normal interactions without at some point scaring whoever I was with. The way I am mental affects people. There's a — I don't know what the right word is, a *seriousness* to what I say — a corniness, even — that drags people down. People would hear me philosophizing about roses or going on about the Beatitudes, or I couldn't help giving them some kind of psychological advice, and I'd lose them."

"So you think you'll lose Mona and E.M. and me if you tell us how you're mental?" I say. "We've seen your heaviness and your corniness, as you call it, and we've heard you give us psychological advice and impress us with all you know, and you haven't lost any one of us. Not even E.M."

"I upset you," he says. "I'm sorry. You see? I do that to people."

I give up on trying to control my irritation. "I don't think it's fair that you don't trust us — trust the group. We've all made ourselves vulnerable in there. You just sit there and analyze us and tell us that we're ill." I'm suddenly angry at Gabriel and I feel like hurting him, almost, and it feels good and terrible at the same time. "You should trust us. Lots of times in the GTH, you encourage me to speak. Why do you think you're so special?"

He lowers his eyes, and I wait. I'm surprised at the words that came out of my mouth. For someone who doesn't care about anything, it sure sounded like I cared about Gabriel just then.

When he looks up, his eyes are moist. "You're right," he says. "All my life, for as long as I can remember, I've had this feeling that I'm special somehow. Because I . . . notice things that no one else does. Because I see divine messages and symbols everywhere. Because I'm so-called spiritual, or I try to be holy, or because I believe I'm called to do something meaningful with my life. I've tried to get rid of this sense of being different — special. I haven't been able to. It's just there."

"Maybe you are special," I say. "You're just not better."

He looks at me for the longest time. I do my best to keep my eyes fixed on his, but in the end I look away. Gwendolyn has quieted down. She's tapping the fingers of her hands on the table, playing a soulful piano concerto. Her demons are giving her a rest.

Finally, Gabriel speaks. "That's good, Vicky. That's good. I'll talk to the group. Thank you. You helped me today."

There's another little silence as I let Gabriel's words sink in. "I helped you?"

"Yeah. You did." He smiles.

I helped another person. Me. My words gave someone something they didn't have before. I feel lighter somehow, as if gravity has lost a bit of its grip on me.

"Hey," he says, making an effort to brighten up, "Dr. Desai said we could go to my grandparents' the day after tomorrow for my birthday dinner. My grandpa is picking us up. You're coming, right? Mona and E.M. are on board."

"I don't know. I'm not very good at parties."

"It's not really a party. Just the four of us, some good Mexican food. Cake. It'll be good. You'll get to meet my grandpa, my grandma. Please come."

"Okay," I say.

Gabriel stands when I stand. "I'll see you tomorrow," he says.

I walk out of the room and hold the door open for Gabriel, but he's not behind me. He stopped by Gwendolyn and is pulling out the chair next to her. He sits very straight and closes his eyes in concentration. He locks the fingers of his hands and stretches them until I hear a crack. With his hands poised over an imaginary keyboard, he waits until he has her attention. She looks at him and slowly imitates him. She sits as straight as she can and lifts her hands parallel to Gabriel's. Then on the count of three, Gabriel begins pounding the imaginary piano, playing what must be a happy upbeat melody, and soon Gwendolyn joins him and they are both bobbing up and down and tapping their feet and swinging left and right and making silly joyful faces.

I stand there watching them along with everyone in the dining room for the two minutes their silent performance lasts. When they stop, we break into thunderous applause, and Gabriel helps the beaming Gwendolyn to her feet. They take a bow.

chapter TWELVE

A sidewalk circles Lakeview Hospital. If you walk it slowly, the way Dr. Desai and I are walking now, you can end up back at the entrance in about fifteen minutes. On our second lap, the clouds part, and we look up to see a patch of pale-blue sky. Today, Dr. Desai is wearing a turquoise sari, and it feels at times as if I'm walking next to a pulsating source of warm light.

Mona says that talking heals, but at times like this, I think that just being next to someone who likes you is all anybody ever needs. Still, the peace radiating from Dr. Desai is not enough to calm my mind. My father is coming to pick me up in four days, and my head is churning with thoughts and questions about what will happen then. After a while I say, "I don't understand how this is supposed to work. How's it going to be different when I go back home? What am I supposed to be getting out of these talks with you or with the group?"

Dr. Desai stops for a moment as if to consider what I have just said and then continues walking. When I see that she isn't going to respond, at least not immediately, I say: "And there are things that don't make any sense to me. Like what you said about pretending, that we all need to pretend to survive. But that's all I've been doing, and it's what I will have to do when I go back home. Pretend to be nice when I feel mean, pretend I like school when I hate it, answer politely when I feel like telling people to go to hell. 'Hi, how's it going? I'm fine, thank you,' when what I want to say is 'I feel like crap.'" I breathe deeply. Why am I so agitated? This is crazy. Now I'm angry at Dr. Desai.

"Go on," Dr. Desai says. We move to the side to let an old man in a wheelchair go past us.

I hesitate and then I let it all out. "If all I'm supposed to learn here is that pretending is okay in some cases, then this is not going to work. Sooner or later I'll . . . I'll be sick of myself." I let Dr. Desai guide me by the arm to a concrete bench on the side of the track. From somewhere in her sari, she takes out a white hanky, and I press it against one eye and then the other. "Sorry. I don't know where all this is coming from," I say, sniffling.

"Is there more you want to tell me?" Dr. Desai asks.

I shrug and shake my head. It feels like my chest is full of feelings that want to latch on to words, but the words aren't coming.

Dr. Desai sighs. "My goodness, Vicky, I don't know if I have the answer to all your questions. There is so much there. Let me see. How does this work? How will it be different when you get back home? What are you supposed to be getting out of the private sessions and the group talks? And pretending. When is it okay and when not? Ooof. You want to make me earn my paycheck today, I see." She is smiling now, her hands folded on her lap. I catch myself twisting her hanky and begin to fold it neatly. What does a person do with a used and borrowed hanky?

"Just now when you were asking me all those questions, you reminded me of when I was a child growing up in a small village in India. There was an old man who lived outside our village. We children called him Mr. Karamachi, although I doubt that was his real name. Mr. Karamachi owned an equally old elephant named Lady Chatterley — don't ask me how she got that name. Mr. Karamachi made his living by renting out Lady Chatterley for wedding processions or to pull a big fallen tree from the forest or to give rides to tourists. I think you reminded me of him just now because I used to pepper Mr. Karamachi with all kinds of questions, and he would grab his head with both hands and say, 'Such big questions, such little brain.' "

Dr. Desai grabs her head and makes a funny face. I laugh first and then she does as well. I feel a raindrop land on my arm. We both look up at the gray clouds. Dr. Desai and I stand and begin to walk toward the entrance of the hospital. After a few steps, she speaks again, so softly I have to lean closer to hear.

"Besides renting out Lady Chatterley, Mr. Karamachi would also go into the jungle and catch small monkeys, which he would then take to Bombay and sell to a man who would send the monkeys to different zoos around the world. We children were fascinated by how he would catch these monkeys. He took a small cage made out of bamboo and put a peeled mango inside it. The bars of the cage were far enough apart to let the monkey stick his hand in sideways, but close enough together to prevent the monkey from removing his hand once he grabbed on to the peeled mango. This cage with the mango, Mr. Karamachi would tie to a tree, and sure enough, now and then, he would come home with a captured monkey.

"I could not believe the monkey could be so stupid. 'But why doesn't the monkey just drop the mango and run when he sees you coming?' I would ask Mr. Karamachi. He would grab his head and say 'Such big questions, such little brain.'"

We are at the entrance to the hospital, where a group of noisy would-be walkers is trying to decide whether it will rain on them. Dr. Desai turns one of her palms up to feel for raindrops. I do the same. "Do you think we can make it around the track one more time before it pours?" she asks.

I nod and we start to walk in the direction we had come. It strikes me that everyone always walks or wheels around the track in the same direction.

"So," Dr. Desai says, once we are away from the noise, "how does this work, you ask?" We are moving slowly, but she slows down even more so that we are barely walking. I see her face flush with concentration, making sure she finds the right words for what she wants to say. "In some form or another, all mental illness consists of our inability or unwillingness to let go of a mental mango that is hurting us. The mango can be an idea, such as the paranoid's belief that people are following him, or it could be an image we have of ourselves, such as 'I'm a bad person for pretending to like school when I really don't.' The mango is a view of reality that is not true, a story about ourselves or about our world that causes us pain and keeps us from being open to life as it is." She pauses. "I suppose what we are trying to do here, in our talks alone and with the group, is to create a safe space where we can reflect on the stories we hold on to in pain . . . so we can let go of them. And of course some people are holding on to more than one mango."

I say, "My mango is thinking that I'm a big, bad phony because I don't like hardly anything or anybody in my life and I have to pretend that I do."

Dr. Desai smiles. "Maybe *pretending* is not the right word. When you are kind to someone, even though you don't feel like being kind, you are choosing what kind of person you want to be in that particular circumstance. Your kind side and your yucky side are both parts of you. Are you being a phony when you choose to override the part of you that wants to be mean and you decide to be kind? It's a sort of pretending, I suppose, but it's a good kind. I think the efforts you made to carry on with your life despite the depression that was bogging you down were good, brave efforts. You were choosing life when everything inside of you wanted you to choose death."

"Until one day I grabbed the mango of death and didn't let go." I laugh a nervous kind of laugh.

Dr. Desai grabs me gently by the shoulders and peers intently into my very soul, it seems. She looks at the darkening sky and then speaks with a quiet urgency I've never heard her use before. "Thoughts are clouds, Vicky. They are not you. The cloud of wanting to die appears, and if you don't grab it, it will eventually float away. The cloud that says 'I'm lazy and a coward and a phony to boot' floats before you, and you can calmly watch it come and go. You are not the clouds or even the blue sky where clouds live. You are the sun behind them, giving light to all, and the sun is made up of goodness and kindness and life."

Then she lets go of me. A drop of rain lands on my head, and when I look up, another falls on my lips. Then all the water in the heavens seems to fall on us all at once.

But that's all right. The sun is still there.

THIRTEEN

The next day, even E.M. seems excited by the prospect of dinner at Gabriel's. Hospital food is therapeutic that way. The more you eat it, the more you want to get well and find someplace else to eat.

Mona fretted all morning about what to wear. Finally, she went to the lost-and-found room and picked out a pair of lime-green pants and a bright-yellow T-shirt. "How do I look?" she asked me.

"You glow," I told her.

"That's the idea," she said.

Gabriel's grandfather is waiting for us in the familiar parking lot below my window. He's a tall, strong-looking man with eyes that crinkle at the edges, as if he were always smiling. He takes off his straw hat and hugs Gabriel for the longest time. Then he shakes each of our hands, bowing slightly as he does so, and tells us to call him Antonio. He's driving a blue truck that has clearly worked hard for many, many years. Mona climbs into the front seat and scoots to the middle so I can sit by the window, but I tell her I will ride in the back with Gabriel and E.M. It's hot, but it feels good to be outside.

The three of us sit with our backs against the cabin, me in the middle. I am tired from a night with little sleep and my mind is . . . tender. I guess that's the best word for it. Still, I decide to make an effort to be social. "How does it feel to be seventeen?" I ask Gabriel at a stoplight.

"So far about the same," he responds.

"Birthdays suck," E.M. says. He has his eyes closed and his face tilted up like a sunbather.

Gabriel and I look at each other and smile. What else would E.M. say?

"When is *your* birthday?" Gabriel asks me. The truck jerks forward and our heads bump against the back of the cabin.

"Is Mona driving?" E.M. says.

"It's the transmission," Gabriel explains. "It's not long for this world."

"Like you," E.M. says, elbowing me. I turn to see if he's smiling, but he isn't.

"Don't listen to him," Gabriel says. "They just let him out of a psychiatric ward. So you were saying, about your birthday."

"January fifteenth."

"That's a good day to be born. Did you do anything?"

"Cecy, my best friend — well, she used to be my best friend. She came over and had dinner with me. Juanita made me enchiladas. She baked a cake."

"Just you and Cecy and Juanita? And your parents?"

"My father and Barbara were on a business trip." It occurs to me for the first time that it was kind of crummy of them to not be there for my birthday. Yes, Mona, my father and Barbara can be jerks sometimes.

"You got sad all of a sudden," he says. "Why?"

"Sorry. I was just thinking about my family. . . . I'll try to be happy. It's your birthday."

"Forget about trying to be happy," E.M. says. "You can't control being happy. Try to be brave. You can control that."

"Out of the mouth of babes and psychopaths," Gabriel says, laughing.

"I heard that," E.M. says.

"What do you know about happiness?" Gabriel teases him.

"All I know, I learned from Huitzilopochtli." E.M.'s eyes are still closed.

"Wee-chee . . . what?" I ask.

"Oh, oh," Gabriel moans, "now you've done it. You'll never get him to stop talking about Huichi."

"Huitzilopochtli," E. M. says. He pronounces it *wee-chee-lo-posh-tlee.* "Alls I've been telling you about being strong, about not feeling sorry for yourself — all that comes from Huichi. Huitzilopochtli was the Aztec god of war. He protected warriors in battle and gave them strength and courage. He fights the night each day so it doesn't stay dark forever."

That sounds familiar, I think. *Except that Huichi appears to have more success than I did.* "So what do you have to do to get strength and courage?" I ask.

Gabriel is about to say something, but E.M. says, "Shh. No more talking. Just act brave even if you're scared. Pretend you're courageous even if you're a coward. That's all you need to know about Huitzilopochtli right now." Then he shuts his eyes and crosses his arms.

"It works for me," Gabriel says, smiling.

The truck goes up a ramp to a highway. Clouds of white exhaust spew out of the tailpipe, and I can see people shake their heads as they pass us. I imagine Barbara driving by in her baby-blue Mercedes and seeing me in the back of the ailing truck between E.M. and Gabriel. The thought makes me smile.

We get off the highway in an area of Austin that I never knew existed. There are restaurants called Tito's and MexDonald's, and a store advertises *BUENA ROPA USADA*. A gas station's roof blinks with red, white, and blue Christmas lights. We turn off the main avenue into a street with small wooden houses. Most of the houses have a front yard and a porch and look like they could use a paint job.

Gabriel's house is a small one-story white cottage with dark-blue trim. It's one of a dozen similar houses on the street, but it is by far the best maintained and the most colorful. White and purple flowers line the brick path from the street to the front porch, and a tall, bushy tree occupies one side of the yard. The grass is dark green and lush and neatly trimmed. We jump out of the back of the truck and wait for Mona and Gabriel's grandfather.

"Dude, this looks like a fairy tale," Mona says to Gabriel as we walk up to the front door.

"Grandpa here works hard to keep it looking good." Gabriel touches his grandfather's back.

Antonio opens the screen door and we enter. Maybe it's the smell of mole, or maybe it's the light that fills the room, or maybe it's the old but comfortable-looking sofa, but as soon as I step in,

I feel as if I have entered a space that is very safe and welcoming. Mona sighs, and E.M. takes a deep breath. I wish I lived in a place like this and I can tell that Mona and E.M. do as well. Then I remember that in two days I will be going home to a place nothing like this, and the air and light leak right out of me.

"I'll get Grandma," Gabriel says, disappearing down a hallway.

"I'll get the lemonade," Antonio says.

"You got anything stronger?" Mona asks.

"Coffee!" Antonio shouts from the kitchen.

E.M. plops himself down on the sofa. Mona picks up a picture from an end table and smiles. "Look," she says. It's a picture of Gabriel, six or seven years old, holding the hand of a young woman. "Must be where Gabriel gets his looks."

I walk over and take the picture from Mona. There is no doubt that the woman holding Gabriel's hand is his mother. She's beautiful, and Mona is right, there is a strong resemblance to Gabriel. I study Gabriel's picture for a few moments. His ample forehead and deep-set eyes, his thin nose, the curve of his lips, they all fit together. Gabriel hasn't changed all that much. His eyes are somehow deeper and sadder, but the beauty of the little boy's face in the picture is still there. I place the picture gently on the table.

Mona looks around the room. "I haven't seen one of those in ages." She walks to the record player and begins to sift through the albums neatly ordered on a shelf above it.

"Why don't you put something on?" Antonio is carrying a tray with a pitcher of lemonade and glasses.

"You sure you can work that?" E.M. says to Mona, who is fiddling with the record player. Mona shoots him one of her killer looks.

"He meant that because you're so young, you may not be acquainted with old-fashioned phonographs." Antonio places the tray on the coffee table in front of the sofa. He fills a glass and offers it to me.

Mona flashes an album at Antonio and Antonio gives her a thumbs-up. After a few minutes of Mona fumbling with knobs, the sound of a mariachi band fills the room.

Gabriel enters, pushing his grandmother in a wheelchair. She is wearing a black dress with white polka dots, her frail, wrinkled arms resting in her lap, a rosary wrapped around her hands. I think of Juanita and the times we said the rosary together.

"This is Chona, everyone," Gabriel announces.

Chona grins a sweet, toothless grin at everyone as we take turns shaking her hand. "Who are these angels?" she asks Antonio.

"They are friends of Gabriel. They came to celebrate his birthday!"

"Birthday? Who has a birthday?"

"Gabriel. Your grandson."

"Ahh, Gabriel." She stretches out a hand toward E.M.

"That's Gabriel's friend," Antonio corrects her. "Gabriel's over here."

Chona grabs E.M.'s hand and places it against her cheek. "Gabriel," she whispers, "have you been a good boy?"

His face freezes, his dark skin turning darker.

"Well, answer her," Mona says. "Have you been a good boy?"

E.M. declares, "No, I've been a bad boy."

"Let's eat!" Antonio claps his hands. "Margarita has prepared a feast."

As we walk into the dining room, I ask Gabriel, "Who's Margarita?"

Gabriel laughs. "She's the daughter of Chabela, the lady who takes care of Grandma during the day when Grandpa and I work. Margarita is an even better cook than her mother, so we're in luck."

"Your grandfather took a day off to celebrate your birthday?"

"Yeah," Gabriel says. "I wish I had known. I would have tried to talk him out of it, not that I would have succeeded. He can't afford to take days off."

"He loves you." The words are out before I know it, and for a moment I hope Gabriel doesn't hear them. In my world, that kind of demonstration of love is unusual. But Gabriel *does* hear my words, and when he touches my arm softly, I know he also hears the sadness behind them.

"Wait until you taste Margarita's mole," he says.

There is mole, thick and reddish brown, and fluffy yellow rice and beans and empanadas and tamales. Mona has to tell E.M. not to drool on the mole and also not to drool on Margarita, who turns out to be yet another beauty. Then when no one can possibly eat anything else for at least a month,

Margarita brings out a chocolate cake, the seventeen candles already lit. We sing "Happy Birthday" first in English and then in Spanish, and Gabriel blows the candles out after making a silent wish.

"What did you wish for?" Mona asks.

He doesn't say anything, but the way he gently touches his temple makes me think his wish has something to do with what is going on in there.

After dinner, E.M. insists on helping Margarita with the dishes. "What?" he says in response to the cynical look on Mona's face. "I like to work. My brain thinks better when I work."

"Brain? Is that what you call the organ you're using?" Mona replies.

"I'll take Grandma to the back porch for some sun," Gabriel announces. "Anybody want to come?"

"Vicky does," Mona says, pushing me toward Gabriel and his grandmother. "Antonio and me are going to listen to some Cuco Sánchez. Grandpa, you dance?"

"Don't be too long," Antonio says to us. "I'm a weak man."

"Whatever I do to you, you're gonna like," Mona coos.

"That's what I'm afraid of," says Antonio. They laugh.

Gabriel pushes the wheelchair through the hallway. "This is Grandpa and Grandma's room," he says when we pass through the first door. We stop in the second room. "This used to be Grandma's workroom. She was a seamstress who worked out of the house." The room holds a queen-size bed with a simple white spread and a dresser, but no pictures, nothing to indicate that it's lived in. "We removed her sewing machine and stuff and bought some furniture at Goodwill," Gabriel explains. "We're trying to rent the room out. Hopefully, we can find someone who can take care of Grandma in return for room and board. Grandpa has been paying Chabela out of his savings, but he's running out." When we are going by the last door, he turns to me and says, "This is my room. You want to see?"

I peek through the doorway. The room is about the size of Barbara's walk-in closet. There is a small cot at one end, the thin camping kind that barely fits in a tent. A desk with a chair, a bureau, and an empty bookshelf are the only other furniture. The walls are bare except for a wooden cross above the cot. It's as close to a prison cell as you can get. I'm about to move away when I see a stack of notebooks beside the desk. They are the exact same kind I use for my journal at home.

"You write?" I try not to sound too surprised.

"Sometimes," he says, pulling me away from the door.

"That was a big stack of notebooks in there," I say.

"Yeah."

"Why are you being so reticent?"

"Reticent?" He laughs. "Did anyone ever tell you that you talk a lot smarter than you look?"

"You're changing the subject. Wait, did you just insult me?" I bop him on the shoulder and he grins. "What do you write? Be serious."

He pushes Chona's wheelchair away from his room. "I put everything in those notebooks," he says, no longer joking.

"Thoughts, poems, stories, observations, prayers. Sometimes I just copy passages from books."

"But there were no books in your room," I point out.

"I gave them all away," he says.

I wait for an explanation, but I can tell that I'm not going to get one.

At the end of the hallway is a porch with screened windows on all three of its sides. Dozens of magenta flowering plants hang from hooks on the ceiling. Sun streams in through one of the windows, and Gabriel wheels his grandmother to a patch of sunlight. "You sleepy, Grandma? You want to close your eyes and take a nap?" He sits in one of the two rocking chairs and invites me to sit in the other one.

"Where's Lupe? Is she home from work yet?" his grandmother murmurs.

"Lupe's my mother," Gabriel says to me.

"Lupe works too much, I always tell her," Chona says.

"She sure does," he agrees.

"There they are again." She points with a trembling finger at a corner of the porch.

"Who?" Gabriel asks, following her finger with his eyes.

"The little kids. What do they want?"

"They just want to keep you company, that's all."

I sit up and stretch my neck to look out the window. Were there little kids out there that I didn't see? Gabriel shakes his head gently and I understand.

"I don't mind them. They're nice," Chona says. "But sometimes they show up when I'm doing my business."

Gabriel giggles. "Tell them you need some privacy. They'll go away for a little while if you ask them."

"I like the way they sing." She closes her eyes, a smile on her face, her head moving from side to side, following the rhythm of some gentle lullaby. After a few minutes, her head stops moving. She's asleep.

We rock in silence. I want to ask Gabriel about the little children, but I decide not to. We hear Mona laugh inside, and we smile.

"Mona and your grandfather really hit it off," I remark. "I wonder what they talked about on the drive here."

"Some things we're better off not knowing," Gabriel says, waggling his eyebrows. He moves Chona's wheelchair a few inches back, away from the direct sunlight. Then he begins to rock again. After a few moments, he asks, "What made you sad back there in the truck, when you were thinking about your family?"

"Oh," I say. "I was thinking about something Mona said once." I'm not looking at him, but I can tell that he's waiting for me to continue. "My father and my stepmother, my sister . . . they can be jerks." I feel strangely guilty at having said this out loud, but Gabriel laughs and I do as well.

"Jerks as in they're mean or jerks as in they don't know any better?"

"Mmm." I think. "I'm not sure." Scheduling a business trip on my birthday probably does not qualify as mean. But what about telling Juanita she cannot live with us anymore? Isn't it mean to fire a person who's lived with you and worked for you for sixteen years, who's part of the family, because they're sick and old and you don't want to take care of them?

"Go on," Gabriel says, "give me one example of jerkiness."

"That's so lame, isn't it? Blaming our parents for our mental troubles."

"Maybe," he says.

"My father and stepmother . . . they have an image of what it is . . . to be happy."

"Which is?"

"I don't know. The usual. Have goals. Do your best to achieve them. Be all you can be. Et cetera, et cetera, et cetera."

"Yeah," Gabriel says. "That's the formula." It is impossible to tell whether he's being sarcastic. When I glance at him, he's staring intently at the same spot where Chona saw the little children. "I don't know what Antonio and Chona would do without me. Antonio can't run his landscape business without me and he can't take care of Chona by himself. They need me."

"Are you going someplace?" I joke.

"Not necessarily," he answers.

I wait for more, but he's silent. Then, "When you're needed, goals and doing your best and being all you can be are not things you think about all that much. You just show up every day because someone needs you."

Is there anybody who needs me? The little elves are asking.

"We need you," Gabriel says, as if answering my silent question.

"Who?"

"Our little group. Mona trusts you. You make her feel smart. I've seen E.M. smile at you when he thinks no one's looking. I can talk to you about anything. We need you."

There they were. The words I didn't know I longed to hear until I heard them. People need me. Despite all the darkness and uglies and the little elves delivering inaccurate messages. I have not felt needed since the days I sat next to my mother's bed and read poetry to her.

I don't know how long we sit there rocking gently in unison. Then Gabriel stands and slowly turns Chona's wheelchair around. He offers me a fist as he goes by me and I bump it.

chapter FOURTEEN

At the end of our next GTH, Dr. Desai says, "Before we leave, I have a proposition for you all. We need more time together outside our meetings, so I've gotten permission from the hospital to have you four spend some time with me at my ranch. We would leave the day after tomorrow, provided I can certify to all administrators and insurance companies and lawyers that you are not in danger of hurting yourselves or others. I feel comfortable that I can do that, based on your outing to Gabriel's house yesterday and what I've seen here and in our private sessions. We'd stay at the ranch for two weeks. Emilio and Mona, you are eighteen, so we don't need to get consent from your parents, but we will need to get the okay from your grandfather, Gabriel, and from your father, Vicky."

"My grandfather needs me," Gabriel says.

"Your grandfather is okay with your going," Dr. Desai tells him. "I talked to him this morning. He's coming this afternoon to sign the waiver the hospital requires."

"Will we have to milk cows and stuff like that?" Mona asks.

"You will have the opportunity to do work assignments just like you have here, but they will be things you feel comfortable doing. Fritz, my dear husband, and our farmhand, Pepe, take care of the animals, and they would love your help, but there are other chores. It's mostly a lovely place by the river where you can relax and reflect. We have good books to read. You can paint. You can go rafting and fishing. Sometimes we go into town to get ice cream."

"Yummy!" Mona exclaims.

"What happens if we don't want to go?" E.M. asks.

"You still have another two weeks of court-ordered observation. So if you decide not to come, you'll stay in the hospital and continue our individual sessions here." Dr. Desai can sound tough when she wants. Then she turns to me and asks, "Vicky, how about you? Do you want to come?"

"It doesn't really matter what I want. My father won't allow it." It's a small miracle that he has allowed me to stay at Lakeview for this long already.

"How do you feel?" Dr. Desai insists. "Could you use another two weeks with us before going home?"

What comes to me at that moment is a rush of memories from the day before: the ride in the back of the truck, E.M.'s jokes, Mona dancing with Antonio, Gabriel and I bumping fists. When was the last time I felt that lightness? But as I look further, I feel beneath the lightness the presence of something dark and heavy and menacing — something old and familiar waiting for me to return home so it can rule again.

This dark thing, I now know, is my depression. It is something I need to get to know, understand, tame if possible, but I don't quite have the strength or knowledge to handle it yet. It has gone into hiding these past few days because I had help — it's been five against one. But once I'm home, the odds will be in its favor.

"Vicky," Dr. Desai repeats, "could you use more time with us?"

"Yes," I say tentatively, "I can use more time."

"Let's see if we can convince your father," she says. "Your father and stepmother are coming to pick you up tomorrow, right?"

"Yes."

"Good. We'll talk to them then."

"What happens if they say no?" I'm surprised to hear that question coming from E.M.

"Then I go home," I answer. "Back to school on Monday."

"Vicky, you have to get them to let you go to the ranch!" Mona says.

"My father will never agree. That's a whole month off from school."

"It would've been longer if you killed yourself," E.M. says drily.

"Much as I hate to do this," Mona says, "I have to agree with Evil Mind here. If you go back to school and the same grind and you're not ready, then sooner or later you'll end up missing a whole bunch more than just school."

"Pretend you're brave," E.M. says. "You can do that."

"Gabriel," Dr. Desai says, "you're awfully quiet today. What do you think?"

Gabriel sits back in his chair and waits for my eyes to meet his. "It's your life, Vicky, and your mental health. If you think another two weeks with us at Dr. Desai's ranch will be helpful to you, you should fight for it."

"That's easy for you to say," I snap.

"It's not easy for me to say," Gabriel corrects me. "My grandfather is paying this friend of his to help him with the landscaping while I'm here. It's hard on him not to have me back, and it's hard on me not to be there. But my grandfather trusts Dr. Desai and he trusts me . . . that I will choose the best way to get well again. Your father needs to trust you, that you are doing what you think needs to be done."

Everyone is silent. I think all of us realize that's the first time we have heard Gabriel admit, even indirectly, that he isn't well. He looks at Dr. Desai and she nods to him encouragingly.

"I owe you all an apology," he says softly. "You all have talked about why you are here and I never have. I've been afraid to say anything because after I talk about . . . it, people see me differently. I . . . didn't want to lose what we have, you know, our friendship."

Mona reaches over and puts her hand on Gabriel's arm. "If I can be quote-unquote friends with Evil Mind here, don't you think I could still be friends with you no matter what you have?"

"Shush your trap and let the man talk," E.M. commands.

"Well, excuse me for living!" Mona replies.

Gabriel smiles at me and I smile back.

"I hear a voice," he says, looking around at all of us. "I started hearing it about a year ago. It was a good voice, not scary. I guess you could call it religious. He — it's a man's voice — wanted me to do things to be closer to God, like getting up early to pray or spending more time with my grandmother. The voice stayed with me, repeating his requests, and wouldn't go away unless I did what he told me.

"The reason I'm here is because six months ago, the voice started to ask me to do certain specific things. He asked me to give away everything I didn't need. So I gave away my laptop, my iPod, my books — all my wonderful books. That one really hurt. Then he asked me to fast for a few days, just bread and water. The last request, he asked me to live on the streets for a week like a homeless person. That's the one that got my grandfather worried. While I was away, he talked to Dr. Desai. She's my grandmother's doctor. When I came back from living on the street, he brought me here to see her. Dr. Desai wants to make sure that what I have is not the beginnings of schizophrenia. My grandmother may have something like that. This is how it starts, they say. First silent, persistent thoughts, then whispered words, then full-blown delusions."

There is silence.

"There are other things too. The sense that I've been singled out for something special." He looks briefly at me and smiles shyly. "Seeing connections everywhere. Signals and messages just for me. Being aware of a reality that others don't see." He stops. His eyes focus on a spot on the floor as if one of those realities just appeared to him. He shakes his head and continues, "These, they say, could also be symptoms of schizophrenia. The onset of it, they call it."

Silence again. I wonder if we are all thinking what I'm thinking — that what Gabriel has is more serious than we ever imagined.

It is Mona who speaks first. "But what if the voice asked you to, I don't know, make the world a safer place by getting rid of Evil Mind here? Would you have to do what it said?"

"He wouldn't ask me that . . . I don't think. The voice is not like that . . . hasn't been like that." Gabriel's words come painfully slow. He is breathing hard and perspiration moistens his forehead. "The voice . . . before I began to hear it, I felt worthless. It all felt worthless. The voice asked me to do something with my life. It told me my life matters."

After another long, uncomfortable silence, Dr. Desai says, "Thank you, Gabriel. Does anyone want to respond briefly? Then I think we'll wrap up this session."

E.M. goes first. "It don't matter much to me what goes on inside your brain. It's what you do that counts. You've done good by me, so . . . that's all."

Then Mona. "I always suspected that you had it worse than most of us. The worst mental illness in the world is to try to be more good and more perfect than is humanly possible. If you got a voice telling you to be a saint or whatever and you're obeying it, that's real bad. Not that I have any experience with trying to be good. So you're a sick human like the rest of us, big deal. I still like you."

"Thanks," Gabriel says sincerely.

It's my turn, and I have no idea what to say. I'm proud of Gabriel for telling us, but I'm also scared. Scared that the voice is too powerful for Gabriel to control. Scared for me too, because I will be alone soon and I don't know if I can fight my own voices.

I look at Gabriel. "I'm glad you told us. I . . . I'm just glad."

Gabriel deserves much more, I know. But that's all I can say.

chapter FIFTEEN

At eight the following morning, Margie tells me that my father and Barbara are waiting for me in Dr. Desai's office. Mona is taking a shower. We didn't say good-bye because she expects me to be strong and convince my father I need to go to the ranch, but part of me thinks I may never see her again.

They both stand when they see me.

"You look good," my father says. "How are you feeling?"

"Better," I say.

"You fixed your hair," Barbara says.

"More or less," I respond, smiling, touching the side of my head.

They sit on the sofa, their legs touching. I sit in the same wooden chair I always use during my sessions with Dr. Desai. My father picks up one of the figures of Ganesh and holds it up to Barbara questioningly. Barbara shrugs. She doesn't recognize it. We look at each other in an awkward silence. Dr. Desai is late.

"What time did you reschedule the meeting with the architects?" my father asks Barbara.

"Nine," she answers, glancing quickly at her watch.

They look at me in unison.

"She might have had an emergency," I say.

"How are you really?" Barbara asks me, meaning it. She is wearing a beige skirt and a white blouse with ruffles. Her golden hair is pulled back and tied in a bun.

"Okay," I say. She wants more, I can tell, something more confiding and intimate, but Barbara and I have never been on intimate terms and I don't feel like starting now.

"Are you ready to come home?" my father asks.

I have anticipated my father's question. *It's your mental health. Fight for it. Pretend you're brave.*

"I think Dr. Desai wants to talk to you about that," I say.

Nice going, Vicky. That's showing them you're brave! Why is it that I'm so afraid to let my father down? I look at the open door, hoping to see Dr. Desai, but she isn't there. Maybe she wants me to face my father and Barbara alone before she comes to my rescue.

"Vicky." Barbara crosses her right leg, the one closest to my father. "Your dad and I talked to that psychiatrist we mentioned the last time we were here," she said. "He really is one of the best in Austin. Dr. Saenz. We made an appointment for you for tomorrow morning. As I said before, he doesn't take any more cases, but he agreed to see you as a favor to your father. He wants to talk to you first, of course, but he says that nine out of ten times, the best way to proceed is to get back to your routine."

"My routine," I repeat mostly to myself. And then I think, *My routine will take me to where I ended up before.*

"Are you still suicidal?" my father asks, concerned.

That's a hard one to answer. The idea does not occupy all my thoughts, the way it did the week before the deed. But the *possibility* is there, like a snake under a rock, and it is real. "Not right *now*," I answer.

"Then you don't belong here anymore," my father says. "You need to come home and get your life back in order."

Barbara rubs his knee, as if reminding him of something they have previously discussed. They both missed the emphasis I gave to the word *now*.

My father continues, "Becca wants to see you. She'll take a few days off from school and come home. She can't believe you haven't talked to her since you've been here."

So Becca hasn't told him about our phone call. I wonder why. Maybe it was an important conversation for her too, one she wants to keep to herself. "Dr. Desai thought it would be better not to have any phone calls or visitors."

"Not even your own family? Does that make sense to you?" my father says.

"Yes." I let the word hang out there long enough for Barbara and Father to read into it whatever they want. Then I add, "I want to stay longer. Dr. Desai has a ranch outside of the city. She wants us to go there for two weeks."

My father looks at me incredulously. Barbara jumps in before he can respond. "Do you really want to throw away your whole sophomore year?" She hurries on, probably afraid that I will answer her question. "We talked to Mr. Robinson, and he spoke to your teachers. They think you can still pass this year if you do some remedial work next summer. We found a tutor for you. A young woman. Becca recommended her. She graduated from Reynard with Becca. She's a law student at UT now."

"You talked to Mr. Robinson? So everyone knows." Becca told me that — that everyone at school knew I tried to kill myself. It's not so much that I care what people think of me. It's more like their knowing will be one more thing weighing against my ability to make it . . . to persist, to keep on living. "I can't go back yet," I manage to say, but my voice trembles.

"You're going to have to see people sooner or later. Later is not going to make it any easier." My father is now ready to resume control of the situation. He waits for me to meet his eyes and then continues, "Right now, if we handle this properly, you still have a chance at getting into a decent college — UT, maybe, if I talk to some people. You throw away this year and you're looking at a community college." He takes a deep breath. "Bottom line: Are you okay now or aren't you?"

"I'm not okay. Not fully. Not yet," I say. "I need more time. I want to go to Dr. Desai's ranch."

It is strange and scary to speak that way to my father. It's as if his strength has sparked my own. He tries not to look upset, but I can tell he is. Barbara places her right hand on his lap.

"Whatever needs fixing can be better fixed in a place where you're surrounded by healthy minds and attitudes," he continues. "I don't like you being surrounded by sick people, by . . . patients in a psychiatric ward."

"These sick people are helping me." I remember my talk with Gabriel in the fifth-floor dining room. "And I'm helping them."

"Vicky . . ." my father says. He's about to speak again when Dr. Desai enters the room.

"Good morning," she says cheerfully. She walks straight to the chair behind her desk without shaking anyone's hands and sits. "Well," she says after studying everyone's faces, "I take it Vicky told you about the ranch."

"We would like her to come home with us," my father says. He moves himself to the front of the red sofa, getting ready to stand up.

"Yes, certainly you have the authority to take Vicky home with you right now," Dr. Desai says calmly. "You're her parents, Vicky is a minor, and I have no say in this at all. But my professional recommendation is that she stay away from her regular environment for at least two more weeks. My ranch is a wonderful place to reflect, and Vicky has already benefited immensely from our group discussions and one-on-one conversations. I think she feels like she needs a little more time before she goes back to her day-to-day life."

"Can I ask you something?" Barbara says.

"Yes."

"Do you have a professional opinion about why Vicky did what she did?"

My father says impatiently, "What she did was a fluke, an impulsive mistake. It's not going to happen again." I meet his eyes when he says this, and I feel as if he is in fact warning me that it better not happen again.

"Vicky." Dr. Desai waits for me to look at her. "Do you want to respond to your stepmother's question?"

Silence fills the room. My father and Barbara are actually waiting attentively for me to speak. It feels strange to see them like that, as if what I am about to say truly matters. It's how my father listens to Becca talk about her victories in debate.

I speak slowly, my eyes glued to the floor. "My thinking is not right. It hasn't been right for a long time, maybe even since Mamá died. It's like I got stuck in the sadness of Mamá's death, and the sadness turned into something worse — an illness called depression. What I'm doing now is understanding how depression works, how it colors everything I see and do. I like some of the things I do here. I like the other kids. I haven't liked anybody or anything for a long time. If I stay a little longer, maybe I can figure out how to like what's waiting for me out there. That's what I need."

There is silence, a loud silence. I see what could be fear in my father's face. Barbara seems confused. She clutches at her tiny brown purse that is just big enough to hold her cell phone and car keys.

Finally, Father breaks the silence. He speaks directly to Dr. Desai. "I can understand why she wants to stay here, protected, taken care of. But what Vicky needs is a future to look forward to. She needs the confidence of overcoming struggles, of accomplishments under her belt. She needs challenges and goals, things to strive for. I'm not talking about challenges that she can't possibly accomplish. I'm talking about objectives that she can reach, given her abilities. Yes, there's some pressure in that, but that's what makes life interesting. You find your dream and then do what it takes to get there. She needs an environment that rewards healthy choices and effort, not illness."

Dr. Desai's dark face turns a darker color. She tilts her chair forward, places both her hands on her desk, and glares at my father. "Mr. Cruz," she says, "your daughter is alive by the grace of God. A few minutes more and she would have been dead. She tried to kill herself. She wasn't joking or asking for attention. She meant to do it, and every doctor worth his salt will tell you that the odds are high that people who try once with that kind of serious intent will try again. Do you understand that?"

She stops and waits for those words to sink in. My father's jaw clenches. He's not used to people speaking to him as if he were a child or an idiot.

"Vicky's assessment of her situation, in my professional opinion" — here she turns to look meaningfully at Barbara — "is absolutely correct. She is depressed. The feelings that resulted from her mother's decline and death turned from a sadness that was natural and even healthy into one that was unhealthy. That unhealthy sadness we call clinical depression. In the last few days, Vicky has had some remarkable insights into her condition. Those insights came with the help of other kids who are also in pain, like her, in some form or another. I urge you to listen to her when she tells you that she needs a little more time to keep figuring things out." She pauses. "It is not only Vicky who needs to understand her depression. Her family must too."

My father speaks slowly. "Understanding is not the only thing she needs right now. She needs to know that depression or no depression, you don't ever quit." He turns toward me. "Do you believe what you did was wrong?"

Dr. Desai crosses her hands on her chest. "Vicky knows that what she did was 'wrong,' as you put it, Mr. Cruz. But fully believing that it is wrong is not going to keep her from trying again. Right or wrong don't matter when you're in pain, and Vicky has been in pain. She needs a little more time to heal before she returns to her regular life. My ranch is on the Natchez River. Over the years, hundreds of kids" — she points at the pictures on the bulletin board — "have spent anywhere from a few days to a few months there. It's a good place for young people." Here Dr. Desai looks at Barbara. Maybe she hopes that Barbara will come to my aid.

"I don't know how much Vicky has told you about her school situation," Barbara says, "but she's in danger of failing this year. The only way for her not to repeat this year is if she gets at least C's in all her finals, which will not be easy for her. Missing so much school is just too costly. We've found a psychiatrist — maybe you know him: Dr. Saenz?" Dr. Desai shakes her head. "I'm surprised you don't know him. He's one of the best in Austin. Anyway, his philosophy is that a combination of medication, individual therapy — daily visits if necessary — and a return to normal life, with some additional support at home and in school, is the best way to treat Vicky. He likened his approach to how we deal nowadays with a sprained ankle. It used to be that when you sprained an ankle, you rested until it healed. Now medical practice recommends exercise immediately — not vigorous, certainly, but some. Healing in the midst of normal life. Being around optimistic, cheerful people. That's what he's proposing, and Miguel and I fully agree. We got Vicky a tutor to help her with her school-work. I also thought she could join me in my Zumba Yoga class." This last suggestion is punctuated with a wink in my direction.

Not in this lifetime, I say to myself.

Dr. Desai turns to me. "Vicky, I'm sorry. I don't know what else to do or say."

My father and Barbara have made up their minds. I feel so defeated just now. I don't think they will understand what I want to say to them, but I go ahead and say it anyway. "I can't go back yet. The first few days that I was here, I was sure that I was going to try again when I got out, and this next time I would pull it off. But now, after two weeks, that certainty . . . now, I don't know. Maybe I can find a way to live out there. I don't know. Maybe I can do it. Before I come home, I want the 'maybe' to be a little stronger, if possible."

"That sounds like a threat," my father says. There is more disappointment than anger in his voice.

"It's not a threat," I say. "It's just the way I feel."

He runs his hand over his neatly combed gray hair. He looks up at the bulletin board and then at me. "Why, Vicky? What's so bad about your life? If you were depressed or what-ever, why didn't you say something?" He turns to Barbara. "I didn't think she was depressed, did you?"

"There were no signs," Barbara explains to Dr. Desai. She sounds almost apologetic. "There were bad grades, but Vicky was never a good student. Then she quit debate in the middle of a tournament, leaving her best friend without a partner. We thought it was some kind of sibling resentment bubbling up. Her sister was the best debater Reynard's ever had." She turns toward me, her eyes fixed on my hair. "The night you took it upon yourself to massacre your hair, I thought you were getting back at us for Juanita."

"Getting back?" Dr. Desai asks.

"She didn't mention that in your sessions with her?" Barbara says, her eyebrows lifting. "Juanita is our maid —"

"My nana," I correct her, "who has taken care of me since I was born, who's been with our family since my father married my mother."

"I know who Juanita is," Dr. Desai says. "She's the one who found Vicky unconscious and called the ambulance. What I don't know is how she's connected to the cutting of Vicky's hair."

Barbara speaks, animated. "Vicky's mad at us because we thought it best if Juanita went back to Mexico. She's got advanced arthritis. She can't work anymore; she can barely make it up the stairs. I discovered recently that Vicky has been doing her chores for God knows how long. Juanita needs somebody to take care of her, but all her family is in Mexico. Miguel and I thought the best thing would be to give her a very generous retirement package so she could go back to Mexico and live comfortably with her younger sister."

"You don't fire family," I say.

"When did you find out about Juanita?" Dr. Desai asks me.

"The week before she tried to kill herself," Barbara answers before I can. "I told her our decision, then she ran off in a huff and cut her hair. Was that when you decided to end your life?"

"No," I say. "I planned on killing myself long before that."

Barbara's eyes widen and my father's face deflates, like some kind of vital air has been let out. It hurts me to watch him. The image of him standing in the receiving line at my mother's wake comes to me — the way he could barely say thank you, as if all he wanted was to go and be with Mamá, wherever she had gone.

I focus on Ganesh.

"Vicky . . ." Dr. Desai says softly after a few moments of tense silence. "Vicky, why don't you go to your room and get your things, and let me talk to your parents alone for a few minutes?"

I get out of my chair without looking at Father or Barbara and leave the room. I walk fast, anger and frustration fueling my legs. In front of my room, I stop and take a deep breath. I need to keep it together so I can say good-bye to Mona. Then I need to find Gabriel and E.M., and I don't want to be angry when I say good-bye to them.

Our room is empty. I sit in the chair next to my bed and put my head between my knees. I think of all the things I should have said to my father that I didn't. *I'm needed here. I'm good at things here, even if it's folding sheets. I'm getting back on that horse of yours but I'm doing it my way, as best I can.*

There is a knock on the door. I don't know how much time has passed. I was supposed to be gathering my things. I stand up so quickly that I feel dizzy and have to grab on to the bed.

"Come in," I say. It's Dr. Desai. "I'll be ready in a minute," I add, heading toward the closet.

"Let's sit down for a second." Dr. Desai lifts the chair next to Mona's bed and places it to face the chair where I had been sitting. We sit, our knees touching. She takes a deep breath. "I don't know how many suicides and suicide attempts by young people I've been a part of, and I am still amazed by the different reactions of the parents. There's guilt, of course, but anger is right up there."

"Like my father," I point out.

"The thing we need to keep in mind is that underneath that anger, there is fear and hurt. In a way, your suicide attempt is a rejection of him, of his way of life, of the way of life he wants for you, of what he has worked hard to give you."

Was there rejection on my part? It felt more like the life my father wanted for me had done the rejecting.

"Anyway," Dr. Desai continues, "your father has given you permission to go to the ranch."

"He did?" I feel my mouth fall open in disbelief.

"Yes. And your stepmother agreed as well."

"That's unbelievable. What did you tell them?"

Dr. Desai makes a devilish face, the one that says a magician cannot reveal her tricks. I feel so many things just now: relief at not having to go back, grateful to my father, glad that I will be with the group, and, surprisingly, fear. It's as if I've been entrusted with something precious for which I am now responsible.

"Please tell me how you convinced them," I insist.

She nods, her face turning suddenly serious. "The important thing to remember is that they put your needs ahead of theirs. They want what is best for you and are trying to give that to you the best way they know how, which may not always be the right way for you. I told them what I believed as a doctor who has treated hundreds of young people. It wasn't much different from what you told them in your own words. In my opinion, although you are stable now and are no longer in the grip of suicidal ideation, there is a likelihood that at the next crisis — and the next crisis is sure to come sooner or later — the suicidal ideation will return."

"And I will try to kill myself again," I say.

"If you are not equipped to resist, yes. In the next few days, we will talk about the need for ongoing medication. My instincts were to hold off on it since you were safe here with us. But now we need to consider it in preparation for your return."

"Will medication make me like my life?" I ask.

A tender smile spreads across Dr. Desai's face. "Medication won't make you like your life. It might help you accept the things you cannot change, and maybe even give you the energy to change the things you can, to paraphrase an old prayer. But to like your life, you're going to need more than medication."

"What else will I need?"

"Ahh," Dr. Desai says mysteriously. "First let's work on making friends with life in general."

"But how?"

Again, her lips form into a smile. "Let's see if we can at least glimpse the answer to that question in the next two weeks."

Dr. Desai pushes herself out of the chair slowly. "Zumba Yoga, indeed," I hear her say on the way out.

CHAPTER SIXTEEN

The next day, Mona, E.M., Gabriel, and I climb into a white van driven by Dr. Desai's husband. His name is Wilhelm, but everyone calls him by his last name, Fritz. He's a bald little man with stringy arms and these intense blue eyes that sparkle when they focus on you. He wears cowboy boots and overalls, speaks with a German accent, and finds everything extremely funny. I have a hard time imagining him and Dr. Desai together. In the van, Gabriel sits in the front seat, E.M. and I sit on the second seat, and Mona sits in the way-back by herself. When I look back, she is punching numbers on Rudy's cell phone.

E.M. notices the phone too. "You need to stay away from that guy. He's garbage."

"I don't tell you how to live your life, do I?" she replies without anger. She takes the iPod out of her pocket.

"He gave you that too?" E.M. asks.

Mona shrugs.

"Are you blind? The guy's an addict. He steals pills from patients, uses half of them, and sells the rest."

I look at E.M. How does he know all this about Rudy, and since when does he care what Mona does? I wait for Mona to respond, but she just sticks the earbuds in her ears and begins fiddling with the iPod. "His taste in music sucks," she says, "but beggars can't be choosers."

The second day I was in the hospital, after Dr. Desai convinced Father to let me stay, Barbara sent over some clothes and my backpack with all my schoolbooks. Somewhere in the backpack, I know, I have my favorite pen, the one my mother gave me for my eighth birthday. I dig through the jeans and underwear and T-shirts until I find it. Then I open the green notebook, and after a while, I write.

On the way to Dr. Desai's ranch. Gabriel is deep in conversation with Fritz. They are discussing a Hindu scripture called the Bhagavad Gita. It amazes me, all that Gabriel knows, and how unconcerned he is about showing off. Mona is in the back listening to music. E.M is staring out the window. Actually, right now he's staring at me.

"What you writing about?" E.M. asks.

"As a matter of fact, just that second I was writing about you."

He gives me a look that probably would have frightened me two weeks ago. I'm about to start writing again when he says, "When you write about me, make sure you say how smart I am. People need to know I'm as smart as Psycho Princess back there or you or maybe even Gabriel. Just different smart."

"It's nonfiction," I say.

He studies my grin for a few moments. "Ha, ha," he says. "That's like a joke, right?"

"A poor attempt at one," I admit.

"That's good," he says. "People are usually afraid to

joke around with me. Could be you're growing some hair on your chest."

I touch my chest instinctively. "Ha, ha. That's like a joke, right?" I mimic him.

He smiles. I go back to my notebook and am about to write when E.M. speaks again. "Make sure you tell people about Huichi."

"What should I tell them?"

"Tell them he was the Aztec god of war. He gave strength in battle to warriors. Those who fought with courage, not just in battle, but everywhere. The Aztec warrior lived with courage. He looked for ways to show his courage, to please Huitzilopochtli."

"Is that what you try to do, please him?"

"Yeah. But not like he's real. He's like an idea. A belief. I don't talk to him." He glances at the back of Gabriel's head. "When you follow Huichi, you know you're on your own. You know you're gonna die and that's it. But that's all right. That's just another fact you need to be courageous about. Huichi warriors are not afraid of dying. But they don't go around killing themselves, either, when it gets rough. That's not the way of courage, the way of Huitzilopochtli."

"You've never been afraid?" I ask.

He looks around as if to make sure no one can hear us. Mona is lost in her music, and Gabriel and Fritz are absorbed in conversation. "I've been afraid. I let my father abuse my mother and the rest of us and I didn't do nothing. For years I didn't do nothing. I thought the brave thing was to put up with it. That's what I told myself. Truth is, I was a coward. Not just afraid. That's nothing. I was a coward."

He watches me quietly for a few moments — or, rather, he lets me catch a glimpse of him without the warrior mask he likes to wear. What I see for the first time is someone who has pain inside of him. Someone struggling against the dark just like me. Then he turns his face toward the window and I know the conversation is over.

After a few minutes, I write:

E.M. *lives to be brave, to please his Huichi, even though he knows Huichi is not real. Huichi is someone he made up, but he doesn't care. The belief gives him strength. What do I believe in? How can I find something to believe in, to give me strength?*

I close the notebook and look out the window. When I could still pray, I prayed for my mother to get well, and then, as her illness progressed, I prayed for her suffering to end. That's the one prayer that did get answered . . . eventually. Then I stopped praying. I wasn't angry at God, because being angry is still a form of talking to Him. All the talking on my part just stopped. That moist place from where words sometimes bubbled up dried out. And now? Now I lie awake sometimes wishing there was someone who would whisper a word to me, something I could hold on to.

I don't know how much time passes before I notice we are off the main road and driving through hills covered with bluebonnets. In the distance, you can see dark-brown and black cows, some of them with calves nuzzling them. Fritz and Gabriel have stopped talking. Gabriel has his eyes closed, but I can tell he isn't sleeping because his back and neck are very straight. No one can fall asleep and keep his head so perfectly balanced.

Then we turn onto a dirt road. Gravel pings the bottom of the van. "There it is," says Fritz. Everyone except Fritz and Gabriel cranes their necks so we can see out the front window.

In front of us is a white house, a red barn, various shedlike structures, and two small log cabins. Big leafy trees tower over all the buildings except the barn. The whole place looks like an oasis of shade. The main house is two stories tall and has a wraparound porch full of rocking chairs painted different colors. Behind the barn, I can see a corral with a sleek, brown horse prancing from side to side. Chickens scatter every which way as we drive up and park under an immense tree next to the house.

Fritz opens his door and steps out. The rest of us stay seated. It's almost as if the peacefulness of the place keeps us from moving, like we're afraid to break the silence with the noise we each carry within us.

"Well, come on," urges Fritz. "No one's gonna bite you."

No sooner has he said this than two dogs come up to the van and start barking. The dogs have long black-and-white hair and bushy wagging tails. Gabriel opens his door first, and the dogs immediately jump on him and begin to lick his face.

Mona opens the side door to the van tentatively. Fortunately, the dogs are not quite as friendly with me and her, and they growl at E.M., which makes Mona laugh.

"Julius! Cleo!" Fritz shouts. He points a stern finger at the two dogs, and they lower their heads, tuck in their tails, and approach E.M. apologetically. E.M. stretches out his hand to pet them, but then changes his mind.

"Coward," I whisper to him, and he gives me a look.

We grab our small bags from the back of the van and follow Fritz and the two dogs. When we are in front of the log cabins, Fritz says that one is for the girls and the other is for the boys. "Make yourselves at home. Lunch is in about half an hour. Then I'll show you around. Lina said we should find you some work." He turns around and walks off toward one of the sheds. Julius and Cleo follow him.

"Lina must be Dr. Desai," E.M. says.

"E.M., you're a genius," Mona says.

Our cabin has two rooms: one big room that is used as a living room and bedroom, and then a small bathroom. There are four easy chairs, a sofa in the middle of the room that looks extremely comfortable, and four bunk beds around the edges of the room. The bunk beds are neatly made with Native American–patterned quilts. The only other furniture is a desk, a desk chair, a bookcase, two lamps, and a small refrigerator. All the windows are open and a crosscurrent of cool air blows through. Mona drops her bag on one of the bottom bunks, and I take one on the opposite wall.

"This is nice," she says. "It's so . . . ."

"Serene," I say, completing her thought.

"Yeah. I was going to say comfy, but serene will do. I can see why Dr. Desai wanted us to come here." She grabs the pillow from her bed and presses it to her face. "Smells like trees. What's that?" She goes over to the refrigerator. "Look at this!" she says when she opens it. "It's full of beers!"

"What?"

"Just kidding," Mona says. "Had you there for a moment, didn't I? Actually, it's got water bottles. Want one?"

"No, thanks." I cross to the bookcase. One shelf has a dozen or so books from the Dalai Lama and other Eastern and Indian authors. Another holds some of my favorite novels, like *Jane Eyre*, *Wuthering Heights*, and *Pride and Prejudice*, along with another of my favorite books, *The Collected Poems of Robert Frost*. A third shelf carries cowboy books.

Mona plops down on one of the easy chairs and takes a swig of water. "I was in the worst mood after talking to Rudy this morning, and the whole trip here I felt like roadkill. As soon as I saw this place, I felt better. This is like another world where all the ugliness out there can't get in."

"Why did talking to Rudy put you in a bad mood?" I ask.

Mona ignores my question. "I bet you no one has ever tried to kill themselves in this place," she says.

I think of my room back home and everything I've done to make it my space, a place where I like to spend time. I placed two of Mamá's paintings of roses on the walls. One of them, the one Juanita and I both love, is of an old white fence covered with pink roses. The mesquite tree outside the windows blocked the sunlight into my room, but I liked it that way. I always kept it neat, with all my books in their proper places. There were never any clothes on the floor, like in Becca's room. I remember Father coming to my room once and saying, "If someone who didn't know you or your sister looked at your rooms, they'd think you were the smart one."

"There you go again," Mona says. "Your mind takes off God knows where all of a sudden. I was watching you on the trip down here. You were in another world after you and E.M. had your heart-to-heart. At least Gabriel closes his eyes. Yours just get glassy, like a dead fish."

"You're funny." I take the book of poems by Robert Frost from the shelf and lie on my bed.

"You haven't said anything about the voice Gabriel hears," Mona says. She holds the plastic bottle in front of her face and examines it.

"You haven't said anything either," I counter.

"I almost wish he hadn't told us." She places the bottle on her lap.

"Why?" I sit up.

"I don't know. I can't help looking at him differently now. Have you ever watched any of those shows where they interview, like, a serial killer or a terrorist, and there you are, looking at this ordinary, boring face, and you know they've got this other life inside of them? Who's the real person there? The nice person you see or the monster inside?"

"That's not the way it is with Gabriel," I say.

Mona grins one of her *I know a lot more than you do* kind

of grins. "He may not be a serial killer, but he's sick. Sicker than you can imagine. Tell the truth, don't you look at him a little differently now?"

"A little," I say honestly. "But I look at you differently than when I first met you. I look at E.M. a lot differently than when I first saw him. Isn't that what happens when you get to know people? You look at them differently? E.M. used to give you the creeps, remember? Does he give you the creeps now?"

"He's still a pain," Mona says. "But we're not seeing him in normal circumstances. When someone gets him real mad, will he be able to control his anger enough not to beat the living daylights out of them? And Gabriel? We're all mental, but what he's got is worse because it's not obvious. You can see him begin to rip if you look carefully. Trust me on that one. He's going to split wide open." There is an edge in Mona's voice I have never heard before.

"Is this really about Gabriel? What's bothering you? What's going on with Rudy?"

Mona takes the last swig of water and then she crushes the plastic bottle. "Nothing. Not one thing."

"Mona?"

"I'm going out for a walk." She stands up, heads for the door, and then stops. "Look, you're new at this, so you don't know jack. We're friendsy and supportive of each other and all that, but ultimately you got to save yourself. You're the only one that can do it. You can't save me and I can't save you, and when Gabriel starts to go, or me or E.M., you have to get out of the way and worry about yourself."

"Mona, wait," I say, standing up as well and moving toward her. "What's wrong?"

She stands in the middle of the room. I wait in front of her until she lifts her eyes and sees me. She seems so lonely, and I wonder if in talking about Gabriel, she was really talking about herself. Warning me to move away, for my own sake, because she's exploding.

I hug her. I hug her without thinking, without realizing that I'm doing it until my arms are around her. This must be what healthy people do with their friends.

"I'm sorry," she says when I let her go. "I'm off today. I have these days sometimes. I'll be all right. Don't worry. I'm nervous about Lucy. I think Rudy is really going to find her. Don't tell anyone about him, all right?"

"E.M. knows about him. He saw you call him. He thinks Rudy's bad for you."

"I know. That was a stupid thing to do in the van. I'm sorry. I don't know what got into me. I'm thinking of you. Be careful. With Gabriel. With me. With E.M. Seriously. You come first. You need to use your head . . . even if it's not clicking right."

"Okay, I hear what you're trying to tell me."

She walks away. I stand in the same spot for I don't know how long.

chapter SEVENTEEN

The following morning after breakfast, Fritz gives us our work assignments. Mona is going to paint the inside of one of the sheds. Fritz gently nixes her color choice, chartreuse, and instead gives her a can of dull Spanish white. Gabriel and Fritz are going into town to buy roses for a garden that Gabriel will design and plant. Starting tomorrow, I will help Gabriel with the garden, but my job today is to help E.M. repair a patch of broken fence on the north side of the property. I look quickly at E.M. when Fritz announces this, and the wicked smile on his face informs me that he's relishing the opportunity to show me what hard work is all about.

Besides those official assignments, everyone will have barn duty every day at six a.m. — milking the four cows, cleaning the stalls for the five horses, collecting eggs, and feeding the chickens and two goats. Starting tomorrow, after barn duty and breakfast, we will have our usual GTH, and sometime during the day, each one of us will have our individual sessions with Dr. Desai.

At the same time we get our work assignments, we also meet the ranch hand, Pepe. He came to the ranch for treatment ten years ago and stayed. He's thirty years old and looks like a kinder, gentler version of E.M.

Pepe drives us to the broken fence in a vehicle that looks like a cross between a golf cart and a heavy-duty truck. I ride in the back, rattling with the tools. It's early but the sky is already a very light blue. In an hour or so, it will be white-hot. I'm glad I was assigned to work with E.M. today and with Gabriel the rest of the week instead of painting with Mona. There's something about being outside that is mentally refreshing, even if the temperature is a hundred degrees.

Pepe shows us the segment of the fence that needs to be replaced. Twelve wooden posts are sagging with rot. Our job is to dig holes for the new posts that Pepe brought the day before. The holes need to be three feet deep so the poles will stand five feet above the ground, the same height as the other fence posts.

"Why can't we just take the old posts out and use the same hole?" I ask.

"Could work," Pepe says, "if they hadn't poured cement down each hole when they first built the fence. People used cement before they realized cement rots the wood."

"What are we going to use to hold the posts in place?" I ask.

"Rocks," Pepe says drily.

"What rocks?"

Pepe and E.M. grin simultaneously, like evil twins. Pepe doesn't answer. After he leaves, E.M. grabs a shovel and tells me, "We take turns. I dig for five minutes and then you dig for five minutes. That way no one gets too tired."

"Wouldn't it be better if we each work on separate holes? That would be faster, wouldn't it?" I wonder if E.M. suggested taking turns because he doesn't think I can dig a hole by myself.

"We only have one post digger," he says. "Anyway, we don't want to go fast."

At first I think he wants to use our full three hours until Pepe returns, but as I watch him work, I realize that he doesn't want to go fast because he wants to do it right. He clears the ground and loosens the soil in a circular area about three times the diameter of the post. Then he takes the post digger and scoops out bits of dirt and rock. I've never used a post digger before, so I watch him carefully. E.M. grabs the two handles, lifts them up a couple of feet, and then brings the post digger down with a force that seems neither too little nor too much. I hear the steel clash against the rocky soil and the grating sound of the digger picking up the loose dirt. Now and then, E.M. grabs a long spearlike iron rod, which he uses to dislodge rocks. He puts the rocks he finds in a separate pile. I can see why E.M. and Pepe smiled when I asked where we would get the rocks to hold the posts in place.

He works for about five minutes and then I tap him for my turn. He hands me the post digger and steps out of the way. The post digger reminds me of a pair of giant chopsticks. The blades close when you pull the two handles away from each other and open when you bring the handles together, but I keep doing the opposite of what's necessary. I look up to see if E.M. is laughing at me, but he isn't. He waits for me to figure it out, which I eventually do. After a while, he lets me know it's his turn. He digs slowly and patiently, conserving his energy, unlike me. I attack the earth as if it's my mortal enemy, and I can already feel a blister forming underneath the leather gloves that Pepe gave me.

We've been working in silence for about twenty minutes when I say, "When Pepe said we had to dig twelve holes about three feet deep, I thought we'd be done in a couple of hours. Now I'm thinking a week may not be long enough."

"This here's called caliche," he says, hitting the ground a couple of times with the post digger. "It's a sandy, rocky kind of clay. I think this is why people prefer to grow cows around here. The trick is to go slow and steady."

Slow and steady. That's the way E.M. works. There's a rhythm to the way he moves, and I have the feeling that he can go at that pace all day long before he tires. By the time we finish the first hole, I'm soaked in sweat and my arms feel like wet noodles.

The hole is beautiful, though. At least it seems that way to me. It is perfectly cylindrical and smooth. E.M. marks three feet on the post with a tape measure, and when we lower it into the hole, the mark on the post is exactly even with the ground. I hold the post straight while E.M. kneels down and carefully places the rocks from his pile around the post. The look on his face is one of pure concentration.

"Why are you being so careful with the rocks?" I ask almost in a whisper.

"If you do it the right way, the rainwater will drain through them and the wood won't rot," he answers without looking at me.

When we finish, we stand back for a few moments to admire our work. Then we walk over to the plastic jug of water that Pepe left us. I drink first and then E.M. takes a turn.

On the way to the next hole, I ask him, "You work in construction, right?"

"Yup."

"You do this kind of thing all day long. Don't you get tired? Bored?"

"You complaining?"

"No. I'm just curious how you do this all day long, day after day."

He studies me for a few moments as if that's the kind of question that only a rich, spoiled girl would ask. "I do it day after day because if I don't do it, we don't eat." His tone is severe, and it takes me a few seconds to realize that he is not being mean. He is simply stating a fact. Then something softens, and he says, "But just because you have to do it, don't mean you don't get tired. Bored, too, sometimes. You learn some tricks for not getting bored."

"What kind of tricks?"

"I pay attention to what I'm doing. I focus on doing it as good as I can. That usually keeps me from getting bored."

"I did that," I say, remembering. "In the laundry room in Lakeview. I liked to concentrate real hard on folding sheets. But I only did it for three hours with breaks, not eight hours a day, five days a week like the rest of the girls. And even then, I could only concentrate for about an hour."

He takes the post digger, lifts it, and brings it down on the dirt. He scoops up a handful of sand and rock and strikes again and again, slowly, methodically, his eyes focused softly, without anger or impatience, on the hole he's attempting to dig. I have the feeling that he's *showing* me how to pay attention, rather than *telling* me how to do it.

When it's my turn, I try to work with concentration as well. I try not to hurry or think about getting the job over with. Instead of getting frustrated by the rocks, I dig gently around them. When I finish, I notice that my pile of dirt and rocks is bigger than it was when I was attacking the hole mindlessly.

After we finish the fourth hole, E.M. grabs the water jug and points to a small tree a few yards away. We sit in a small patch of shade. I take off my gloves and begin to peel one of the blisters.

"You like to work," he says. There's a hint of surprise and admiration in his words, or so I choose to hear.

"Thank you," I say. "I like this type of work."

"What type is that?"

"Manual work." I pause, and then add, "I'm not so good with work that requires me to think, like schoolwork. My mind goes kind of blank when I have to think under pressure."

He considers this for a few moments. "So you want to dig ditches when you grow up." Then he adds with a knowing smile, "If you grow up."

"Yeah," I say, "if." Our eyes meet and I look quickly away. "Tell me more about Huichi," I say to change the subject.

He shrugs. "I only just started thinking about him."

"Why? I mean, how did you start thinking about him?"

"One day I was carrying boxes of books people donated up to the third floor in Lakeview for that little library they got, and I saw this book about the Aztecs on top of one of the boxes. It was a kid's book with lots of pictures. On the cover, it had an Aztec warrior with a jaguar head dancing. That night when I read the book . . . it just came to me that I wanted to be like Huitzilopochtli — even if he was someone I mostly made up."

"So you believe in Huichi?"

"I told you, I don't believe like the guy is real or out there someplace. I imagine what he's like and try to be like him."

"He's brave."

"Yeah. Huichi is about being brave. About not being defeated by anybody or anything. Rising up every day and doing what you gotta do. Shining your light so that people and things around you can live. The fight is hard, else you wouldn't need to be brave. It's all caliche, so what's the use whining about it? The rocks are everywhere. You have to dig around them without getting pissed at them. I expect the rocks to be there. Sometimes I think they're put there on purpose so I can learn not to be angry about them." He stops. He seems embarrassed to be talking so much.

"You've really thought about this a lot," I say.

"I never used to think about stuff like this. But . . . here and at the hospital, I think about things I never thought before. Besides, I got Gabriel for a roommate, remember?"

"Yeah," I agree, smiling. "That would do it."

He picks up a pebble, examines it, tosses it away. "Did Dr. Desai ever tell you the story about the elephant and the stick?"

"No. She told me a story about monkeys once."

"This old man in India owned this elephant . . ."

"Lady Chatterley," I say, remembering.

"Yeah. That was the name. Anyway, this old man, Mr. Mariachi . . ."

"Mr. Karamachi," I correct him.

"Thought you said you didn't know this story."

"He's the same old man in my story . . . with the monkeys. Your story is different."

"So, anyway, this Mr. Mariachi used to rent Lady Charlie out for weddings and things. But it was a problem, because when the elephant walked through the streets, she would steal stuff from the stalls, like bananas and coconuts. She'd swing her trunk out there and grab stuff and the owners would get mad and Mr. Mariachi had to pay for the fruit . . . What? Why are you laughing? I'm talking to you serious."

"I'm sorry," I say, erasing my smile as best I can. I tell myself not to think of Mr. Karamachi dressed in a *charro* outfit.

"So Mr. Mariachi came up with this idea of giving Lady Charlie a bamboo stick to hold in her trunk, and to raise it up in the air when she walked like it was something special. So that solved the problem."

I wait a few moments. He's trying to tell me something that is important to him, but I don't know exactly what. "So . . ."

"So I didn't know why Dr. Desai told me that story. She just said to think about it. So first I thought she was trying to tell me that I needed to have a stick, something to think about when I started to get angry, something different from whatever was making me angry, so I wouldn't lose my temper. But then I found that book about the Aztecs, and it came to me that the bamboo stick was more than just a way to keep me from getting angry. The stick is like a picture of who I want to be. Huichi is my bamboo stick. We all need one like that to hold on to."

A ladybug is crawling on his pants. He watches it for a few seconds and then puts his finger in front of it. The ladybug climbs on his finger and then takes flight. "You got an image of who you want to be?" he asks.

"No," I say. I feel a sad kind of emptiness at that answer. Then the image of my mother comes to me. When my mother was ill, I watched her fight for life until the very end — or almost the very end. The last month, her life was filled more with acceptance and peace than with fight. I believed she was right to fight and I believed she was right to accept the inevitable. Can I be like her in her fight and her acceptance?

E.M. leaves me alone with my thoughts for a few minutes and then he stands. It's time to go back to work. As we are walking to the next post, he says, "Lots of people spend their lives digging holes, or mowing lawns, or folding sheets."

"Yeah."

He goes on, "Maybe there are jobs out there where people enjoy what they're doing, but those jobs have their boring moments as well. Do you know people who love their jobs every single minute of the day all their lives?"

"My father," I say, without thinking.

"That a fact?"

"I've never heard him complain about his work. He loves wheeling and dealing and making money. My stepmother is that way too. They like what they do. Or at least they need to keep busy. They would end up on the fifth floor of Lakeview if they didn't have work."

He laughs. I don't know why I feel something like pride in myself whenever I get E.M. to laugh. I wonder if I can put that in a college application. "Yeah," he says. "Guess I'd go crazy too if I didn't work."

"You dropped out of school to work?"

"Made it all the way to the eighth grade. Then I had to work. I wasn't much for school anyway. But . . ."

"But . . ."

"I like carpentry, and for some carpentry jobs, you need a high school diploma."

"Maybe in the future you can find a way to go back to school," I say.

He stops and looks at me and there's a flash of anger in his eyes. "You shouldn't talk to people about the future if you don't believe in one for yourself."

Then he speeds up and grabs the post digger, leaving me behind.

CHAPTER EIGHTEEN

When Pepe comes to get us two hours later, the twelve holes have been dug and the posts are solidly in the ground. Tomorrow E.M. and Pepe will string the posts with new barbed wire and remove the old section of the fence. I look at our work with pride one last time as we drive back to the house.

During lunch, Gabriel suggests a trip to the river, but the blue skies turn suddenly dark, and then the rain comes. The river trip is postponed until tomorrow and we spend the rest of the afternoon reading. Mona sits with a romance novel, the cell phone by her side. Every few minutes she checks to see if a text has come in or if she has missed a call, even though the polka ringtone she chose can probably be heard by the horses grazing in the north pasture. Other times she stands up, looks at the deluge outside, and sighs. Whenever I ask if something is wrong, she says she's fine and then changes the subject.

Seeing her like this, so restless, so unable to be in her skin, makes me think about the conversation I had with E.M. earlier. There is something about the future and hope that is a mystery to me. People say you need hope to live, but hope also makes things worse. Lucy is Mona's hope. The loss of that hope made her try to take her life. Ever since Rudy told her he could help her find Lucy, here is Mona, miserable, no longer satisfied with her present circumstances, anxious about not getting what she hopes for.

I can't think of anything to hope for. When I try to think about the future, I run into a dark, thick, impenetrable wall. Am I better off than Mona? I don't know. What's better? To hurt from your wants or to be so dead inside that you don't want anything? I don't want anything. I don't even want to die, I suddenly realize — so maybe that's something.

The next morning, Gabriel and I set about creating a rose garden. The soil in the front of Dr. Desai's house, where the garden is to go, is not quite as rocky as it was in the north pasture. Gabriel and I work mostly in silence. At one point, as I'm patiently digging around a rock with a hand trowel, I notice him looking at me and smiling.

"What?" I say. "Never seen someone work?"

"You learned a few things from working with E.M. yesterday, didn't you?"

"I learned not to ask silly questions," I say, trying not to smile.

That afternoon we finally are able to walk to the river. It's just Gabriel and me. E.M. decides to go target shooting with Pepe. Mona says she has cramps and wants to lie down, but I think it's the fear of a lack of a cell phone signal by the river that keeps her from coming with us.

Gabriel is waiting for me on the front porch of his house. He comes down the wooden steps with the dogs beside him, clamoring for his attention.

"You made some new friends," I say.

"I love dogs," he says. "I've tried to get my grandpa to get us one ever since my mother died, but he's always said that he can only take care of one wild creature at a time." He laughs. "Do you have a dog?"

"A cat. His name is Galileo." I instinctively raise my hand to my chest. Galileo's scratches are still there.

"Wow! Look at that." Gabriel stops in front of the corral where the brown horse is penned. When I look at it more carefully, I realize the horse is actually a mixture of red, gold, and brown.

"What color would you say he is?" I ask.

"She," Gabriel corrects me. "That there is a bay horse." He climbs the lower rung of the fence and motions for me to climb up next to him, then begins to make a clicking sound with his tongue. The horse twists her head as if she were somewhat interested and then slowly and cautiously begins to approach, shaking her head as if to convince herself that it's a bad idea. When she's just within reach, she lowers her head in front of me. "She wants you to touch her," Gabriel says.

"Me?"

"She's shy. She'd prefer it if a girl touched her. Go ahead. Rub her right between the eyes. They like it when your touch is firm."

I hesitate for a second, and then I touch the horse with the tips of my fingers. As soon as I do that, the horse neighs and trots away.

"How did it feel?" Gabriel's eyes are filled with curiosity.

"It was soft but strong. I've never touched a horse before." A memory comes to me.

"What did you just think of?" Gabriel asks.

"Why?"

"A shadow came over your face."

"I thought about the time I quit debate. When I told my father, I expected him to be angry at me, but all he said was 'You can't ask a mule to be a racehorse.'"

Gabriel's face turns serious, as if he's weighing the import of what I just said. He stoops to pet Cleo. Julius has gone off someplace.

We walk in silence. Ahead to our left we see a large fenced-in area with only a few trees. Four horses and two cows munch grass in the shade. To our right we can see a dirt path that leads to a formation of rocks in the distance. We take the path, and for a moment I'm reminded of the walk up the mountain that Jaime and I took, only I don't feel any of the apprehension I felt then. Gabriel picks up a broken branch and throws it for Cleo to fetch. After a while I say, "Last night, after everyone went to their cabins, I went to the main house to get Mona a glass of warm milk. There you were in the den, writing away in the notebook that Dr. Desai gave us."

"Why didn't you come up and say something?"

"You looked like you were so into what you were writing. I was afraid to disturb you."

"Seeing you write in your journal inspired me."

"You've been writing for a lot longer than you've known me," I say. "I saw the notebooks in your room. Remember?"

"Oh, those. I probably should have gotten rid of those when I got rid of my books. But the voice wasn't specific about that. He said books. So I kept the *note*books. . . . What? You just shook your head disapprovingly."

"I'm sorry, it just doesn't make sense to me why your voice, or anyone for that matter, would want you to get rid of your books."

"I liked them too much. That's all I can think of. I was spending all my money on books. One time, Margarita — you met her. She wanted to borrow a book she saw when she was cleaning my room. It was one of my favorites, *Saint Francis of Assisi* by G. K. Chesterton. And when she asked me about it, I had these really selfish thoughts that she was not smart enough or educated enough to understand the book. And then I felt possessive, greedy, like a two-year-old who doesn't want to share a toy — a toy he's not even playing with at the time. It was ugly."

"And you say I'm hard on myself!"

"Really, you think I'm hard on myself?" He sounds surprised.

"*Duh*, as Mona would say. Those kinds of thoughts come to all of us."

Cleo finally brings Gabriel the stick. He wiggles it out of the dog's mouth and tosses it. Cleo goes after it.

"So what did you do?" I ask.

"Mmm?"

"Did you lend Margarita the book?"

"Of course."

"Well, then, that's all that matters, that you didn't let the selfish thoughts stop you. Who cares what happens inside your head? It's what you do that counts, as E.M. says."

Gabriel looks up. "A storm is coming." I follow his gaze and see several black clouds coming together to form one dark mass.

"Maybe we should head back," I say.

He studies the clouds. "We have time. Let's take a look at the river. It has to be over by those rocks and trees. Come on!" He starts to run.

"I'm wearing flip-flops!" I yell at him.

"Take them off!" he shouts and keeps running.

I take off my flip-flops and run. The earth is hard and warm and smooth under my feet. My legs feel weak and unused, and by the time I reach the first clump of trees, I'm panting. I make my way through red, dusty rocks that look like they've been left over from some prehistoric volcano. Then, around a bend, there is an opening, and I almost fall into the river.

The water moves slowly on the banks, but I can tell that the current is stronger in the middle of the stream, where there are rapids. Gabriel is standing in a small clearing a few yards away with a rubber raft, a couple of kayaks and oars, and some kind of storage shed. Thunder cracks the sky, and rain begins to pelt us. There aren't even a few drops of warning — just thunder followed immediately by buckets of rain. "We have time, huh?" I bump his shoulder.

Gabriel tilts his head back as far as it will go, shuts his eyes, opens his mouth wide, and extends his arms to the heavens.

He's like a child who's spent his life locked up in some dark room and is feeling the wetness and coolness of rain for the first time. How does he do that? See newness everywhere? I hate the dark space where I live, but I'm too afraid to step out.

There's a flash of lightning and another clap of thunder. I tug his arm. "Shouldn't we head back?" I yell so he can hear me.

"Not while there's lightning," he says. He pulls me away from the edge of the river. Then he lets go of me and motions for me to help him turn over the rubber raft. He props it up with one of the oars, and we duck under the shelter it provides.

We lie on our backs side by side. The rain hitting the raft makes a hollow sound, as if we're inside a drum being played by a maniac. There's something exhilarating about listening to the thunder and rain with only a rubber lining for protection. I turn briefly to glimpse Gabriel's face, and the smile I see there makes me smile as well.

A thunderbolt explodes almost on top of us, and Gabriel shudders, pretending he's terrified. I laugh. I remember how I felt when Becca and I shared a room and we crawled into the same bed and covered our heads with the quilt at the sound of thunder. There was a time when I was not alone, before something invisible and hard came between me and others. But here, next to Gabriel, there's no wall.

I say, "One time you said, I guess it was in one of our group meetings, that you knew about depression. Why did you say that?"

His face turns serious again. "I've had it."

"What was it like for you? I mean, what did it feel like?"

"I don't know. The image that always came to mind was of a basketball with not enough air. You try to bounce it and it just sticks in the ground with a thud."

I smile. I've been a basketball with not enough air. "And you're okay now?"

"I moved on to bigger things," he says with a grin. "The depression went away."

"When?" I ask.

"When I started hearing the voice." I can see his mind working, chewing on some new realization.

"What are you thinking?" I ask.

"I was wondering what would happen if I stopped hearing my voice. Would I go back to being depressed?"

"But when you were depressed, you kept on going, working, mowing lawns."

"Yes, I kept on mowing the lawns. I had no choice. Plus moving around and having something to do helped me."

"I asked E.M. when we were out digging holes how he managed to work at construction day after day. He said it was easier if you had to do it or else you and your family didn't eat. He also learned some tricks not to get bored, like concentrating on what you're doing."

"That's hard to do when you're depressed. But medication helps with concentration."

"Were you on medication?"

"Yes, for about three months."

"What was that like?"

"There are no 'happy' pills. All the things that are hard in your life remain. All the things you don't like to do, you still don't like. But at least you'll have the energy to do them."

"Dr. Desai wants to wait a while, see how I do when I get back home before I start taking antidepressants."

"She would have already put you on medication if she thought you weren't getting better or you were still suicidal. Dr. Desai is very slow to put people on medication, if it's not urgent. Depression is bad, but it can teach us some things."

"Like what?" I say.

"There's things you see when you're depressed that you don't see otherwise. You see how silly the world is sometimes and the craziness around you. You see all the things that people strive for, like money and success and popularity, and you realize that those things don't make us happy."

The image of my father and Barbara and myself sitting at the dinner table comes to me. The conversation always seemed to center in some form or another around making money or not losing it. But they didn't look happy. They seemed anxious and worried, as if they were afraid that money would run out before they got their share. "You almost make it sound as if it's good to be depressed," I say.

"No. Depression's bad, and you have to do all you can to get out of it. But I learned how to persist when I was depressed, how to go out and mow the daily lawns even when I didn't want to or thought I couldn't."

We remain silent for a long time. I'm thinking about the days following my mother's death. My father had the special hospital bed, the oxygen tanks, and all her medicines removed the day after we placed her ashes in a cemetery vault. He went back to work the following day, and Becca and I returned to school. A few days later someone from the Salvation Army came to take all of my mother's clothes. My father wanted us to get back on the horse of daily routine, get on with life. "The best medicine for grief is to keep busy," he said.

I wish my father would have let me feel sad, really sad, as sad as I could get for as long as it took. Then maybe there could have been a new beginning for me. And what would have happened if he too had let himself feel sad? Would he be different now?

Lying here next to Gabriel, I feel sad again, for my mother's death, for her absence in my life. Only there's something about this sadness that is moist and cool, like a summer rainstorm. It's a sadness that has been knocking at my door for a long time, and I finally let it in.

We stay like that until the rain stops. Afterward, we put the raft on the ground and walk back toward the house. The rain has given the earth, the trees, the rocks a shimmer of newness. Cleo suddenly joins us out of nowhere, completely dry and happy.

When the corral with the prancing bay horse is in view, Gabriel says: "Mules are cool. They're patient like a donkey, strong like a horse. They work hard. They carry loads, pull plows, wagons, do whatever needs to be done. They don't want to be racehorses. They're happy being mules."

I think I understand why Gabriel is telling me this, but I still say, "You're going to have to translate that into regular English for me."

"If Vicky is a mule and not a racehorse, then so what? She's still needed."

In the distance we hear the dinner bell.

"Come on," he says. "Let's run."

We run.

NINETEEN

On Saturday morning, we get ready for our outing to Fredericksburg. Mona is digging in her green canvas duffel bag when I hear something rattle.

Her medication, I think. When we were at Lakeview, a nurse would bring Mona her medication every morning and every night and stand around until she saw Mona swallow the pills. Here at the ranch, Dr. Desai gave Mona two opaque orange vials and told her she would be responsible for taking her medicine. Could she trust her? Mona said yes, and I saw her take the pills the first morning and the first night, but not since then.

"Why haven't you been taking your medication?" I ask. The anger I just felt at myself for not noticing comes out in the way I ask the question.

She keeps sifting through her bag, and I can tell she's deciding whether to lie to me. She holds up a wrinkled white T-shirt with a picture of a puppy and a kitten kissing. "You like? My Lucy loved this shirt. We bought it at an arts fair in downtown Austin. I tried to find one just like it for her, but they didn't have any her size. But I used to let her wear this one to sleep. You know, like a nightgown." She puts the shirt back in her bag. "The lithium makes me draggy and sleepy and the Lamictal is basically useless anyway. I just wanted to go off the stuff for a while. I need the energy. Every once in a while it's good to have a little oomph, know what I mean? It feels good. Have I been edgy?"

"Yes," I say. She's been acting strange all week long. I thought it was Rudy and the possibility of finding Lucy that had unsettled her, but it was clearly more than that.

"But only you've noticed because I let my guard down with you. That's a compliment, by the way. I control myself at the GTH and when I talk to Dr. Desai. You're not going to tell her, are you?" She puts her shirt on.

"Yes, I am," I say firmly. "You've told me — you've told all of us what happens to you when you're manic."

"Yeah, but the trick is not to get fully manic, which is what I plan to avoid by just going off the medication for a week or two. I need to feel alive, Vicky. Rudy's finally on track again with finding Lucy. This guy he knows that works with Welfare, he wanted a thousand dollars to help us find her, and Rudy came up with the money on his own. For *me*. He's doing it for me. I'm excited. Do you know what it's like to be full of hope after not having it for so long? I don't want that to be dulled by some medicine. I just want to enjoy it for a few days. Look, tell you what, tomorrow night I'll start with the lithium."

"And the other one? The one you take in the morning?"

"Okay, I'll take that right now. But let's just settle down about all this, all right?" She goes into her bag and comes up with one of the plastic bottles. She uncaps the bottle, takes out one white pill, holds it in front of me like a magician about to make it disappear, and then pops it into her mouth.

"You usually take two of those," I say.

"Ughhh!" She groans and repeats the same procedure with another pill. "Happy?" There's a honk outside. "Oh, we gotta go."

"Mona," I say, "what will you do if Rudy finds Lucy?"

She's lifting the quilt on her bed, looking for something. "Have you seen my phone? I have to buy a charger for it. It went dead three days ago and it's driving me nuts. Here you are, you little devil. I don't know, Vicky," she says, opening the door to our cabin. "I'll have to cross that bridge when I get to it. Try to sneak a peek at her, for starters."

She rushes ahead of me toward the waiting van. I can see Gabriel and E.M. in the backseat. Pepe is in the driver's seat. Fritz is holding on to Cleo, keeping her from jumping into the van. Dr. Desai stands on the porch in a light-yellow sari, her arms crossed, smiling.

When we get to the van, Fritz hands first Mona and then me three fifty-dollar bills.

"Awesome," says Mona. "What's this for?"

"I believe in paying people something for their work, even if it's not as much as they deserve. I figured if I paid you ten dollars an hour times five days of work, that makes one hundred and fifty dollars."

"I like the way you do math," Mona says.

"You do more than three hours a day when you count the morning chores and whatnot. It's just a little something."

"He doesn't want the authorities to accuse him of slave labor," Dr. Desai pipes up from the porch.

"That's true, that's true," Fritz acknowledges. "Now go. And if you can, have lunch at one of the German restaurants. I recommend the knockwurst and sauerkraut with a nice tall glass of Beck's."

"Fritz!" Dr. Desai admonishes.

"Beg your pardon. I meant to say lemonade. It was a Freudian slip," Fritz says, winking at us.

I sit in the middle seat by myself and Mona sits up front with Pepe. As we are pulling away, Mona says, "No offense, but I'm glad we're going to some civilization for a change. I'm tired of sitting under a cow pulling and squeezing those rubbery things."

"They're called udders," E.M. says from the back.

Mona turns around. "Listen to you! Put you on a farm for a few days and you're speaking cowboy."

"It's a ranch, not a farm," E.M. corrects her. Before Mona can respond, he asks, "Hey, Pepe, do you know if there's a bookstore in town?"

There's a moment of stunned silence, and then everyone except Pepe twists around to see if those words really came out of E.M's mouth.

"What?" E.M. says before nonchalantly glancing out the window.

I'm waiting for Mona to make some comment, but she seems to be deep in thought, as if trying to figure out what E.M. could possibly want with a book. Pepe says, "I know they sell comics at the drugstore. You want real books?"

"Yeah, the real kind, with no pictures," E.M. replies.

"Let's see. They got to have one. You can find anything in Fredericksburg."

"How about cell phone chargers?" Mona asks.

"Walmart probably has those. Come to think of it, I've seen books there too."

"Oh, oh, oh," Mona says, excited, turning to E.M. "I figured it out. I know why you want to go to a bookstore."

"What you talking about now?" E.M. says.

"I seem to remember overhearing a conversation not too long ago at a certain birthday party where a certain someone found out that the person he was drooling over liked to read."

"That's why you were asking for my address this morning," Gabriel says. "You want to send Margarita a book?"

We all observe E.M.'s face turning a very dark shade of red.

"I . . . ah . . ." he stammers.

"Pretend to be brave!" Mona shouts. "Think of Huichi-whatever."

"Leave him alone, you," I say, poking Mona in the back. "You're embarrassing him."

"Big macho man like him, he's not afraid of a pretty girl, is he?"

"That's a great idea, giving her a book," Gabriel tells E.M. "That will really impress her."

"It's very thoughtful," I add.

"Yeah, E.M.," Mona says, half-mocking, half-serious. "It's very thoughtful. I didn't know you had it in you."

"You're just jealous," E.M. tells her.

"Pff!" Mona waves him off. But I can tell that maybe she is just a tiny bit jealous.

Pepe says, "I'll drop you off on Main Street; there's gotta be a bookstore there. Then I'll take the rest of you to Walmart."

"I think E.M. might need a little help picking the right book," Gabriel says to me.

"Me? You're the one who knows what Margarita likes to read."

"Pepe and I need to keep an eye on Mona. Protect the male population of Fredericksburg and all that."

"Oh, please," Mona says, "as if there's anything here that would interest me."

Pepe drops E.M. and me on Main Street to look for a bookstore, while he, Gabriel, and Mona go to find a cell phone charger. We agree to meet in front of the post office in two hours to go to lunch together.

"What kind of book do you want to get?" I ask E.M. as we walk down Main Street.

"I don't know," he says, rubbing the black bristles on his head. "What kinds of books do girls like?"

"They like every kind. Why don't we get her a book you like, so she'll get to know you better?"

"A book about the Aztecs?"

"Mmm. Let's see. Why do you want to give her a book?"

"She said back when we were doing the dishes together that she liked to read."

"She didn't say what?"

He shakes his head, discouraged. "Maybe the book thing is not a good idea. What do I know about books? I read two my whole life. One of them was mostly pictures."

"You feeling sorry for yourself now?" I tease.

E.M. stares at me like he's considering whether to let me live. He reminds me of what lion tamers say of the lions in their circus act: It's always good to remember that they can bite your head off at any moment. Still, it's hard to pass up the opportunity to turn the tables on E.M.

E.M. steps in front of a man with pointy boots and a black cowboy hat. I watch the man's Adam's apple go up and down rapidly. "There a place around here where they sell books?" E.M. asks.

"There's a bookstore at the end of Main Street," the cowboy says, pointing over his shoulder with his thumb.

"And a post office?" My tone is a few notches friendlier than E.M.'s.

"At the other end," he says, nodding in the direction he's walking.

"Thank you," I say. Then, when he walks away, I say to E.M., "You scared him."

E.M. shrugs. "What kind of book would you like to get if and when someone gave you a book?" he asks.

"Me?"

"Like if you got the book you'd think, 'This guy likes me but respects me also,' you know?"

I consider the question. "Well, for me, a book of poetry

would make me think that about the person who sent it. It would have to be written by a good poet and it would have serious poems, not just silly love poems. That would be corny."

"Yeah," E.M. says. "I don't want corny."

"But that's me, because I like poetry. So getting a book of poetry from someone would mean the person is accepting me as I am, in a way." I gather from the somber expression that comes over E.M.'s face that this is probably not what he wanted to hear. Then I remember the story Gabriel told me about how hard it was for him to lend Margarita one of his books — a life of St. Francis of Assisi. "I think I know what kind of book to get her."

E.M.'s face brightens. "How?"

"Something Gabriel told me."

The bookstore turns out to be at the very end of Main Street, but we don't mind the long walk. It's in an old, ordinary-looking house with a bookcase on the porch. Inside the house, there are rooms filled with carefully organized shelves of books and colorful sofas and leather chairs inviting us to sit and read. I leave E.M. alone in front of the religion and spirituality shelves. I'm pretty sure Margarita would appreciate any book from there. "Pick a title you like," I tell him.

For the first time since I met him, E.M. actually looks scared. But I leave him alone to face his fears while I head over to the poetry section. I pull out a small volume with a red cover. The book's title is simply *Emily Dickinson*. I remember one of her poems from English class and I look for it until I find it.

"Hope" is the thing with feathers —
That perches in the soul —
And sings the tune without the words —
And never stops — at all —

And sweetest — in the Gale — is heard —
And sore must be the storm —
That could abash the little Bird
That kept so many warm —

I've heard it in the chillest land —
And on the strangest Sea —
Yet — never — in Extremity,
It asked a crumb — of Me.

I like that poem. What would it be like to have the "thing with feathers" perch on my soul? Can you hope for hope?

I put the book back where it was, go to the porch, and wait for E.M. When he comes out, he shows me the book he bought for Margarita: *The Four Loves* by C. S. Lewis. "What you think?" he asks, nervous.

I take it from him, open it, and read the table of contents out loud: " 'Affection, Friendship, Eros, Charity.' It's perfect. Why did you pick this one?"

"It looked good," he says, putting it back in the bag. Then, after we start walking, he says, "The old lady who owns the place said I couldn't go wrong with a book that talks about friendship."

I nod. I can't really add anything to that.

We stop at a drugstore and buy an envelope and a postcard with a picture of a buffalo, of all things, which E.M simply signs with his full name and sticks in the middle of the book. Then after we find the post office and mail the package, we buy chocolate ice-cream cones and sit on a bench, waiting for Pepe and the crew.

E.M. displays total childlike concentration, licking around and around the ice cream, catching brown drops before they slide down the cone. The sunlight is on my face and it is soft, caressing. The chocolate ice cream is rich, smooth, cold. Sitting on that bench, not wishing for tomorrow, or being afraid of it, feels a lot like the little bird in the poem by Emily Dickinson. It's come out of nowhere, perched on my soul, and begun to sing a tune.

TWENTY

Sunday morning — about fifteen minutes after Mona finally falls asleep, or so it seems — Fritz knocks on our door and tells us it is time to milk the cows. I don't know how I manage to make it through the next hour. No matter what I do, I can't get any milk to come out, and Rosie the cow keeps looking back at me with growing annoyance. Pepe kneels beside me and shows me again how to hold the udder between my thumb and index finger and how to tug gently but with strength.

After breakfast, which includes two mugs of black coffee, we head to the river, wearing swimsuits we borrowed from a trunk in the big house. We drag a big rubber raft to the shore and are about to climb in, when Gabriel says, "Wait, we need to put on life jackets."

"We're not going far, are we?" Mona says. "I just want to go where we can jump in. Besides, it's not that deep. I can see the bottom."

Gabriel walks over to the wooden shed and comes back with four life jackets. "According to Fritz, the river is twelve feet at its deepest part," he says. "That's plenty deep to drown for someone who doesn't know how to swim."

"Who doesn't know how to swim?" asks Mona.

"I don't, for one," says Gabriel. "E.M. doesn't either."

"How you know I don't?" E.M. says.

"Because I grew up in the same kind of neighborhood you did. The only deep water we saw was in the kitchen sink."

Mona reluctantly puts on her life jacket, and E.M. slips his on without buckling the front. The life jackets are bulky and discolored. I can barely breathe with mine on.

Mona and I climb into the raft, and Gabriel and E.M. push us into the water. The rubber raft has three seats: One up front facing the back of the boat, a middle slab for two people, and a rear seat. Mona takes the one up front. Gabriel settles into the middle seat next to me and hands me an oar. E.M. makes himself comfortable in the back. I peer in the water and see hundreds of baby sunfish.

"Why we going upstream?" Mona asks. "Let's float down the river."

"The rapids are downstream," Gabriel answers. "Fritz said we should go upstream and then we can float back to where we started. It's been raining hard and the rapids are strong. We're not experienced enough to handle them."

"Oh, phooey!" Mona says. "Fritz is a worrywart. I've been locked up in a room all week painting walls almond cream. I need a little excitement. Enjoy life while you can 'cause you never know what's gonna happen. Let's just go down a little ways, and when we see the rapids, we can turn back."

"What do you think?" Gabriel says, looking at me.

I look downriver. It seems calm enough, and I can see unusual rock formations not too far from where we are. "We can go down to those rocks. Mona and E.M. can paddle back." The caffeine from the coffee is finally kicking in.

"Very funny," says E.M. "I'm gonna sit back here and work on my tan."

"Okay, but only to the rocks," says Gabriel. "We might have to carry the raft on land on the way back."

"I didn't bring any shoes!" Mona protests.

"I didn't bring any shoes!" E.M. mimics her.

"You shut up," Mona says.

Gabriel begins paddling to the middle of the river and I try to do the same. Soon we are moving slowly downstream.

Mona lies back in her red bikini to soak up the sun. A few minutes later, she says, "Stop ogling me. Why get yourself all worked up? It's not going to do you any good."

"Are you talking to me?" E.M. asks.

"Yeah, you. Why do you always ask me that? Stop ogling my body."

"What the hell is ogling?" E.M. says, unperturbed. "Why can't you speak a language people understand? Anyways, you're not as hot as you think you are."

"Ogling is when you stare at somebody's body parts with your tongue hanging out and slobber dripping, like you've been doing."

"Children, children, let's be harmonious," says Gabriel. We have caught a gentle current, so we are steering more than paddling.

"Harmonious? Don't anybody speak normal in this group?" E.M. says.

"Just 'cause your vocabulary matches your mental age," Mona answers.

"Maybe we should put the oars in the oarlocks." Gabriel points to the plastic hooks on each side of the raft.

Mona turns sideways on her seat and rests her head on the side of the raft. She unbuckles her life jacket and sighs. "Wish I had sunglasses," she says.

We float in silence, the only sound the murmur of the river and the gentle splash of the oars. On the banks, trees dip their branches as if to drink from the water. I think about the day before: helping E.M. buy a book, the knockwurst and sauerkraut we all had for lunch and hated. Sauerkraut reminded me of those days when every second dripped with bitterness. It's so peaceful on this raft, and yet so vibrant. Is this what happiness feels like?

When we get to the rocks, the current unexpectedly begins to pick up speed. "Okay, let's turn around," Gabriel says. "Vicky, you paddle forward and I'll paddle backward." We manage with some effort to turn the raft sideways, but by then we are past the rocks and going even faster. The raft begins to heave up and down as if going over small bumps. There is a distant sound of water rushing. We row harder and harder, but we are still moving in the wrong direction.

"This reminds me of my life," Mona says.

Gabriel looks back toward the sound, which is getting louder and louder. "We're gonna hit the rapids!" he shouts. "Vicky, let's turn the raft back around and row to that clump of trees there before the rapids."

My arms ache with the effort of fighting the current. By the time we turn around again, we are almost past the trees. Ahead of us the river ripples and gurgles as it snakes around the rocks. Mona sits up to look and says, "Those are the famous rapids? I've been in bathtubs more dangerous than that."

"Tighten your vest," Gabriel tells Mona.

I see that E.M. is gripping the edge, a look of paralyzed fear on his face. His life jacket is lying on the bottom of the raft. "Put on your life jacket," I say to him.

"Vicky, do you see those two rocks?" Gabriel asks. "We need to steer the raft around them or else try to maneuver between them."

"We have to go between them," I say. "The current is too strong to steer around."

"You're right," says Gabriel.

"Hold on, Mona," I yell, "we're going to hit the rocks with the side of the raft."

"Yeah, let's do it!" she screams.

We pick up speed. The raft begins to bounce on the surface of the water, and then it dips into a trough that's unexpectedly deep. When we rise again, Mona is on the floor of the raft sliding toward us and we are heading straight for the rock.

"Paddle backward!" Gabriel shouts, but we are going so fast and bouncing so hard that I forget which direction backward is. Before we know it, we have crashed head-on into the rock.

The jolt lifts Gabriel and me out of our seats and into the bottom of the raft. We scramble back to our places as the bumps over the water diminish. Mona is on her knees soaking wet and laughing, and it suddenly occurs to me to that we have not heard a peep out of E.M.

I look back. There is no E.M. His life jacket is on the bottom of the raft.

"E.M. fell out," I say weakly. Somehow Gabriel hears me. He turns around and utters a word I did not think was in his vocabulary.

"Let's paddle to the side so we don't drift farther down," I say. We get ourselves out of the main current and stop between the roots of two trees, then we turn back around to look for E.M. After a few seconds, a hand rises out of the water.

"I see him!" I yell.

"Where?" Mona and Gabriel ask at the same time.

"He went under. There." I point to the place I saw his hand.

Gabriel moves to the edge of the raft and gets ready to jump into the water. I put my hand on his shoulder. "You don't know how to swim," I say as I unbuckle my life jacket.

"I'll be okay with the life vest," he says.

"You'll never reach him with a life vest. He's upstream." Before he can say anything else, I dive in. I dive flat because I don't know how deep it is and I don't want to hit my head on the bottom. I swim toward a spot ten or so yards ahead of where I last saw his hand. The current gathers force and my arms begin to feel heavy, so I switch to a breaststroke. When I get to the place I aimed for, I tread water, feeling with my arms and legs for E.M. Then I dive under as far down as I can.

Gabriel said that the river at its deepest was twelve feet. The water is so murky that I can barely see. I stay underwater, still groping for E.M., until I begin to feel the way I felt half an hour or so after I took Barbara's sleeping pills, when the tunnel I was falling through grew darker and darker.

Then I see E.M. about ten feet away from me. His arms float straight up, like a puppet's held by strings, and his legs are moving in slow motion, as if he's walking on the surface of the moon.

I go up for air, then dive under again. I grab him from the back, one arm around his chest, and use my free arm and legs to push us toward the surface. As soon as our heads pop out, I put my hand under his chin to keep his head above water and let us float a little. My limbs are so weak I can hardly move them.

Gabriel and Mona are shouting for me. They stand in the shallow water, extending the oars toward us. I make one final effort and somehow get close enough to grab Gabriel's oar. He pulls us in, and he and Mona drag E.M. to shore. I sit in the shallow edge of the river, too weak to stand.

"He has a pulse," I hear Gabriel say.

"Should we give him mouth-to-mouth?" Mona says.

"Not if he has a pulse. He's going to be okay. We just have to get the water out of his lungs. Help me turn him on his side."

I get to shore just in time to hear E.M. cough and see water gush out of his mouth and nose. Gabriel is patting him softly on his back.

It occurs to me, as I kneel next to them, that I have just acted as if life is worth living.

CHAPTER TWENTY-ONE

Gabriel runs back to the ranch to get help. Mona and I stay with E.M.

"I'm okay," E.M. groans, looking anything but okay. He insists on getting up, but when he tries to walk, his legs wobble. We help him over to sit in the shade of a willow tree.

"Thank you," he says, coughing.

"Now I know you're delirious," Mona says. "That's the first time I've ever heard you say thank you."

He tries to respond, but a coughing fit interrupts him.

"You shouldn't talk now," I say.

But words gush out of his mouth uncontrollably. "I was down there and all I could think of was who's gonna protect my little brother from my father. I shoulda killed the old man when I had a chance, then I wouldn't have to worry about it. That's what came in my mind. Then everything went black, man, black, and I saw this Aztec warrior, he had one of those — like a head of a jaguar on his head, you know, like you see in pictures. Then he starts speaking to me in Aztec, 'cause I don't understand what he's saying. And I'm like, I wanna know what he's saying. I got so frustrated that I didn't understand. I got mad at myself. Like I was supposed to learn Aztec when I was at school or something and I didn't because I didn't like school or didn't think it was important, and now I was regretting it and wishing I had."

"The dude was probably giving you instructions on how to float up and get some air," Mona tells him.

E.M. ignores her. "All I could think of is that the warrior was Huitzilopochtli. Then I began to understand what he was saying even though he was still speaking Aztec. I don't know how it happened. I didn't understand the words, but I knew what he was saying, know what I mean?"

"Yup, I do," Mona says. "Lucy made up her own language when she was about one and a half, but I knew exactly what she was saying."

E.M. continues, "At first I thought he was telling me I was a coward because at the last second I had felt sorry for my old man and not finished him off, but that wasn't it. I don't know how he knew what I was thinking or how I understood him, but I knew he was mad at me for something else. He wasn't angry at me for something I'd done, he was angry about something I hadn't done, and he wanted me to get off my ass and do it. The only part I didn't get is what I was supposed to do. He went on and on like I was supposed to know. Then he said that if I didn't know, then I sure as hell better find out, and he grabbed me by the chest and he started to pull me out of the hole where I was."

"That wasn't Huichi-whatever, you bonehead," Mona says. "That was Vicky here dragging your sorry butt out of the bottom of the river."

"I know it was her that saved me, but in my mind she was Huitzilopochtli. All I'm telling you is what I saw. This guy was as real as you sitting there."

"Or it could be that you've been spending too much time with Gabriel," Mona says. "Him with his voices and now you with your Huichi."

"Maybe I'm just as nuts as you guys now." A wicked-looking smile comes over E.M.'s face as he looks at Mona. "I even had a nightmare you wanted to give me mouth-to-mouth resurrection."

"It's resuscitation!" Mona screeches. "Man, you're as dumb as that cow you tried to milk this morning! Mouth-to-mouth, in your dreams. How could you be so stupid as to take off your life jacket after everybody told you to keep it on?"

"Maybe I wanted to die like you guys." E.M. turns serious. He says to me, "Why did you save me?"

"I didn't think about it," I say.

"I could've pulled you under."

"You weren't thrashing about. You were just floating there like a log. It wasn't that hard to pull you out."

"Not too bad for a spoiled rich girl," he says.

I figure that's a compliment, coming from E.M. I thank him with a nod.

"That's all you're going to say? After she risked her life saving you?" Mona whacks E.M. on the shoulder, nearly knocking him over.

E.M. looks straight at me and says, "I owe you one, Huichi."

Fritz and Gabriel arrive in the same vehicle that Pepe used to take E.M. and me to the north pasture. We tie the rubber raft to the roof. Gabriel and Mona ride in the back with E.M., and I ride up front with Fritz. When we get to the ranch, Dr.

Desai insists on taking E.M. to the hospital outside of Fredericksburg. She wants to make sure there's no water left in his lungs and the lack of oxygen hasn't damaged his brain. Mona gives me a meaningful look when she hears this, but she restrains herself from wisecracking for once.

Dr. Desai pulls me aside to ask if I'm all right. I tell her I'm exhausted but otherwise fine. She says, "Vicky, someday you will receive what you gave today." She puts her arm around my shoulders, then she heads out the door.

Gabriel, Mona, and I walk silently to our cabins. When we get to our door, Mona says, "I'm going to sleep till tomorrow," and goes in.

I turn to say good-bye to Gabriel and see him standing there, a lost look on his face.

"You okay?" I ask. He doesn't answer. I touch his arm gently.

"Hey," he says, as if waking up.

"Where were you?"

He shakes his head, embarrassed.

"Did you hear something just then?" I ask.

"I don't know. Something's happening in here." He taps his head.

"What?" We begin to walk toward his cabin.

He shakes his head again. A few seconds later he says, "What you did was so dangerous. It should have been me jumping after him."

"You don't know how to swim, and you never would have been able to pull him up with a life jacket on."

"You could have died."

"But I didn't."

He grimaces and covers his ears with his hands.

"What is it?" I ask, worried now.

He stays like that for a minute or so, pain convulsing his face. It occurs to me that in the past few days, I've started to believe that maybe his voice wasn't all that bad. How can someone who says the sane things he says not be sane? But now I feel the same fear I felt when he first told me about the voice. This force that is gripping him now is not healthy or normal or good.

Finally, he removes his hands from his ears. "Wow," he says. "That was unusual."

"I should get Fritz," I say.

"I'm okay," he says. "I need to rest. Too much excitement. I'll see you. You were out of this world today." He squeezes my arm, then opens the door to his cabin. He turns and waves good-bye at me. I wave back.

Then, after he has entered his cabin and closed the door, I hear him say, "Okay, okay! I'm here."

TWENTY-TWO

When I get to our cabin, I feel a current of energy coursing through my arms and legs. I can even feel my heart beat at a quicker, more alert pace, and I slowly begin to feel myself wanting things. I want Gabriel to be well. I want Mona to be safe. I want E.M. to be fine. I want to keep Juanita from going back to Mexico. I even want to go back to school and finish the year with passing grades. I can get the necessary C's to move on to the next grade, and I will somehow make it through the next year, and then what? It is a fragile, tentative kind of wanting and there is sadness in it, but it is still wanting and it is new to me.

I remember Gabriel showing me the room in his house where his grandmother used to work and telling me that they were looking for someone who could move in and help take care of Chona. What if Juanita goes to live with Gabriel's grandparents? I finish the school year at Reynard and get a summer job somewhere, anywhere except my father's firm. I get my certification as a lifeguard and work at a public pool. I take driver's ed and get my license and drive Becca's car to work. I drive to see Juanita on the weekends. Mona is okay. She finds out Lucy is better off where she is and leaves her alone. E.M. is dating Margarita and they are immensely happy together. Gabriel has found a way to go back to school. After that, the images get hazy, but just seeing a few months into the future feels like a small miracle.

I sleep the rest of the afternoon. Around six p.m., I walk over to the main house to get something to eat. "Is E.M. back?" I ask Mona. She's making a peanut butter and jelly sandwich. Her eye is twitching at a faster rate than usual, and she keeps shifting her weight from one leg to the other.

"Dr. Desai decided to keep him at Lakeview for observation. He'll be there a couple of nights," she says distractedly.

Dr. Desai comes in from outside, a worried look on her face. "Gabriel has a fever. Not very high now, but . . ." The way she stops makes me think that she is worried about Gabriel for more than just the fever.

"I can take him a sandwich," I say.

"Let him rest for an hour or so," she tells me. Her eyes drift to Mona, who is putting half a jar of peanut butter between two slices of bread and then bites into the gooey mess as if she has not tasted food for a month. "How are you doing on your medication?" she asks Mona pointedly.

Mona looks up with her mouth full, a guilty expression on her face. "I've been good," she says after swallowing. "Ask Vicky."

Dr. Desai turns to me and I nod. I saw Mona put the lithium pills in her mouth yesterday and this morning. But now it occurs to me that I did not see her swallow them.

"Let's talk tomorrow after I get back from the hospital," Dr. Desai says.

Mona stays in the main house to watch TV with Fritz and Pepe. I go back to the cabin and sit on an easy chair to write, but I can't keep my eyes open, and after a few minutes I fall asleep again.

The next morning, I'm fixing a bowl of cereal when Dr. Desai walks in and asks me to check on Gabriel later. She has an emergency at Lakeview and has to leave, but he still has a fever, and I should make sure he drinks plenty of liquids. His temperature is 104. If it increases, I should call her on her cell.

After breakfast, I hurry over to see Gabriel. I knock but he doesn't answer, so I go in. He's in bed, his eyes wide open, staring at the ceiling. I pull up a chair next to his bed, and he turns to look at me.

"Are you okay?" I ask.

He nods and smiles feebly. I go to the bathroom and bring back a glass of water. He sits up to drink it, looking dazed. He lies back down, and I cover his bare, perspiring chest with the sheet.

"You're hot," I say, touching his forehead.

"Thank you," he says.

I smile at him. "I meant as in temperature."

"Oh." He pulls himself up, and I fix a pillow for his back.

"I should have jumped. I hesitated," he mutters to himself.

"Are you still stuck on that?" I place the glass next to his bed and say patiently, "You couldn't have gone underwater to get E.M. with your life jacket on. And if you took it off, you would have drowned because you don't know how to swim. I was the last person who saw him. You didn't know where he was. Is that what's bothering you, that you didn't jump in?"

"You could have died."

"So could you. So could E.M."

For a moment I think he has forgotten that I am sitting next to him. He's someplace else, some sad place. I try to cheer him up. "You should have been there to hear what E.M. had to say when we were waiting for you to come back with Fritz. He had this vision that Huitzilopochtli was angry with him because he hadn't done something he was supposed to do, and he wanted E.M. to get back to earth and do it. Then he thought that Huitzilopochtli was saving him, and it turned out it was me, so now he calls me Huichi."

Gabriel smiles. When he speaks, his voice is different, quieter. There are pauses between words and I can't tell whether another word will follow. "I thought I lost you and E.M."

"But you were wrong," I say.

"Then. Now it feels weird, like you are going away. Gone."

"Gone as in I'm going back home, you mean."

"Yeah. But more. Like you're far away. You'll be gone. Soon."

"I was planning to keep in touch. Weren't you?" The truth is that I have not thought about how I would stay in touch with Gabriel or E.M. or Mona. I've been trying not to think about going home.

He's silent. Then he says, "What if . . ."

"What if what?" I have a feeling that I will not like what he's about to say.

"What if I'm like Gwendolyn or my grandmother?"

"Gabriel, where is this coming from? What is the voice saying?"

"It . . ."

"Tell me."

"I'm afraid. The voice. I've never been afraid."

"What is the voice asking you to do?"

He massages his temples. "Nothing," he says, but the way he says it, I know he's hiding something. "I'm just scared."

"Why are you talking like this? What are you feeling? What did the voice say to you?"

He shakes his head and closes his eyes. He doesn't want to tell me. "I'm sorry, Vicky."

"For what?" I say.

"For this." He touches his head. "I didn't want you to see this."

"You didn't want me to see a Gabriel who is mentally ill?"

His eyes stay closed.

"Gabriel. So what? We're all ill. We're all in this together. We'll make it."

I watch him a few more minutes. Some kind of frantic activity flickers beneath his eyelids. There's a desperate fight going on in there. Finally, his breathing deepens and the twitches and jerks stop and I leave.

I spend the rest of the day painting walls with Mona and thinking about my conversation with Gabriel. There is something about him that is different, dimmer. He saw me as far away. But it is Gabriel who is pulling away, disappearing.

Mona is even more jittery than usual. Her brushstrokes look like what Van Gogh would have painted if he'd been plugged into an electric power source. Every five minutes she steps outside to smoke from a pack of cigarettes she must have bought in Fredericksburg. At one point she disappears for an hour, and when she comes back, she's more irritable than ever.

"What's wrong?" I ask.

"Nothing," she says. "Stop asking me that. Why do you ask me that?"

"You don't seem yourself. You haven't been yourself since . . . Rudy."

"This is me!" she snaps. "I'm being me. Sometimes I wish people would just let me be." She dips the brush in the paint can and begins to paint. "Damn it!" she shouts a minute later. "I got to make a phone call."

Through the window, I can see her walking briskly toward our cabin, lighting another cigarette.

I don't know what to do about Gabriel. I want to check on him. I know I should. It's been a couple of hours since I last saw Fritz go to his cabin with a tray of food. But maybe it's better if I leave him alone. Or am I being a coward? What impulse should I obey? The one that cares for him or the one that is afraid?

Huichi would say that it's okay to be afraid. I smile to myself. Will I ever be able to be afraid and not think of Huichi? I take a deep breath and walk to Gabriel's cabin.

His temperature is still 104. He makes an effort to talk, but I can tell his mind has trouble generating words. He said this morning that he was afraid for the first time. I want to ask Dr. Desai if that's how schizophrenia works — a voice that begins with persistent suggestions and gradually increases in intensity until it ends up shouting commands.

Just before I leave him for the night, I ask him the question that's been on my mind since this morning. "Gabriel, who's speaking to you?"

He swallows and waits a few moments before he answers: "God."

A chill runs through my body. Then I ask, "But if it's God, why are you so scared?"

"God is scary."

"You were not scared before. This voice is different, isn't it?"

He hears my question. I know he does. But doesn't answer. He doesn't want to. Then he closes his eyes.

TWENTY-THREE

When Fritz knocks on the door the following morning and tells us the cows are waiting, Mona is not in her bed. I have been awake for hours but somehow did not see her leave the room. I lie there looking at her empty bunk and a feeling of dread comes over me. It reminds me of the day Mamá died: I woke and knew immediately that something bad was going to happen.

I get up and dress and go over to the barn, where Pepe has already started on one of the cows. "I'll milk, you shovel," he says, pointing with his head to the wheelbarrow and shovel in the corner.

"Have you seen Mona?" I ask as I bend to grab a pair of black rubber boots.

"Walking," he says, shaking his head. "She's got the ants."

"The ants?"

"In her skin. I seen it lots of times."

After I finish cleaning the stalls, I go to the main house to look for Mona, but no one is inside. There's a note from Fritz saying Dr. Desai stayed overnight in Austin. I walk outside and am on my way to Gabriel's cabin when I hear Mona call me. She's on the front porch, pacing nervously.

"There you are," she says when she sees me. "You were asleep when I got in last night. I didn't want to wake you. I watched this old movie, *Night of the Living Dead*. Have you seen it? It's like the first zombie movie. I love zombies, but then I couldn't sleep. I had this dream that Lucy was in a room by herself. She spilled a box of Cheerios on the floor and was picking them up and eating them, her little fingers having a hard time grabbing them off the floor. Then someone came in, a man, I couldn't see his face. He was wearing these boots that motorcycle people use, big black ones with that buckle across the front. He started stomping on the Cheerios, and Lucy began to cry. She was sitting there stretching her arms out for someone to pick her up, and then the man took the box of Cheerios away and left her there all alone, terrified, crying and bawling. My God, Vicky, it was horrible. I woke up screaming."

"Mona, Mona, slow down. You're going a hundred miles an hour." I sit on a rocking chair and point to the one next to me. She sits and begins rocking so fast I think the chair will launch her over the porch rail. "What's the matter with you?"

"I ran out of cigarettes sometime last night. I'm like *dying* for a cigarette. I swear I'm going to roll up some of that hay those cows eat and smoke it. I was doing pretty good until that dream. I've been calm, you've seen me. But why would I dream something like that? That dream was telling me something about Lucy, that she's in danger. Dr. Desai is going to be mad at me because I stopped taking the lithium, but it was making me too tired, and I honestly thought the crisis was over. I was normal again. You know how I've been laughing and everything? The GTH meetings and the private sessions with Dr. Desai were working, they really were. When I first got here I was like, wow, this place is so peaceful, and now all of a sudden I can't stand how quiet it is. I'm going nuts. I have to get out of here. I'm walking over to the highway and hitching a ride back to Austin. I need to see Rudy and find out what's happening with Lucy. I've never had any problem getting from one place to another. Men are so predictable."

"Wait! Wait," I say. "Remember how in one of the GTH meetings you described what it was like to be manic? You're like that now. You lied to me about taking the pills."

"Don't mother me, okay? I hate it when people mother me. But don't take it personally about me lying to you. I haven't lied to you about anything else. I'm not manic. You should see me when I'm manic. I'm a little revved up, that's all. I went off the pills for a while because I need to be ready. I've been talking to Rudy and I have a feeling, a real strong one, that we're going to find Lucy. I need the energy to do what it takes to get her back."

When she stops to take a breath, I jump in. "I'm going to call Dr. Desai." I stand and take a few steps toward the door.

Mona springs out of the rocking chair. "I'm going to take the van. I'll leave it in a place that's easy to find. Tell Dr. Desai thanks for everything, nothing personal. I have to find my Lucy."

"Mona, do you know how dangerous all this is?" I say. "You had a bad dream, that's all. And what are you going to do when you find Lucy? There's no way you can get to her without breaking the law. And think about *her*, if you love her so much. Maybe she's happy now and you'll upset her."

There's a flash of anger in Mona's eyes. "You don't know

that! You don't know anything about my dreams. Those kinds of dreams are messages. I've had them tons before and they've always been right. Remember what I told you about mental people being smarter and more perceptive? It's true. You should know that by now. I wouldn't have had that dream if something wasn't wrong. She's with a family that's not hers. And even if she's happy, she belongs with her family, and that's me."

She brushes past me into the house. I stand there paralyzed, not knowing what to do. A minute later she comes out with the van keys dangling in her hand. She runs down the porch steps and then stops, turns around, flies up the steps again, and gives me a hug. "Okay, yes, I'm kind of mental this morning, as in I got upgraded, and I know it doesn't look like I'm in control, but I am. I've never felt better. I'm not going to hurt myself or anyone. I'll find Lucy. Without Lucy, I have nothing." She looks at me intently for a few moments, pleading for me to understand. Then she runs to the van.

"Wait, wait!" I say. "At least give me a number where I can call you."

She digs Rudy's phone out of the back pocket of her jeans and hurriedly reads out a number. I look around for Fritz, for Pepe. How can I stop her? She starts the van, backs it out of the side yard, then turns around and heads down the long gravel driveway, leaving a cloud of dust behind her. Julius and Cleo begin to bark.

I go inside and write the number Mona gave me on a napkin, then call Dr. Desai. She's on her way back to the ranch when she picks up her cell phone.

"Mona's left," I say. I feel suddenly out of breath, like I've run up three flights of stairs to get to the phone. "She took the van. She's going to meet this guy named Rudy. He works in the cafeteria. At Lakeview. She thinks he can help her find Lucy."

"Do you think she's a danger to herself or others?" she asks me.

"No," I say, remembering what she said to me just before she left. "I don't think so. But I've never seen her like this before."

Dr. Desai sighs. "There's not much we can do other than arrest her for taking the van, and I don't want to do that. She's eighteen. She's in treatment voluntarily. I'll call her mother." Her voice sounds tired, defeated, as if she's lost a battle she was hoping to win. "Let Gabriel sleep until eight, and then could you check on him?"

"Yes." Then I add, "It's more than just a fever. He said God was speaking to him." There is silence on the other end. "Hello?"

I think maybe we've been disconnected. Then I hear Dr. Desai exhale: the sound of someone whose worst fears are turning out to be true. When she speaks again, she sounds discouraged. "I'll be there in an hour or so. Sooner if I can."

I look at the clock in the kitchen. It is seven forty-five. I step outside. The bay horse I touched with Gabriel sticks her head over the top of the corral. She's nodding at me, inviting me to come. I approach the corral slowly with my hand outstretched so she can run if she wants to. But she doesn't move, and when

I'm close enough, I place the palm of my hand on her forehead between the eyes. I reach between the rails and rub her neck and feel the breath from her nostrils on my hair. Then I touch her neck. There's so much strength, so much life in this horse.

Sadness slowly fills me, but there's something about this sadness that is different, more real somehow, than the sadness I felt before I came to Lakeview. While that sadness was everywhere, floating, this sadness is attached to people and places. It comes from watching Mona pull away in a cloud of dust, E.M. being gone, seeing Gabriel slowly sink into a world I don't understand. The brokenness out there seems so much greater than the strength and life given to us.

chapter TWENTY-FOUR

I walk to Gabriel's cabin and see that he is still asleep. I pull a chair up next to his bed and watch. The in-and-out motion of his chest seems so fragile, the whole machinery of life so delicate. And then I am on a chair next to Mamá's bed, watching her struggle to breathe. She is unconscious, but now and then she opens her eyes and looks into the distance as if she's seeing something only she can see.

This is what I'm thinking when Gabriel opens his eyes. He looks at me fully alert, as if he has only been pretending to be asleep.

"Hey," I say.

"It came again. The voice. A real voice."

I reach out and place my hand on his forehead. "Your fever seems to be going up." I stand. "Let me get you a wet washcloth."

"Stay," he says. I sit down in the chair again. He covers his face with his hands. Then he lowers them and speaks, his voice quivering.

"It told me that I must give up my life so that another may live."

It takes me a few moments to register what he says. "What does that mean?"

He doesn't answer me. He's looking at something inside his head.

"Gabriel, you had a fever. It was a delirious dream."

"It wasn't a dream. It was real."

"Tell me exactly what the voice said."

" 'You must give up your life so that another may live.' "

"Must or will? There's a difference."

"Must. This time the voice was more than just a thought. The words were clear, like actual sound, only inside my head." Gabriel seems more alert, more present, than the last time I spoke to him. He's come back, a little, from where he was going.

"And you must *die*?"

"So another may live." He completes the statement.

I feel cold all over. "Remember when you told me that with schizophrenia, persistent thoughts turn into sounds. You have to look at this not as a command to be obeyed but as a thought that needs to be looked at and treated."

"This is real. I'm not ill." His voice reminds me of a little boy trying hard not to sound scared.

"Gabriel," I say. "Yesterday you were afraid you were going to end up like Gwendolyn or your grandmother. You recognized that you might be ill. Don't you still see that? You have a fever. You very likely have a mental illness." I wrap my arms around myself. "What is happening to everyone? First E.M. nearly drowns, then Mona goes manic, now you believe a crazy, scary voice."

"What about Mona?" he says.

"She left this morning — took the van back to Austin in search of Lucy. Rudy knows someone who can find her. She didn't look well. She stopped taking her medication."

He narrows his eyes. Something inside his brain clicks.

"What?" I say.

"Maybe . . ."

"Maybe what?" I ask. I already know what he's thinking. "You think Mona's the life you're meant to save — by dying?" He doesn't answer. I go on, "You must promise me to tell Dr. Desai about the voice, about what the voice told you. About the fact that it's more a voice than a thought this time." His eyes are closed and his lips are moving as if repeating something only he can hear. He is drifting farther and farther away from me, shutting me out. "I'll tell Dr. Desai if you don't," I say firmly.

He opens his eyes and slowly focuses on me once again, and for a moment he is there with me — the old Gabriel. "Since when did you become so tough?"

"Mules are tough. You're going to tell Dr. Desai?"

He nods. Then he shuts his eyes and his hands fly to his ears as if he's just heard some shrieking noise. He stays like that, shaking his head, electrified by some inner horror. I'm afraid to touch him, in case interrupting whatever is happening inside of him will only make things worse.

Then he begins to whisper something, and I lean closer and hear him repeat, over and over again: "Not my will but yours."

TWENTY-FIVE

A few minutes later, there's a knock on the door. I open it and Dr. Desai steps in and looks at Gabriel. His eyes are still shut tight, his lips trembling. "Let me talk to Gabriel," she says to me. "I'll come see you in a few minutes."

I walk to my cabin and move around the room in a daze, picking up Mona's things and putting them in the large shopping bag she used to carry them. How is it possible for Gabriel to believe that he should die? I argued with him as if the voice were real. But the voice is imaginary, the product of a mental disorder. It has to be. What happens to people with schizophrenia? Can they function? Do they end up on the upgrade side of the fifth floor for the rest of their lives?

I continue to pack up Mona's things. There isn't much. A pair of shorts, an orange T-shirt from the University of Texas, an extra pair of jeans, a romance novel I have never seen before, a sad-looking bra. I bend down to pick it up and I feel suddenly an empty, sad place in my chest, the empty place that Mona left, that Gabriel is leaving. Is there any way to avoid the emptiness of people's absence?

Dr. Desai knocks and asks if she can come in. She sits in one of the desk chairs. I sit in the armchair and wait.

"I'm going to drive Gabriel to the hospital. His fever is at a hundred and five. I'm worried about that and —"

"He told you about the voice?"

"Yes." She folds her hands on her lap. She's wearing a turquoise sari, so her hands seem to float on the surface of a calm ocean. "Well, this stay at the ranch did not work out as I expected."

"No," I say, agreeing.

She sighs and then says, "I'll start with Emilio. He's fine and was released from Lakeview this morning. I wrote a letter to the judge telling her that there were no psychological disorders, no signs of mental illness in him. He faces assault charges, but given the circumstances, that he was defending himself and his family, I doubt he will be incarcerated. He's agreed to attend anger management classes."

"That's good," I say.

She shrugs. "He's returning to the same volatile situation. What will he do the next time his father attacks his mother or his little brother?" Another sigh. "As for Mona, I expected that at some point she would discontinue her medication. I didn't think it would be so soon. She's got a lot on her plate, including fighting the demons of addiction. When I finish talking to you, I'll alert the social worker who is helping the family that she may go looking for Lucy. I'm afraid there's not much else we can do."

"Mona said things like 'Without Lucy, I have nothing.' Can't you put her back in the hospital for that?"

She shakes her head. "You can't confine someone to a health facility on a suspicion that they might be suicidal at some point in the future. Not being able to help is the hardest part of this job. I don't want you to get involved trying to find her. Let me take care of that, okay?"

Her eyes fix sternly on me until I nod.

"Now, about Gabriel," Dr. Desai continues. "I've never had a case so perplexing. I'm telling you this because I know he confides in you. I'm a physician trained in the scientific method, but I am also a spiritual person, someone who believes that we are more than flesh, bones, and gray matter. For a while I've been conflicted as to how to deal with the voice he hears. Usually, when someone hears voices, there are other symptoms, other instances of disorganized thought or aberrant behavior. I've never met anyone for whom the total opposite was true, someone whose thoughts, at least until now, have been *more* ordered and whose behavior is *more* exemplary than the majority of us poor humans."

"But the voice he is hearing now —"

"Is different. It scares him. And his thoughts are becoming more disorganized. He is in touch with our reality one moment and then he's someplace else, another reality. There will be two Gabriels from now on: one who knows he's ill, and another who believes the voice is real. He'll come in and out in waves."

"How can he believe that God wants him to die?"

Dr. Desai chuckles. "I'm glad you've come around to that perspective!" She continues, "The voice he hears is connected, for him, to his spiritual search, the life he has been trying to live. The kind of sacrifice he is being asked to make by this . . . voice . . . is part of that search. Anyway, I'm going to treat the voice as a hallucination. At Lakeview, we'll do some tests to make sure there is no organic cause such as a brain tumor. And if there isn't, I will proceed to treat him with medication, assuming that the voice he hears is a symptom of mental disorder. I just hope I can convince him to accept treatment."

"Is it schizophrenia?"

"I'm hoping that it's something we call brief psychotic disorder, a one-time condition that is temporary. But even if the symptoms persist and it turns out to be full-fledged schizophrenia, we can treat it. There are many, many schizophrenics out there, functioning in society and doing well."

I hesitate for a moment. "He thinks it's Mona's life he needs to save."

"It's understandable that he would think that. There's no such thing as coincidence for him right now. The voice, Mona's departure, everything that happens to him right now is part of a plan that is leading him to what he thinks he is being asked to do." Dr. Desai looks around the room. Mona's bed is unmade and the clothes I haven't picked up are still strewn all over the floor. Her gaze returns to me. She smiles. "Let's talk about you," she says. "You're welcome to stay here until next Sunday as originally planned, or you can come with me to Lakeview when I return there with Gabriel this afternoon. I can take you home later in the day."

I think about this for a few moments. I haven't thought about home or school for days and now, suddenly, there they are looming before me. What will it be like to go back to Reynard, to be in my house alone, to face my father and Barbara? Cecy? Jaime? Those are the rocks in my life that I must find a way to dig around, and I don't know if I'm ready. But staying here at the ranch without Mona or Gabriel or E.M. will not make me stronger or more prepared. It will just be lonely. "I should probably go home," I say.

"You don't sound too sure," Dr. Desai points out.

"It scares me."

"Why?"

I always like it when Dr. Desai asks a question to which she already knows the answer. Instead of telling me what she knows, she wants me to discover it in the process of saying it out loud. "I guess I'm afraid I will feel the way I felt before. These past few days I've felt . . . different. Like I've wanted things I've never wanted before, hoped for them."

The expression on Dr. Desai's face means she is proud of me for being honest. "I've noticed a bit of rebirth in you as well. It's not an uncommon occurrence in people who have attempted suicide to bounce back and appreciate their life and the world in a new way. This is especially true if the person is in a new environment, even a place as drab as a hospital, as long as it's away from all the stressors that triggered the attempt. But then . . ."

"When they go back, they fall into the same rut." I finish her thought.

"In many cases, yes. What will happen, what usually happens, is that the person who has attempted suicide will feel a depletion of the new energy. But sometimes the person finds a way to manage and function in the midst of the old problems. You'll need to be careful. We talked once about the possibility of medication for your depression. I didn't see the need to start you on it while you were here, but we need to keep an eye on how you feel when you're back home. I would like to see you at Lakeview next week and at least once a week for a while so we can make sure that you don't 'fall into the same rut,' as you point out."

I imagine for a moment what my father and Barbara will say about that. Will my father see my visits with Dr. Desai as a failure to get back on the horse? Will Barbara insist I see the fancy doctor that her friends recommended?

"Would you like to continue seeing me?" Dr. Desai says.

"Yes, I would," I answer quickly, "but . . ."

A knowing grin appears on Dr. Desai's face. "You are sixteen, a mature sixteen. You have some rights when it comes to your mental health. You can insist on the treatment that you think is best for you. I will support you."

The prospect of confronting my father scares me. Dr. Desai must see that. She says, "You've stood up to your father before, Vicky. You told him you didn't want to take debate. You insisted on coming to the ranch."

"Look how well that worked out," I say, trying to be funny.

But Dr. Desai doesn't laugh or even smile. "I know you said that because you're anxious. One of the things I was hoping to do in one of our group meetings was to try to bring together and understand everything that we learned from each other at Lakeview and here at the ranch. I'm sorry that our stay is ending so abruptly and we won't have an opportunity to do that. But you can do it when you get home, Vicky. What did you learn from E.M., from Mona, from Gabriel, from me? Each person gave you something you needed, a tool you can use when you return to your everyday life. Will you try to figure out what those tools are?"

"Yes," I say.

"And I want you to think of this ranch as a place you can always stay for as long as you want. If you ever need to get away, just come. There's a Greyhound bus from Austin to Fredericksburg that you can take."

"Thank you."

"I expect to see you next week, then. And Vicky" — she pauses and looks straight into the deepest part of me — "the thought of suicide may return. It's okay. It's just a thought. It's a cloud passing by. It's not you. If it comes, go for a brisk walk, exercise, think good thoughts. If it gains strength in force and frequency, I expect you to call me or hop in a cab to Lakeview or on a bus to Fredericksburg."

I nod. I'm glad Dr. Desai knows the thought is in me. It makes me feel like less of a liar and a fake.

She lifts herself slowly from the chair. I have a feeling she has aged a good ten years since the first GTH meeting. "So," she says. "I'll drive my truck over to the boys' cabin and you can help me with Gabriel." She laughs a short, sad laugh as she bends to pick up Mona's purple notebook from the floor. "Purple is for royal pain."

"I'll get it," I say.

"We'll take her things and I'll keep them at the hospital just in case. You're a very kind person," she says.

"And Gabriel?" I ask. "How long will he be in the hospital? Will I be able to see him?"

"Let me take care of Gabriel and Mona and you concentrate on your reentry. It's like what flight attendants tell you about the oxygen masks that plop down in an emergency: First you put yours on, and then you put it on the child next to you."

She waits for me to nod and then she walks out the door, the weight of the world on her shoulders.

chapter TWENTY-SIX

Dr. Desai drives us back to Lakeview in her truck. I sit in the middle and Gabriel sits by the window with a pillow under his head. I don't think anyone says more than ten words the whole trip.

When we get to Lakeview, Dr. Desai offers to give me a ride home as soon as she gets Gabriel settled, but I tell her I will call my father and ask him to come and get me. She repeats her offer to call her anytime and that she wants to see me next week. She says she will do what she can to get in touch with Mona, then gives me a serious look, as if to remind me that I should not get involved. Then the serious look melts into a warm smile and she hugs me. Dr. Desai tells Gabriel she'll be right back and she disappears behind a set of swinging doors. I have the impression that she wants Gabriel and me to have a few moments alone to say good-bye.

I sit down on a green plastic chair next to Gabriel and take out my notebook. Gabriel looks at me with a wan smile. I tear out the last page and write my cell phone and address. Then I fold the page and stick it in the front pocket of his shirt.

"Vicky," he says weakly.

"You shouldn't talk," I say. I can see in his eyes that he is the sane Gabriel right now, the one who knows that the voice is an illness.

"It's hard . . ."

"I know," I say, thinking he's referring to the voice.

"When you see me like this."

"Gabriel, we're friends. There's nothing to be embarrassed about."

"Please. I ask you. Don't come visit me here. It hurts." There's a desperate, insistent look on his face that I've never seen before.

"Okay," I say. It will be better for him if I pretend to accept what he asks. But there's a place inside of me that agrees with him as well. It hurts Gabriel for me to see his illness get worse, but it also hurts me and scares me to see him this way. I wish that wasn't true, but it is.

"Bye," he says quickly, without looking at me. He stands up and walks toward a nurse approaching with a wheelchair. He sits down in it, they turn around, and I watch them walk away.

I'm filled with the feeling that I will never see him again, that through some cowardice on my part, I have lost him and all my friends, and I cry. I cry for Gabriel, for what he's going through, for Mona and her pain, and I cry for me, because after all this, after Lakeview and the ranch and countless hours of talking and listening and befriending, after all this, I'm still not sure that I have changed all that much, or that I want to live any more now than I did a few weeks ago. There were moments of light in the past three weeks when I could see a future, moments of laughter and belonging and courage. But all I can feel right now is that someone turned on a light just long enough for me to see what I could never have, so that it would hurt me even more than if I had never seen it.

I weep and I weep in the green plastic chair — green, the color of life, life that is all around us, like Gabriel said. And maybe I'm not as bad as I was before Lakeview, and maybe there's a part of me that wants to live, a part that wasn't there before, because it makes me strangely happy in the midst of the tears to remember his words, to think that the force that makes so much green life must be in me too, if only a drop or two.

After I don't know how long, after the tears stop and my eyes dry, I feel something in my chest, some kind of consolation and peace and resolve. It's as if I'm a sail and a gentle breeze comes and fills me up and moves me. All I need to do is decide where to point the boat.

I ask one of the nurses if I can use the phone behind the reception desk, and I call my father at work. He's in a meeting and so is Barbara, but his secretary asks me to wait. When she returns to the phone, she tells me that neither my father nor Barbara can get out of their meeting, but they have arranged for Ed from IT to pick me up. Ed is out on an errand, but as soon as he returns, he'll come get me. It might be an hour or so.

I'm disappointed that my father can't come to get me. Would I feel different if he rushed out of his meeting to pick me up? No, it's all right. My father is my father and part of me is glad that he is not treating me differently than before I came to Lakeview. I have not thought about this, but now it comes to me: My father taught me how to swim. Every day he'd come home from work early so we could have our swim lesson before dinner. The pool in our first house was smaller than the one we have now and shallow enough for him to tiptoe through the deepest part. I remember the way his hands supported me on the surface of the pool as I learned how to float. It was a gentle, solid touch that I knew would be there until I felt completely safe. I was scared to go in the deep end without my inflatable wings, but he was so patient with me, so calm, so careful, that soon I was more comfortable in the water than anywhere else.

There was a warmth to my father once that is no longer there, a softness that hardened, a care for me despite all my flaws that turned into impatience. Now he has a fear, almost, of warmth and gentleness, which hurts me, and there's no use denying it. That's one of the rocks ahead of me that I have to face.

I sit back in my green chair and wait, and then a few minutes later I take the elevator to the third floor and find the hospital library, where E.M. discovered his Aztecs book. And there on a bottom shelf alongside the other children's picture books is a thin book with a picture of a jaguar-clad warrior on the cover. I sit on a child's chair and read about floating gardens and precise calendars and great temples and Huitzilopochtli, the god of the life-giving sun, who rewarded his followers with victory in war.

Two hours later, Ed from IT arrives. He apologizes for taking so long, but he was installing a Wi-Fi system in a new building and no one told him to come get me until he returned to the office. We ride in awkward silence for the first half of the trip. Finally, he starts to tell me about how fun and challenging it is to work at Cruz Real Estate and Construction. He's in the midst of explaining how he managed to get hired out of dozens of applicants when I interrupt him.

"Did my father tell you why I was in the hospital?"

"Uh. Well. Not exactly."

"Not exactly?" I ask.

"I mean," he mumbles, "your father didn't tell me. Actually, I don't think your father's spoken to me since I've been there. Of course, I'm in IT, so we don't have any reason to interact unless his computer goes on the blink." He laughs a kind of nervous, timid laugh. "Marybeth, his secretary, asked me to come get you." He grips the steering wheel so tightly that his knuckles turn white. "But people know about . . . you. We feel bad."

"Thank you," I say.

"Do you . . . want to talk about it?" he ventures.

"No," I say in a way that stops all further conversation.

The rest of the trip home, I wonder how I'm going to deal with people who feel sorry for me, who are embarrassed to talk to me, not knowing what to say. Am I embarrassed myself? Ashamed that even Ed from IT knows I tried to kill myself? I decide that no matter what I feel, I'll keep my head high in front of others. I think of Mona and her theory that people with mental illness are smart in a special way. When I deal with people, I'll remember this intelligence is now mine.

It's around four in the afternoon when I get home. I thank Ed, get out of the car, punch the code that opens the iron gates, and run to Juanita's room in back of the house. The door is unlocked, so I walk in.

I know Juanita is gone as soon as I enter. The bed is made, and all of her saints and images of the Virgin Mary are still on the shelves and the small table in the corner. But there is an emptiness about the room that scares me. I go over to the only closet and peer in. The few dresses, blouses, and skirts that Juanita owns are missing, and the brown suitcase that she keeps on the top shelf of the closet is gone.

I have an incredible urge to scream. How is it possible for Barbara and my father to send Juanita back to Mexico without letting us say good-bye to each other? I take a few deep breaths so I can gather my wits, and then I remember Juanita telling me that she would not leave without saying good-bye. I rush out of her room. We stash an extra key to the house inside a fake rock in the garden. I use it to open the back door, and then I climb the stairs as fast as I can.

My room is dark and somber. It reminds me of the first time I entered Mamá's room after her funeral — like someone recently died in it. *Or should have died,* I think. I look at my bed and see myself after I took the pills, lying there with my hands folded on my stomach. I turn my head quickly away from that image, draw open the shades and window, and go to my desk. There, just as I had expected, is Juanita's note, written in pencil on one of the index cards I used for debate.

Mi Niña.
  I'm at Yolanda's. I wait for you before I go back.
  Your Nana.

I remember my daydream after our rafting trip. In the midst of all the wanting that came to me, I thought about Juanita renting the room in Gabriel's house. What if that wasn't

228

just a silly daydream? What if it were possible for Juanita to stay in Austin, if that's what she wants?

Yolanda's number is stored in my cell phone. I plug my phone into its charger and sit on the edge of the bed, thinking. Yolanda, her son, his wife, and their four children live in a three-bedroom house with three of the children crowded into one room. Juanita won't be able to stay there for too long.

Maybe it's being back in my room for the first time after the deed, or the strain of trying to figure out what to do about Juanita, but as I sit here, waiting for the phone to charge, I feel as if someone opened a valve in the back of my neck, and a thick gas the color of an egg yolk begins to infiltrate my head. Dr. Desai warned me that depression could return, but I never expected it to be so sudden or so soon. How long have I been home? Half an hour? What is it about this place that's so toxic, and how will I ever survive here?

I jump off the bed, shaking my head, trying to clear the invading fog. I stick my head out the window. The mesquite tree reminds me that I have not seen Galileo anywhere, so I start calling him. "Here, *gato, gato*," I shout. A mixture of Spanish and English is Galileo's preferred language. "*¿Dónde estás, gatito?*" But there is no response. His favorite spot is under one of the camellia bushes that surround the pool. I decide to go look for him. I'm sure that no one fed him after Juanita left, and God only knows how long she's been gone.

He's not in his favorite spot or under any of the other bushes. The gaseous substance in my head has turned into a fluffy, sticky material like cotton candy. I can feel my thoughts slowing down. It's hard for the brain elves to move in the gummy mess.

I peel out of my T-shirt and dive in the pool. The cold water revives me a little. I float on the surface, facedown and arms stretched out for a few minutes, and then I swim until the movement of my arms and legs clears my head. I sit on the steps to the shallow end of the pool, taking deep breaths, searching for one word or image from the past weeks that I can grasp, hold on to, a memory that will keep me afloat through the minutes, hours, and days that lie ahead. The only one I can think of is what E.M. said to me after I rescued him and the pride I felt when he said it: "Not too bad for a spoiled rich girl."

I pick up my clothes and walk back into the house, take a shower in the hall bathroom that Becca and I use, and put on a pair of jeans and a white short-sleeve shirt that reminds me of the one Gabriel wore every day. I grab my phone and tap the screen. It has enough power now that I can find Yolanda's number and call.

"Oh, Vicky, it's you," she says, immediately recognizing my voice. "Just a second, just a second. Juanita is here. She's been waiting for you to call."

Juanita's voice is joyful, tearful, grateful. "My *niña*. I so afraid I leave without talking to you."

"How long have you been at Yolanda's?"

"Eh?"

"How long? *Cuánto tiempo estas con Yolanda?*" The only Spanish I know is what I learned from my mother and Juanita and from classes in school. My father insisted on talking only

English to Becca and me and got mad at my mother and Juanita when they lapsed into Spanish.

"Ah! Since Sunday. I told your father that Yolanda take me to the airport, but I come to her house. He say it better for me, for you, if I leave before you get home. But I wait for you. Yolanda change ticket."

"Did Father give you the money, the twenty thousand dollars?"

"Yes, he gave me check. More. Twenty-five thousand. So much money."

"Nana, listen to me. *Escúchame un momento.*"

"*Sí, mi niña.* What is it?"

"Do you want to go back to Mexico to live with your sister, or do you want to stay in the United States, here in Austin?"

"What? *Qué dices?* I have to go back. Your father want me to. Mexico maybe better for me with my sister. Who take care of me here? I no walk anymore. I problem for you."

"But what if you had a place to live? Where you didn't have to walk so much. *Qué prefieres?* Mexico or here?"

"*Qué prefiero?*" There's silence on the other end of the line. "Here. With you. But is not possible."

"Yes, it is, Nana. It's possible. I found a good place for you, okay? Don't go anyplace. I'll come see you very soon."

"But, *mi niña.* I'm like, what you say, a heavy load on you. I don't want be to you like that."

"Nana, trust me. It will work. I need you to stay in Austin. For me. Can you stay with Yolanda a few more days?"

"Yes. I help her here with Lucio's baby."

"I'll call you soon, Nana. I love you."

"Okay, Vicky. I love you."

I tap my phone off and stare at it. Why did it never occur to me before to fight for Juanita to stay? Was I really that powerless, or did I just feel that way? I got angry, but deep down I accepted my father's decision. I never really thought I could do anything about it.

I wonder if Huitzilopochtli ever got depressed. So much caliche. There's no getting around it. Gabriel said once that if the depression is chemical, it never really goes away, but I could manage it. I could learn to live with it. Exercise, good thoughts. I got to find me some good thoughts.

My cell phone rings. It's Barbara. *So much for the good thoughts.*

"Welcome home," she says. "I figured you probably charged your phone by now. How are you?"

I feel like crap, I want to answer. Instead, I say, "I'm fine." I'm lying again. Do I want to start lying again?

"Good. Glad you're back home. Listen, couple of things. You caught us a little bit by surprise, so Miguel and I have this dinner with some Japanese investors that we can't get out of, but there's a frozen pizza that you can microwave. We might be home late. These guys expect to be taken out for drinks. You know how it is."

"Okay." That's good. By the time she and Father get home, I can pretend I'm asleep.

"But your dad wanted me to tell you to get ready to go back to school tomorrow."

"Tomorrow?" I can't hide the dread in my voice.

"Yes. Tomorrow. Might as well get in a couple of days of school this week, he says, now that you're back. What happened? Things didn't work out at that ranch you went to?"

"Things worked out okay," I say distractedly. Tomorrow I will go to school, where everyone knows what I have done. I will be looked at with what kind of eyes?

"Great. We talked to Mr. Robinson as soon as you called earlier. Miguel and you have an appointment with him first thing in the morning before classes begin."

I flop back on the bed and sigh.

"You still there?" Barbara asks.

"Why?" I say.

"Why what?"

"Why do we have to meet with him?"

"Well, there's the small matter of your flunking grades, for one. I guess he also wants to make sure that the school wasn't somehow responsible for what you did by letting someone bully you or maybe teachers putting too much pressure on you. You know how it is these days. Everyone's worried about lawsuits. Well, have a wonderful evening. Get some good sleep. We'll see you in the morning."

She hangs up before I can say anything. I lie there on my back with the phone dangling in my hand. I feel like an old-fashioned scale, like the kind Lady Justice holds in her hand in front of courthouses. On one tray there's everything good I have gathered at Lakeview and the ranch, and on the other are those parts of my life that are not changing, that I will need to live with — the things that drove me to the deed in the first place. Guess which way the scale is tilting?

I open my laptop and check my email. I don't know why I do this. It's probably just habit, even though the only emails I ever got were from Cecy and that one from Jaime. I have three now: one from Cecy, one from Jaime, and one from Liz Rojas, the editor of *The Quill*.

I stare at them for a couple of minutes, trying to gauge whether I have the emotional stamina to open them and read them. It has been a long, long day.

Emily Dickinson's poem about hope comes to me as I sit there with those emails. I took the poem to say that hope, the thing with feathers, comes or it doesn't come of its own accord. But what if *I* need to create the thing and feather it and perch it in my soul, in such a way that it will live in the chillest land, the strangest sea? What is my thing with feathers? What is my hope? And how can it survive the months and years ahead of me in this room, with this family, in this life?

I'm not sure I can. It seems like an impossible task, and it occurs to me that what is still perched in my soul, what is still there, is that familiar feeling, hopelessness.

TWENTY-SEVEN

I close my laptop and lie in bed in the same spot, in the same position, as the night I took the pills. *Do you want to live?* Has anything changed since Gabriel asked me that?

I feel lonely, I realize. I feel *so* lonely. I didn't feel lonely the night I tried to take my life. You have to be somewhat alive to feel lonely, and that night I was already dead. But I feel lonely now. I miss Mona and Gabriel and E.M. I miss Mamá. I miss Becca. My sister. I have a sister.

I search for my cell phone in the bed beside me, pick it up, and push Becca's number. It rings only once, then she answers.

"Becca, it's me."

"Vicky. This is crazy. I was just about to call you when the phone rang. Barbara texted me that you were home. Are you okay?"

"I'm okay." *Really? Am I really okay?* "Actually, it's a little hard."

"I can imagine. I wish I was there. Guess what. I just went online and bought a plane ticket. I'm coming Saturday afternoon. I can stay for a few days."

"Really?" I say. "What about school?"

"School will still be here when I get back. I'll be home until the following Tuesday, but I can stay longer."

"You'd stay for me?"

"Of course I would."

There's something about Becca's voice that sounds different from our last phone call. I can't exactly pinpoint how. Less afraid to be talking to me, maybe. More like . . . she cares. Or maybe she just feels . . . "Becca, it's okay. You don't have to feel guilty. We're okay."

"I'm not doing it because I feel guilty. But you're wrong. I should feel guilty. Guilt is exactly what I need to feel. I let you down, Vicky. I'm not going to let it happen again."

"You didn't let me down."

"No? You know what I did right after we hung up last time we talked, when you were in the hospital?"

"No," I answer tentatively.

"I checked the missed calls on my cell. I didn't have to because I already knew what I was going to find, but I finally had the guts to do it. You called me that night when you tried to . . . Eight p.m. Know why I didn't pick up when you called?"

"Stop. You don't have to do this." I don't know what I would have said to her if she had picked up. I wanted to let her know — what? I wanted to let her know I loved her.

"Yes, I do. I was at a party given by this very special, elite, secret society that I wanted to get into. I was at that very moment trying to impress a guy with a suede jacket and horn-rimmed glasses. I saw your name on the phone and ignored it." I hear her voice quiver. She's crying.

"It wouldn't have made a difference if you had picked up," I say, trying to console her. "I didn't want you to feel responsible for what I was going to do. I wasn't going to tell you . . . what I was planning."

"I was the person — the last person you called."

"The only person. You should feel honored," I say, hoping to make her laugh.

"I am honored," she says, not laughing. "When you called me from the hospital, I was afraid to tell you how bad and guilty I was feeling, because that would be admitting what I didn't want to admit."

"But you weren't responsible."

"Yes, I was. Yes, I am. We're responsible for each other. We're sisters."

"Yes. We're sisters," I repeat. I feel a warmth, a warm breath, rise from my chest and settle in my throat.

"I've done some soul-searching since we talked," Becca says.

"You have?" That's how her voice is different from the last time we talked. Her voice is what a voice sounds like after soul-searching.

"I couldn't figure out why I was so cold and distant to you. There you were in the hospital for an attempted suicide, and I couldn't bring myself to be warm and accepting. Why was it so hard for me to tell you how I felt?"

"You did tell me. I didn't think you were cold and distant."

"And what I figured out is that, ever since our fight at Padre Island, I've been scared of you."

"Scared? Of me?"

"Yes. When Mamá decided to not go for that last round of chemotherapy, the one that would have extended her life for maybe six more months, you were the only one who understood and let her know that was all right."

There is silence at the other end of the line.

"Becca, are you there?"

"Miguel and I didn't get it," she says softly. "We wanted her to fight for life till the last drop, even though I couldn't bear to see her die. I was staying away from her, like you said."

"But —"

"No, let me finish. Miguel and me, we're alike in many ways. We don't like to feel weak."

"I know," I say. "I mean, I know you and Father don't like to feel weak."

"The thought of someone not being in control, like when they are dying of cancer or trying to kill themselves — that drives us up a wall. Remember the time I sprained my ankle in that soccer game when I was in eighth grade?"

"Yes." I do remember. A girl the size of Arnold Schwarzenegger stepped on Becca's ankle accidentally on purpose. I hear the bone crack once again.

"Mamá couldn't come because she was already sick, and you and Miguel were on the sidelines. I was on the ground writhing with pain. The game stopped and Miguel came onto the field, and he started yelling at *me*. He was angry with me for being in pain, for getting hurt, for letting a kid hurt me, of all things. I couldn't believe it. Angry! Do you remember?"

"Yes." I was embarrassed for my father. Coaches, teammates, even the Arnold look-alike stared at him like *What is wrong with you?*

"I finally figured out why this past week."

"Why?"

"Why he yelled at me. He — I mean me too — we don't like the way other people's pain makes us feel. We turn into unfeeling robots to protect ourselves."

"You're never a robot."

"Don't defend me. I'm on a roll. I want to get all this out before I see you because, like I said, I'm a coward and it's a lot easier to say all this on the phone than face-to-face."

"It's going to be good to see you." The lump in my throat melts. I'm getting my sister back. She's coming back to me.

"So. Where was I?"

"You were calling yourself names."

"Okay, no more name-calling. Maybe just one more. Miguel is not a robot deep down either. We just get angry when we hurt, when we're vulnerable or scared. The anger keeps us going. It got me into Harvard. Miguel was so angry after Mamá died, he went out and married Barbara."

I'm silent, thinking. *You can't ask a mule to be a racehorse.* I sensed the disappointment in those words, but not the anger or the hurt.

"Vicky, are you still there?"

"Yes."

"You trying to kill yourself must have reminded him of Mamá saying no to more chemotherapy, saying no to six more months of life. If he didn't want you to stay at Lakeview or go to that ranch, it's because he saw that as you giving up, like Mamá."

"It was different. Mamá gave up, if you can call it that, because she wanted to live more fully those last few weeks." I swallow. "I gave up because I . . ."

"Vicky?"

"It was different. Mamá accepted a death that couldn't be stopped. I brought death on myself."

"In Miguel's mind, it amounts to the same thing. There's no *accepting* in his vocabulary. Giving up is giving up no matter why. I agree with you that it was different, but it might take Miguel a little longer to see that too."

"So . . ."

"So keep that in mind when he comes at you with his all-business, no-pain-no-gain face. And . . ."

"And?"

"Remember that the guy is hurting. He's been hurting since Mamá died and he doesn't even know it." We are both quiet. I know what she wants to say next, and then she says it. "Just like me."

"Like you?"

"You're like the only one in this family that stayed with the pain and hurt of Mamá dying. Miguel and I couldn't stand it. We'll do anything to not feel the pain of losing her. But —"

"It doesn't work," I say, finishing her sentence. One of the things I learned at Lakeview is that pain that is not acknowledged, talked about, shared even, doesn't ever go away. It hides for a while and then comes back in a different form.

"Yes."

"Becca . . . thank you . . . for the soul-searching."

"I know this is a lot. But this is my first step. This phone call is more for me than for you. This turning hurt into anger is not good, Vicky. I need to work on that."

"I'll help you."

"I think Miguel also needs to work on the hurt that's turned to anger. It'll be harder for him because he's so set in his ways. See if you can manage to pierce through that, though. I learned not to take his anger personally. I learned to give it back to him and stand my ground. I'm not his favorite daughter, Vicky. You are. You're the one who reminds him of Mamá."

"No," I protest. How can I be my father's favorite when we are so different, when I'm such a failure in his eyes?

"Yes. Trust me on that one. Okay, okay. I'm done. I'll let you go. What are you doing tomorrow?"

I'm still thinking about my father. Is it possible to be loved and not feel loved? Isn't love supposed to be felt by the beloved?

"Vicky, are you there?"

"Yes. I'm sorry. What did you say?"

"What are you doing tomorrow?"

"School."

"Oh, God, are you ready?"

"No. But tomorrow I will be."

"Listen, don't let Miguel push you into doing things you're not ready for. His instinct is to push, and he will keep doing it until you push back. Tell him what you think, what you really feel. Let him get angry. Don't be afraid to negotiate with him. If he asks you to do something you don't want to do, offer to do something else, something in the direction of what he wanted but also something that you can live with. Or ask him for more than what you need, and when he says no, settle for what you wanted all along. Negotiate."

"Okay. I'll try. And Barbara? Any words of wisdom there?"

"Yeah. Go shopping with her. You'll suddenly appreciate her multiple talents. Let her buy you whatever her little heart desires. I discovered early on that nothing makes her happy like buying me stuff. It's a tough job, but someone has to do it."

I laugh. "Bye, Becca. I'm glad I called you."

"Are you?"

"Yeah. Can we talk like this when you're here? Will you be brave and talk to me like this face-to-face? I'm good at talking about deep stuff now. All those therapy sessions."

"I could use some of those. Yes. We'll talk. See you Saturday."

I place the phone on the small table next to the bed and go over everything that Becca said. I stop when I get to the part where she says that she's not my father's favorite daughter, that I am. How can he love me when I'm so different from him? But Mamá was different from him, and he loved her. Have I been getting it all wrong? Was it a case of not feeling, not seeing, not understanding what was always there?

I should confess to Becca how much I resented her. I should tell her all those uglies I saw in myself that night at Lakeview after Mona told me about them. The uglies. That's what Mona taught me. Dr. Desai asked me to think about what each person taught me, about the tools Mona and Gabriel and E.M. gave to me. Don't lie to yourself, from Mona. How to be brave and concentrate and work with the rocks that are always there, no matter if you wish they weren't. That's from E.M. And from Gabriel? The small things. That's where the green of life is, which is all around us. A phone call with my sister. The look on Ed from IT when I asked him if people knew. Juanita. Knowing someone needs you. Maybe that's enough. That's good enough for one day.

Close my eyes. Sleep.

TWENTY-EIGHT

I wake up around six a.m., my head full of a poem. It isn't the first time I've had a dream in which I write a poem and then I wake up remembering it word for word. But the poem I dreamt this time is different. The subject matter, the meter, the style, all of it is new. I amble over to my desk, still drowsy with sleep, and write it out on the last page of the notebook Dr. Desai gave me.

> *You hardly see me in the sun,*
> *My sparkle's in the stars.*
> *When all is dark around you,*
> *I'm the memory of light.*
>
> *I'm not the fruit of summer.*
> *I'm not the blooming rose.*
> *I live in roots of trees*
> *And in the seeds of love.*
>
> *When all is lost around you,*
> *When life's last dream is gone,*
> *I'll be the breath you breathe,*
> *The next step that you take.*

When I finish writing the poem, I pick up the picture of Mamá I keep on my desk. In the picture, I am six and she's pushing me on a playground swing, my legs pointing toward the sky, my mother's face full of joy and mine full of terrified delight. Is it possible to transform the yearning that you have for a loved one into the energy needed to dig around the daily rocks? *I miss you, Mamá. You're my memory of light.* I hold the picture in front of me. *Help me to be brave, like you.*

I glance at the digital clock on my desk. It is almost six-thirty. The whir of the blender comes from the kitchen. Barbara makes a protein shake for herself after she finishes her Zumba Yoga. I slept with my clothes on, so I quickly change into a plaid skirt and a pink blouse. It's the outfit I wore when I took Juanita to Mass. I step in front of the full-length mirror that hangs on the back of the closet door. It has been so long since I last saw my reflection that it's almost like looking at someone else. The girl in front of me looks older, calmer, kinder than I remember. It's the reflection of someone who can go unnoticed, someone ordinary. Even her hair looks tamer and more at peace. It has lost some of its anger.

I grab my phone beside the bed to call Lakeview and ask about Gabriel and also to try Mona one more time. I'm about to leave my room when I remember the emails I have not read.

I stop. *What would Huitzilopochtli do?* I ask myself. I turn around and walk to my desk. I read Cecy's email first.

Hi Vicky,

I don't know if they let you keep your laptop over where you are so maybe you'll be reading this when you get back. I'm sorry we didn't get to patch things up before you did what you did. The thought that you might have died with us still being mad upset me so much, you don't even know. I know it's selfish to say this, but I felt so guilty, and then I got angry at you all over again. I also know you didn't do it to make people like me feel guilty or angry. You tried to make up after the debate thing. It was okay to be mad at you for about three days max but not for so long. What's worse is that I was pretty much set on never speaking to you again.

Don't get me wrong. I still think you quitting debate was inconsiderate and immature. It really sucked for you to do that. All I can think now is that you were going through stuff I had no idea. So then I got mad at you again for not telling me how you were feeling, for not trusting me. I was your only friend, remember? You and me are so different, I don't even know how we became friends and now I'm wondering whether we were ever really friends.

But anyway, when you come back, you want to try again? We can just hang out at lunch and on weekends sometimes and see what happens. Maybe we're just meant to be regular friends and not best friends who share deep secrets etc. That would be fine too. I'm not saying this because I feel guilty or because I feel sorry for you or anything. I know I told you once that I only took you on as a debate partner because I felt sorry for you. The truth is that I thought the whole thing would be more fun to do with someone I liked, even if we didn't win all the time. Of course, I never expected to lose every single match! No, seriously. I knew you were God awful bad. You need a mean streak like the one

I have to be good at debate and there's not even a mean spot
in you. That's probably the kind of friend someone like me
really needs. Welcome back, Vicky. I'm glad you're still around.
     Cecy

I stare at Cecy's email for a few minutes. Read it again. I
like the part where she says that maybe we were just meant to
be regular friends and not best friends "who share deep secrets
etc." It is hard to imagine talking to Cecy about the uglies like
I did with Mona. But it could be that regular friends are nothing to sneeze at. The thought that I can hang out with her at
school makes me dread my return to Reynard a little less.

Then I read Jaime's email.

Hey Vicky!
     I know I'm probably the last person you want to hear
from, but I had to write you. I called your father or your mother
almost every other day to see how you were and also to find
out if I could come see you, but they said they weren't letting
in any visitors where you were. Your dad was worried about
people in school knowing. I told him I wouldn't tell anyone. I
didn't want to tell him that word got around on its own, I don't
know how. Let me know when you're back. I really would like
to talk to you. I've recovered from you not liking me. It took a
while! I didn't do a very good job at getting to know you. Can
you call me as soon as you get back, please? No pressure.
Honest. Just talk.
     Jaime

P.S. I'm attaching a poem I wrote the day I found out about what you tried to do. What you did made me realize what really matters in life. The poem is not about you but it is because of you. It's probably the last poem I will write. I'm sticking to engineering, you'll be happy to know.

There's a Word document attached to Jaime's email with his poem. I don't open it. I wonder what I will say to Jaime when I see him. Maybe when I get to Reynard, I can imagine the whole school as one big psychiatric ward and everyone there as mentally ill in some form or another. We are all mental in our own peculiar ways, all grasping on to hurtful mangos that keep us imprisoned. The world is full of Gwendolyns and Jaimes and Cecys and Vickys, and we should know that we are ill and be kind to one another.

I click open Liz Rojas's email.

Dear Vicky,

I was wondering if you'd like to come work with me at The Quill. We need an assistant editor and I think you'd be great. Mrs. Longoria says really good things about you, and I loved your poems that we've published. The assistant editor is pretty much a worker bee, but usually the assistant editor becomes the editor their senior year. One downside you should know about is that it's against our policy for the work of staff to appear in the magazine, so you wouldn't get to publish your poems. Can you send me an email if you're interested?

Liz

I check the date of the email. She sent it the first school day after the deed, a Monday. There was no way she could have known what I had done, which means that she did not send her email out of pity or because someone asked her to help the sad suicide girl.

Someone wants me to be a worker bee. It makes me smile inside. I close my laptop, grab my backpack, and head downstairs.

Barbara is standing by the toaster, waiting for her bagel to pop, and Father is sitting at the kitchen table, reading *The Wall Street Journal*.

"Hi," I say.

"Hey there!" Barbara says, turning. She walks over and gives me a hug — or, rather, she leans over and pats me, making sure that the only points of contact are her hands and my back.

Father waits for Barbara to finish her show of affection before speaking. "Good to have you back," he says. "Grab some cereal, we're running late." He folds the newspaper, pushes his chair back, and stands. "I'll get the car out. See you outside."

"You're lucky," Barbara says while I look for the bread to make two peanut butter and jelly sandwiches, one for breakfast and one for lunch. "You get to ride to school in the Spider."

The Spider is a convertible, which means Father and I won't be able to talk. The car's motor and the rushing air are so noisy that it makes conversation between the passengers impossible. It occurs to me that maybe this is why Father picked this particular morning to take the Spider.

As I make my sandwiches, Barbara tells me about a new Indian restaurant where we can eat with Becca on Saturday. Becca also wants to go shopping, and Barbara wonders if I would like to go with them. She glances quickly at the blouse and skirt I'm wearing. "You can use some new clothes," she says, not unkindly.

"Okay," I say. I'm trying to stuff the two sandwiches into a bag designed to hold one sandwich.

"Really?" Barbara asks, shocked. "You'll come?"

"It could get expensive. I basically need a whole new wardrobe." *Some pretending is necessary and even good,* I remember Dr. Desai saying. Besides, Becca will be there.

"Then you're talking to the right girl," Barbara says. She looks happy.

Father is honking in the driveway. "Bye," I say.

Outside, I open the passenger door and slink in. Father adjusts the Dallas Cowboys cap he always wears when he drives the Spider. I don't have to worry about my hair flying all over the place. We take off with a jolt as the iron gates open.

We drive in silence, as expected. Once, we stop at a red light and the motor stalls. "Damn," my father says as he turns the key and pumps the accelerator. "I had this car tuned up last month and I've driven it once."

I feel sorry for the mechanic, who will get an earful sometime soon. There is nothing worse in my father's moral universe than people who do not do what they are paid to do.

At school, he pulls into a parking spot right in front of the building. The spot is probably reserved for teachers, but

Father always acts like he owns the place whenever he shows up at Reynard. He is, after all, one of its biggest financial supporters.

It's about fifteen minutes before the first-period bell rings, and students are standing in small groups and sitting on the concrete backless benches on the sidewalk leading to the front entrance. Reynard is a small school, so everyone knows one another, if not by name, then certainly by face. As soon as I get out of the car, I can feel heads turn toward me. There's no doubt in my mind that everyone is either thinking or saying, "That's the girl who tried to kill herself." I keep my eyes straight ahead and try to walk as erect as possible.

Father must have noticed the stares as well, because he says, "Don't worry about it. Tell yourself that you're better than they are."

I smile. I have just received from Father as much encouragement as I am going to get.

Mr. Robinson, the principal, has someone in his office, so Mrs. Rogers, his secretary, asks us to sit in the two chairs outside the door. "Can you tell him we're here?" my father says in a way that would make anybody else nervous.

But Mrs. Rogers ignores him. "Are you okay, honey child?" she says to me, her eyes moistening for a moment. Mrs. Rogers is older than the state of Texas and used to seeing all kinds of pushy parents.

"I'm okay now," I say, grateful.

My father takes my arm and leads me to the chairs. We sit at the same time and he waits for Mrs. Rogers to occupy herself with some folders. Then, "What's the plan here?" he says to me, leaning close as if to share a secret.

"Plan?"

"What do you want to do the rest of the year? Do you want to try to salvage what's left of the school year?"

"Sure," I say. Then it occurs to me that I'm always saying yes to my father even when I don't know what he's asking. If "yes" is the response I sense he is expecting, then "yes" is the response I give. "Wait. What do you mean by 'salvage' the rest of the school year?"

My father looks at me, perplexed. I don't know whether he thinks I'm dumb for not understanding the question or whether he's shocked that I asked for a clarification. He speaks slowly and carefully. "Are you going to do what it takes to not flunk out? That's what I mean."

This time I do not automatically say yes. I think about it. Answering yes means that I will need to put in the necessary effort, and that means determining whether I have enough energy and motivation to carry it off. I will need to get A's from this moment on in order to end the year with passing averages. I will even need to get an A in geometry. Two days ago, when I was at the ranch, if someone asked me if I was capable of going all-out in school, I might have said yes. But at this moment, I'm not sure I have what it takes. I don't want to promise my father something I can't deliver.

"I'm not sure," I say. I feel his shoulders sag a little. "I'm not sure I have the drive or the energy to do that. I wish I did, but I don't."

He raises his hand and smooths his distinguished gray hair. I can see his mind clicking through the various responses that are available to him. The more he thinks, the more I know that anger is not going to be one of those responses. What remains is disappointment, resignation, maybe understanding. "Well," he finally says, looking at Mr. Robinson's door, "let's see what the next-best offer looks like."

About two minutes later, the door opens and Mr. Reyes, my geometry teacher, steps out. He stops when he sees me and glances quickly away as if embarrassed. Then he says, "Good to have you back," nods, and hurries away.

Mr. Robinson is the only man I've ever met who uses old-fashioned suspenders to hold up his baggy pants. Reynard students call him Santa because of his white hair and beard, his paunch, and his constant jolliness. Father and I sit on a very worn, tan leather sofa and he sits on a straight-back chair. The sofa is soft and low and places my father in a very unimposing position. The frown on his face says that he does not relish looking so powerless.

"How are you doing, Vicky?" Mr. Robinson asks. I imagine the real Santa would have asked the question the same way.

"I'm better, thank you."

"Good," he says. "Are you sure you're ready to come back to school? Do you need more time?"

"It's better if she comes back," my father answers for me. "Too much time to think at home is not good."

Mr. Robinson completely ignores my father's remark. He waits for me to answer.

"I'll be all right," I say. *Let the day come.* I want to see what my days will be like here and know if I gathered enough strength these past four weeks.

"Well, go easy on yourself until you feel up to speed," Mr. Robinson says. "I suppose we should talk about how we should proceed, what would be best for you as far as the remainder of the school year."

My father tries to push himself forward on the sofa. He's getting ready to negotiate. "What are the options?" he asks.

Mr. Robinson turns, grabs a folder from the edge of his desk, and flips it open. I can see him looking at my transcript with every single bad grade I have ever obtained at Reynard. "It's not impossible to catch up," he says, closing the folder. "But I wonder if that's the wisest thing."

"What are the options?" my father says again, an edge of irritation in his voice.

"Catching up will be very demanding." Mr. Robinson looks at me as if my father isn't there. "What do you think, Vicky?"

"I'm not sure I can pull it off," I answer truthfully. I'd have to take in an enormous amount of material and digest it in just a short time. My brain doesn't work that way, even when it's working well.

"So here's what I'm thinking." Mr. Robinson acknowledges my father's presence for the first time since we came in. "Vicky continues the rest of the year with a reduced load. She stays in Mrs. Longoria's English class, where she's doing well, and in her world history and economics classes. She will need to work hard in those classes to bring her D's up to, say, a B-minus, but I think she can do it."

"What about next year and the year after that? What does that do to the requirements she needs to graduate?" My father sounds anxious.

"So, Vicky." Now Mr. Robinson is talking to me again. "This would mean that you take geometry during the summer. I talked to Mr. Reyes. He can meet with you once a week this summer, and if you pass, that grade will count for this year's requirements. As far as the other two classes are concerned, you'll have to retake them over the next two years, which means that your junior and senior course loads will be heavier than usual. But I have the feeling you'll be able to handle it."

I look at my father. He seems to be processing the fact that this is as good a deal as he is going to get, given what he is trying to sell. He turns to me and asks, "Is that right? You'll be able to handle the increased workload next year?"

"I think so," I say, with as much conviction as I can muster.

"There is one other option," Mr. Robinson says. He waits for my eyes to meet his. "I want you to understand why I am saying this, because I don't want either of you to misinterpret me." He pauses. "This school is not for everyone. I've seen lots of good, smart kids who would do well elsewhere flounder at Reynard. We're high-pressure, competitive, fast-paced, extremely structured. We have more required courses than other schools. Science and math are mandatory every single year. Not everybody likes or does well in that kind of learning environment. That's perfectly fine."

"What are you getting at?" Father interrupts, impatient.

Mr. Robinson speaks directly to him. "That maybe a public school would be better for Vicky. Westgate High is an excellent school. There would be more electives for Vicky to take, courses that she might like. Westgate offers courses in Russian and Latin American literature, for example, which is impossible for us. It's a large school, so there would be more of an opportunity for Vicky to —"

"Are you kicking her out?" Father asks incredulously.

"Not at all," responds Mr. Robinson. "I'm thinking about what is best for Vicky."

"Let's go," Father says to me, standing.

I dig myself out of the sofa with some effort.

"So." Mr. Robinson stands as well. "Something to think about. Oh, Vicky. I would like you to go see Mrs. Reisman. Just to talk."

"Who's Mrs. Reisman?" my father asks.

"She's one of our counselors — also a psychologist. I just think it would be a good idea, to make sure you're okay."

I immediately glance at my father, expecting him to object. He makes a slight movement with his shoulders as if to say he doesn't care.

"Okay," I say.

Mr. Robinson puts his hand on my shoulder and guides me to the door. My father follows. Just as we are leaving, the principal says, "You know, on second thought, I think it would be better if you started tomorrow. I'll get your teachers to email you what has been covered in class in your absence and where they are. That way you won't completely lose your first day. Do you need to get your books?"

"No, I have them." I show him my backpack.

My father says, "I think it's better if you start today. You're here. Tomorrow's not going to be any easier."

I look at Mr. Robinson and he tells me with his eyes that it's my decision. But my father's right for once. Tomorrow is not going to be any easier.

"I'll start today," I say.

TWENTY-NINE

As I walk down the stairs, I remember the first time Mona took me to Dr. Desai's office and how she warned me that if I turned right instead of left, I would end up in the morgue. When I turn right toward my locker, I get this feeling that I just took the wrong turn.

I have seen TV shows and movies where the high school halls are chaotic places, with kids shouting and jostling each other. That's not the way it is here. Reynard kids don't shout or jostle. They stand in front of their lockers, quietly trying to figure out what books they need for the next three hours, and when they get them, they close their lockers, snap shut the combination locks, and move on. It's not as if you don't hear laughter or people talking to each other. You do. But the laughter and the talk are subdued, like the laughter and talk you might hear at a wake.

I stare at my locker, feeling the little elves in my brain slowing down. How can I forget a combination that consists of my and Becca's and Mamá's birth dates? 15-16-24. The message finally arrives. Now the hard part. It's fifteen to the right and sixteen to the left. Right? The first warning bell for class rings. That means I have five minutes to get to class. But it is not fifteen to the right and sixteen to the left. Fifteen to the left and sixteen to the right and twenty-four to the left. No, that's not it either.

I manage to open my locker just as the second bell rings. I study the schedule taped to the door. Today is what day again? Thursday. That means my first-period class, the one that is starting right now, the one for which I am going to walk in late is . . . economics with Mr. Lindsay. *Wonderful. One of my favorite subjects.* Did I sound like Mona just then? Mona. How is she? And Gabriel. What am I doing here?

Just dig around the rocks gently, Vicky. Be a mule. Do what you need to do.

Everyone is seated and Mr. Lindsay is writing something on the blackboard when I enter. "Sorry," I say when he looks at me.

He nods and smiles and I make my way to an empty desk in the back. At Reynard, the good desks are up front — ambitious students try to get them by coming early. Needless to say, I always preferred the back. Kids try not to look at me, but they do. One or two smile a sugary smile full of pity. I do not smile back. I sit and dig for a book and notebook, and then I look at Mr. Lindsay and pretend that I understand what he is saying. I see his mouth open and close and words come out and reach my ears, but that's as far as they go. The words themselves I can understand. What I can't figure out is what the words mean when they are put together. I know what the word *balance* means, and *trade* and *payments*, but what does *balance of trade* and *balance of payments* mean?

It takes me a good fifteen minutes to finally realize that we are now in the part of the textbook that deals with international economics. I find that chapter in the book and read the first paragraph. Then I read it again. I can more or less under-stand what the author is saying, so I decide to read the chapter rather than listen to Mr. Lindsay's lecture. Now and then, I hear him ask a question, but the nice thing about Reynard is that there is always someone else who knows the answer and is eager to give it.

The same thing happens in my world history class. It's like the lessons are being taught in a foreign language and I am completely lost. At one point, it all seems so incomprehensible that I almost burst into tears. Somehow I hold it together. When class is over, I walk to Mr. Roark's desk.

"Nice having you back," he says. Mr. Roark is probably the youngest teacher at Reynard. He's twenty-eight or so but looks like he's about fourteen. He always wears a tie and a blue blazer, and I don't think I have ever seen him smile.

"I have some catching up to do," I say. "I'm lost."

"I know," he says. Our eyes meet briefly, and I wonder if he noticed that I was about to cry in class. He opens up a large appointment book. "I have an hour free on Tuesday at three. We can go over what you've missed then." He looks up at me expectantly.

"Okay," I say.

He writes down the time on a yellow sticky note and hands it to me. "So you don't forget." I put the sticky in the front pocket of my backpack and am about to walk away when he says, "What kind of grade are you hoping to get?"

"Pardon?"

"I think we should be realistic. I don't believe an A or a B is attainable at this point."

Boy, would I like to introduce this guy to E.M. What would I give to see Mr. Roark in the north pasture telling E.M. in his squeaky voice, *I don't believe a three-foot hole is attainable in this kind of soil?*

"Is it still possible to get a passing grade?" I say, holding back a rising wave of anger.

"With a lot of effort, perhaps."

There's something in the tone of his voice, an arrogance, a self-importance, that I haven't heard in the past four weeks. God, this is my world. This is the world I have to live in, and I don't know if I can make it.

"Thank you," I say. I don't say those two words gratefully. Those two words are really a substitute for two other words, and I say thank you the way I would have said those two other words.

I walk slowly out of his classroom and plod my way to the library. Mrs. Longoria's class is not until ten, so I have some time. My favorite desk is empty, on the second floor next to the poetry section. I'm tired. I put my arms on the desk and use them as a pillow for my head. Time is going so slowly. It has a different feel than it did at Lakeview or the ranch. I wish I were folding sheets or digging holes or planting rosebushes. Here you can feel the seconds tick by and they don't seem to go anywhere. *Tick. Tick. Tick. Tick.* How many seconds left in this class? In this day? In this semester? In this life?

I close my eyes and am counting tick, tick, ticks when someone touches my shoulder. I raise my head and see Cecy.

"Hi, Vicky," she says, as if afraid to disturb me.

"Cecy!" I stand and hug her. She seems surprised at first, but then she hugs me back, and I can tell she is relieved.

"May I?" She points to an empty chair at the next desk.

"Sure." I pull out my chair so that it faces hers, and we both sit.

"So," she says, "it's good to see you."

"It's good to see you too," I say.

We look at each other, wondering what more there is to say.

"How's it going so far?" she asks.

Something is different about Cecy, but I don't know what it is. Then I realize she changed the color of her hair. It used to be a light brown and now it's totally black.

"I know," she says, when she sees me looking at her hair. "I needed a fiercer, more menacing look for debate. Studies show that women with dark hair are more intimidating and are taken more seriously than women with lighter hair."

I stare at her for a few seconds, wondering if she's serious, and then I see her laugh and I laugh too. "I thought you were serious for a moment," I say.

"I *was* being serious," Cecy says, still laughing. Then she stops and reaches out for my hand. "I'm sorry, Vicky." Her eyes fill with tears.

"You're sorry? Cecy, there's nothing for you to be sorry about. I'm the one who caused you pain. I read your email this morning. That was so nice of you. Thank you."

"I wasn't much of a friend to you." She's found a package of tissues in her backpack and is wiping her eyes with one of them. "I knew you were quiet and sad sometimes, but I never imagined it was that serious."

"I did a pretty good job at pretending I was all right. It's not like I shared with you anything that I was feeling."

"And now?" she asks.

"How am I feeling now?"

She nods. "Are you better?"

"Yes," I say. That's the truth, isn't it? I am better. But that's not the whole truth. The whole truth is that even though I'm better, I can tell just by how this morning is going that I'm not well, not fully. So I say to Cecy, "I'm not out of the woods yet. I have to continue seeing the doctor I saw at the hospital. I'll probably need to take medication. But I'm in a better place than where I was before."

"Was staying at Lakeview horrible? With all those people?"

I look at Cecy and I know for sure at that moment that she will be a regular friend, not a special one with whom I will share deep secrets. But that's okay. "It was good, actually. Lakeview was good. I made some good friends there."

"Oh," says Cecy, a little taken aback. "That's awesome."

"You found a new debate partner?" I ask.

"Yes, yes. Regina Thompson. You know Regina."

"I know her," I say. Regina is in Mrs. Longoria's English class with me.

"She's incredibly fast on her feet and has a very nice streak of nasty in her."

"That's good. I'm glad you found her," I say, and I mean it.

"We've only been to one tournament so far but we kicked butt. Listen, I'm meeting her during lunch to go over our case for the next tournament. But, Vicky . . ." She pauses. "Can I see you? Can we still be friends?"

"Yes," I say. "I'd like that very much."

"Have you talked to Jaime?"

"No."

"He's been real worried about you. He called me . . . a few days after . . . to see if I had heard from you. I told him I hadn't." Cecy takes a deep breath, and I have a feeling she's about to get something off her chest. "We . . . I mean, we've been calling each other and emailing now and then. He showed me a poem he had written after he found out about you."

"Cecy," I say, reaching over and touching her arm. "That's good. I'm glad you and Jaime have been in touch."

"Really?"

"Yes."

"I think he still likes you, Vicky. He's a nice guy, you know."

"I know."

"Jaime said you told him you didn't like him," Cecy says.

"It's true. I did." I wait a few moments, and there's a tiny part of me that enjoys keeping Cecy in suspense. She likes Jaime a lot. I can read it all over her anxious face. "Jaime is a very nice boy, but . . . I don't think he's for me, Cecy."

The muscles in her face relax. "You may feel differently

now, Vicky. Talk to him at least," she says to me, not too convincingly.

"Okay," I say, feeling suddenly exhausted. "But I wouldn't worry."

"Don't get me wrong. I'm not worried," she says quickly, defensively. Then I see her stop to consider whether her tone of voice might have hurt me. I have a feeling that people will walk around me on eggshells for a while, afraid to say something that will push me over the edge. I have to find a way to let them know how much I prefer honesty. "I better get going. I'll call you tonight?" Her voice is kind, friendly again.

"Okay," I say. "Bye, Cecy. Talk to you tonight."

Tonight seems an eternity away.

I stay hidden in the library until it is time to go to Mrs. Longoria's class. I get there ten minutes before the final bell rings so I don't have to make a grand entrance like I did in Mr. Lindsay's class. Mrs. Longoria's eyes light up when she sees me come in. She is a large woman and she struggles to lift herself out of her chair, but when she finally does, she embraces me. I'm lost for a few seconds in warmth and oranges, the smell of Mrs. Longoria's perfume.

"I've been so worried about you," she says, still holding me. "I'm so happy to have you back. I ran into Mr. Robinson and he told me." A couple of students enter the room and she lets go of me. "Can you stay for a few minutes after class? We can talk then."

"Sure," I say.

"I'm glad you're here," she whispers to me.

The way she says "here," I have a feeling she means more than this classroom.

Jaime rushes in a few seconds after the final bell stops ringing. He's wearing white shorts and a pink polo shirt, carrying his backpack in one hand and the bag for his tennis racket in the other. He stops when he sees me, a shocked look on his face. I wave at him. He sits behind me. Mrs. Longoria asks us to open our books to the page she has written on the blackboard.

The class is studying the poems of Emily Dickinson. I look for her poem about the thing with feathers, but that's not one of the selections in our anthology. Instead, I am struck by a poem I have never seen before. While Mrs. Longoria talks about the poet's solitary, reclusive life in Amherst, Massachusetts, I read words and images that I understand intimately because I have lived them:

> *I felt a Funeral, in my Brain,*
> *And Mourners to and fro*
> *Kept treading — treading — till it seemed*
> *That Sense was breaking through —*
>
> *And when they all were seated,*
> *A Service, like a Drum —*
> *Kept beating — beating — till I thought*
> *My mind was going numb —*

And then I heard them lift a Box
And creak across my Soul
With those same Boots of Lead, again,
Then Space — began to toll,

As all the Heavens were a Bell,
And Being, but an Ear,
And I, and Silence, some strange Race,
Wrecked, solitary, here —

And then a Plank in Reason, broke,
And I dropped down, and down —
And hit a World, at every plunge,
And Finished knowing — then —

It strikes me when I finish reading the poem that you need images to properly convey what depression feels like. I call it a sticky, thick, smelly kind of fog. Emily felt boots of lead creaking across her soul. Gabriel's was a deflated basketball.

I have depression, I say to myself. Saying "I am depressed" makes it sound like that's all that I am. But that's not all that I am. I have depression, but I am not just depressed. Maybe the night I tried to kill myself, that's all I was. Depression took over and became my all. But I'm a good worker at the right job. I like to write. I like American Beauties and the soft-hard feel of a horse's forehead. I'm a friend. I have memories and . . . hopes? Why not be like Emily? Can I hope to write like her someday? Can I make that my hope? My bamboo stick. What if I set out to learn to work with words and images and rhythms so others can see and feel what they could not see or feel or understand before?

When class is over, I talk to Mrs. Longoria. There are two five-page essays and a twenty-page research paper that I have to write in addition to a couple of tests I need to make up. "You can take all the time you need to catch up," she tells me. "And if you want to get an Incomplete this semester and finish the course during the summer, we can work something out."

"Thank you."

"Vicky," she says, "is everything okay now?"

That's a question that I'm going to be asked a lot. I'm not going to be able to tell everyone how I really feel. But I wonder if I can tell some people. Some of them, like Mrs. Longoria, might understand.

So I say, "I have depression . . . but I'm getting help." It feels strange to say the words out loud, and I don't know why I feel slightly ashamed when I say them. But there's nothing to be ashamed of. Gabriel and Mona and E.M. and Dr. Desai — all of them, for different reasons, would be proud of me just now.

"I know what that's like," Mrs. Longoria says. "Reynard can be a hard place for people with depression . . . like us." She stops to make sure I fully understand what she's telling me. I nod to let her know that I do. "We can help each other. Okay?"

"Okay," I say gratefully.

I walk out of the classroom, wondering how Mrs. Longoria, who is always full of energy and optimism and kindness, can have depression. Mrs. Longoria loves teaching, I'm sure of it.

Yet there must be days when it must be so painful to do her job. I can't imagine standing in front of people, talking, listening to them, smiling at them, and all the while feeling depressed.

"Vicky!" Jaime is waiting for me outside the classroom. I brace myself. I wish these reentry conversations would occur slowly, maybe one a day, not all at once.

"Hello," I say.

"Cecy texted me that you were back. She said she talked to you." Jaime looks at me as if he's afraid I will be mad at him.

"Yes," I say. "I talked to Cecy." I smile at him and he seems relieved.

"We were very worried about you." We start walking toward one of the exits. I need to get some air.

"Thank you. I got your email. I didn't get a chance to read your poem."

"No problem," he says. "I just wanted to give you that. To let you know that . . . it really affected me when . . . I found out. I thought that maybe what happened between us had something to do with —"

"No," I say quickly. "It didn't."

"Oh, good. I mean. I wouldn't think it would. You're the one that gave *me* the brush-off." He laughs a nervous kind of laugh.

"I'm so honored, really, that you . . . showed me your poems and told me that you liked me. Thank you. I probably wasn't able to say back then how grateful I was that you thought of me that way. But I can tell you now." The words as I say them feel right, truthful.

"Well, I'm sorry things didn't work out. My loss." He opens a door for me to step outside. "I've been calling your house every couple of days. I think your dad and I have become good friends. Somehow I mentioned to him that I loved sports cars and he invited me over to take a look at his Spider."

"He did?" I can see how my father and Jaime would get along great. How happy my father would be if I brought Jaime home as my boyfriend.

"He and my dad know each other. Some Latino business-men's association."

"That makes sense," I say. I'm running out of words. Lead boots. I feel them creaking across my soul.

"So," he says, "I guess I'll see you around." He pauses, and then, "Would you like me to lend you my notes from Mrs. Longoria's class? I have them in my laptop. I can email them to you, or come over to your house and go over them with you."

Jaime looks at me expectantly, and I know that underneath his offer, he's asking if there's any chance that he and I can be more than friends.

"Thanks," I say. "I worked out a schedule with Mrs. Longoria for catching up. I'm good."

I see a flicker of something hard and piercing in his eyes. "Okay," he says. He points with his chin in the direction of the Athletic Department. "They're waiting for me. Big tournament against Westgate this afternoon. Time to go kick some butt. Wish me luck."

"Good luck," I say.

There's a concrete bench a few steps away. I sit and watch Jaime run toward a white van. He runs with a kind of aristocratic elegance, I notice. Even though kids in the van are yelling at him to hurry up, he refuses to go full speed. When he gets to the van, he turns around and looks back in my direction, and I get the impression he wanted to make sure I was watching him. He waves, and I wave back.

I'm tired. The conversations that I've had today with my teachers, Cecy, and Jaime have depleted me. There's an intensity required here that wasn't needed at Lakeview. It's the difference between talking to people who accept you and talking to people who are evaluating you, judging you. I'm not being very fair to Cecy or Jaime, who I know mean well. But that's how I feel.

This strange feeling of not belonging, this sense that every task, even the smallest one, is unpleasant and requires effort — this is how my days will be here. And how many days like this will there be? Will I make it? Do I have it in me to wiggle through the crushing rocks? Right now it doesn't feel like I do. I feel as if a week, a month from now, sooner or later, I will say no to life again. I will say no to these days.

These thoughts are clouds. They come. They go. I am not the clouds or even the sky. I'm the sun that shines on clouds and sky.

I stand up quickly and walk in the direction of the Arts Center, where all the extracurricular activities at Reynard have their offices. I'm trying not to think. I'm trying not to sink. I need to hold on to something, a bamboo stick that will keep my mind steady and give me a purpose.

The door to the offices of *The Quill* is open. From the entrance, I can see a front room with two desks and computers and another room in the back with the door slightly ajar. There's no one in the front room, so I walk to the back door and knock.

"Come in," I hear from the other side. When I open the door, I see Liz Rojas sitting in an easy chair by a window, holding a large red book on her lap. She puts the book down and smiles the kind of smile you give someone you weren't sure would show up and does. I'm searching for words, but I can't find any, and my eyes fill with tears. She stands up and takes the backpack from my hand.

"Do you still need an assistant?" I ask.

chapter THIRTY

During dinner that night, my father tells me that he would like me to work in his office on Saturdays. "You need to keep your mind occupied," he says. My job will be to describe the properties for sale on the company website in a way that makes them irresistible to buyers. Ed, the young man who picked me up at Lakeview, will handle the technical part.

"It's the perfect job for you," my father tells me. "You like to write, don't you?"

I have no idea how my father knows I like to write. I wonder if he went through my notebooks when I was at Lakeview.

"What about schoolwork?" I say.

"This will only be for a few hours on Saturdays. You can take your books and work on school stuff afterward," my father says. He looks at Barbara. This is something the two of them have discussed.

Barbara says, "It will be good for you to be around fun, motivated people."

"I have so much to do just to catch up," I say weakly. I don't have the strength to argue.

"The more things you have to do, the more efficiently you will do them, and the happier you will be for having accomplished what you set out to do." My father pours red wine into his empty glass. "And you will be getting paid for your work."

He waits for me to ask him how much. When I don't ask, he says, "The job pays one hundred dollars an hour."

He expects me to be impressed and grateful. I smile, because I recognize what he is trying to do. He wants money, the fun of earning it, the pleasure of having it, the thrill of wanting more of it, to light a spark in me. It's my father's answer to depression.

When I came home from school this afternoon, Barbara was in the kitchen cooking. She left work earlier than usual to make a "welcome home" dinner for me, and now we're having chicken cordon bleu, garlic mashed potatoes, green beans with almonds, and a salad with grapes, croutons, and tiny pieces of orange. Father brought a bouquet of yellow roses for me. They are trying. So I listen to their plans and their hopes for me. They are not my plans and they are not my hopes, but maybe they will do. I'm too tired and too deflated to tell them that going to the office on Saturday mornings to work on a website will just about do me in. I eat as much as I can of Barbara's dinner, which is not much, and then I ask if I can be excused.

"I don't feel all that good," I say, which is true.

When I get to my room, I call the hospital to ask about Gabriel. The receptionist tells me that he has been moved to the fifth floor and transfers me to a nurse who tells me the usual, that Gabriel is stable. I know by the way she says this that there is more to Gabriel's condition than simply stable. But if he's on the fifth floor, out of the ICU and back on the mental ward, it means that his fever is better. I try Mona again and still no answer. Then I call Dr. Desai. I leave a message for her to call me so we can set up an appointment. I haven't told my father that I want to continue seeing Dr. Desai and I don't know how that will go. I will have to cross that bridge soon. I couldn't do it today. There's only so much that a day can hold.

I have one more thing I need to do before the day is over. I search the Internet for the telephone number of Romero Landscape.

"Hello?" It is Gabriel's grandfather. I recognize his voice.

"Mr. Romero, this is Vicky Cruz. I'm Gabriel's friend from the hospital. I went to your house for Gabriel's birthday."

"Yes! Vicky, I remember. How are you?" He sounds happy.

"I'm all right, Mr. Romero. How is Gabriel? I called the hospital, but all they will tell me is that he's stable."

"Ah, yes. I don't know. I think Dr. Desai wants more tests. To see, you know, if it's something like a tumor."

"Have you seen him?"

"Yes. I went to see him. He seems okay one moment and the next like he goes someplace else."

"Mr. Romero . . ."

"Please, call me Antonio."

"Antonio. I called about something else too."

"Yes."

"My nana. She's sixty-eight years old and has bad arthritis. I need to find a place for her to live. Gabriel mentioned that you were looking for a boarder. Someone to rent the room in your house. And I was wondering if I could maybe bring my nana over to meet you and your wife someday to see if maybe she could live with you. She has a little trouble walking, especially going up the stairs. But she can help take care of your wife. She's a very good person. Her name is Juanita." It feels good to get that out. It feels like the right thing, but I am still nervous.

"Yes! Yes!" I hear Antonio say and his enthusiasm almost makes me cry. "Come with Juanita to see the room and we all meet. When can you come?"

"Soon," I say, "soon. I still have to work some things out." *I have to work a way around my father.* "But thank you. That means a lot to me."

"Where's Juanita now?" he asks.

"She's staying with a friend."

"Does your friend have a phone? I will call her."

After I give him Yolanda's phone number, Antonio says, "You don't worry. I will take care of this. I will get the room ready. Gabriel will be happy."

"Bye, Antonio." I hang up. Juanita will be good for Chona, and a help to Antonio and Gabriel. And Juanita will like living there. I know the Gabriel who is healthy will be okay with this too.

I am amazed. I just acted on the hope that things will turn out well.

I walk to the window. I open it and call Galileo again. He doesn't come. But I leave the window open. I know he will return.

THIRTY-ONE

On Saturday morning, I drive with my father to the offices of Cruz RC to work on the firm's website. We are in the Spider with the top down so conversation is not possible, which is probably just as well. I thought that he had forgotten the famous website because nothing was said about it yesterday, but this morning he knocked on my door at seven and told me we were leaving in half an hour.

I lay in bed for a few minutes, wondering whether this was one of those instances where I should push back like Becca told me. I decided it wasn't. How hard can it be to make a house sound like the one spot on this earth where the sum of all happiness will be found? I also didn't have the energy to argue with him. The deal is that I will work on the website until noon, and then I get to work on schoolwork until the early afternoon, when we'll go to the airport to pick up Becca.

In my backpack, I have a stack of poems, stories, and essays that Liz gave me to review for possible publication in *The Quill*. Yesterday, after my classes were over, I went to the *Quill* offices again. Liz gave me a key so I can go and hang out whenever I want. There must be a hundred books of poems and about the craft of poetry lining the shelves of the reading room. I sat in one of the wing chairs and closed my eyes. It was so peaceful in there. I felt protected, like when Gabriel and I lay safe under the raft while the rain raged outside.

As we cruise along the highway, I remember how much Mamá liked to go for drives around the city and out past the city limits, often not knowing where she was going. I would sit next to her and we would drive aimlessly for an hour or so, commenting on what we were seeing or whatever came to mind. Mamá used to say that driving was great for conversations because you didn't have to look at the other person. Both of you could just stare at the road ahead, and somehow this made it easier to communicate. Driving was especially good when you had something to say that might make the other person angry. People had to stay in control, otherwise you'd crash.

It was on one of those drives that Mamá first told me she had cancer. The concentration required for the driving kept her calm and even upbeat as she spoke. She described the type of cancer she had, the treatment she was going to receive, and the side effects. When I asked her if she was going to die, she explained that the survival rate for her type of cancer was forty-two percent after five years and much higher before then. I asked if she had told Father and Becca about the cancer, and Mamá said that she wanted to tell me first, that she wanted to practice what to say with me because I was the strongest one in the family.

Wow, I think now. *How can Mamá have been so wrong?* But . . . Mamá was never wrong about people. What if I am strong and I don't even know it? What if I'm not strong like Father or Becca or Barbara, but strong in a different way? Why did Mamá say that? How am I strong? I make a mental note to think about that.

After about fifteen minutes, my father pulls into an auto repair shop for foreign cars. He turns off the engine and says, "Why don't you come in? I'm going to leave the car here."

"How —" I start to say.

"They'll loan me a car while they're fixing this one." Then he gets out, opens the glass door to the shop, and disappears past a row of new, shiny cars inside. Off to the side is a glass-enclosed waiting room with fancy-looking chairs and a television mounted on one wall. I go in there, sit in one of the chairs, and hunt for my cell phone inside my backpack. Dr. Desai called me back yesterday while I was at school and left a message. I tried calling her when I was at *The Quill* but couldn't get through. I try again, and this time I reach her.

"Vicky!" she says. "So good to hear your voice. How have you been?"

"So-so," I say.

"Tell me."

I tell her everything that's happened since I returned home. "I feel this pressure in my head, like a thick fog," I finish. "Everything seems so difficult. It's like the way I felt before Lakeview. But there are more good moments. Times when I do things that will help, when I remember what I learned from you and the others."

"I think it's time to consider medication," she says. "It sounds as if you're finding ways to be positive, and now you need the strength and energy to carry out your good intentions. Can you come in today? I'll be here at Lakeview most of the day."

"I don't know. I'm on my way to my father's office to help him this morning."

"I'm going to leave a prescription for you on the fifth floor in case you can come and pick it up. Follow the instructions on the label carefully. We'll start with a small dosage. Will there be a problem with your parents?"

"I haven't talked to them about seeing you yet. I've been trying to avoid conflict."

"Don't avoid," she says, her voice firm. "It just makes it that much worse . . . while you're waiting for the confrontation and when you finally get there. I have to go now, Vicky. If you can't come get the prescription, call and give the nurses the fax number for your pharmacy and they will fax it. Okay?"

"Okay. Doctor, how's Gabriel?"

Silence. Then, "Gabriel's fever went away, thank goodness. We still don't know what that was all about. But I'm afraid the voice is more intense, more frequent, more persistent. He's in the secured section of the ward where he can be closely observed."

"Will he be all right?"

There are a few more moments of silence. "I would like to get him started on antipsychotics. He has moments of lucidity and moments when he's lost to his voice. But he doesn't want to stay at Lakeview any longer, and he's refusing medication." She pauses. "Vicky, it sounds as if you are struggling, but out of that struggle, finding ways to live at home. You need to concentrate on that. I'll take care of Gabriel. I think the medication will help you, and I want to see you on Monday. It is important that I see you if you start taking the medication. Okay, I have to go now."

"Bye, Dr. Desai."

The line goes dead but I keep my cell phone glued to my ear. Gabriel is in the secured section of the ward. He has been upgraded. Should I try to see him? Could I convince him to stay at Lakeview, to take the medication he needs? Did I ever in all those debate tournaments convince anyone of anything? I have to try. I want to see him. He's my friend. He needs me.

There's a rap on the glass. It's my father, motioning for me to come out. I follow him out of the exhibit room into the parking lot, where a smiling man opens the door of the loaner car. It's another sports car, but this one has a roof, so I'll be able to talk to my father while we drive, for a change. But that means I have to decide what exactly I want to tell him.

It strikes me that if we were a normal family, I would be able to ask my father to take me to Lakeview to see Gabriel. But I feel unable to ask him to help me. Why? What keeps me from asking? What makes me so sure that if I ask him, he will say no, and then it will be harder for me to see Gabriel?

One of the things I felt that week before the deed was this nausea at all the lying and pretending in my life. I pretended I liked debate when I didn't. I pretended I was happy when I wasn't. What would happen if I were truthful and honest with myself and others? Would I feel better?

Father starts the car and backs out. When we get to the

exit, he puts his right blinker on, in the direction of downtown Austin.

I take a deep breath. I feel a little like I felt on the edge of the raft, getting ready to jump in after E.M. "Dad, I'm sorry, but I can't start work right now. I really need to go to Lakeview."

He turns right and pulls out into the street, then shifts gears and speeds away from an oncoming truck. The truck honks angrily at us. Father glances in his rearview mirror and grins at the hand signal the truck driver sends him. "Why?" he says.

"I need to see a friend who is ill." There. It felt good to get that out. I said it nicely, without fear. I imagine that's the way a daughter who has a close relationship with her father would say it.

"A friend?"

"A boy I met when I was at Lakeview. His name is Gabriel and he's sick. I need to see him."

He fiddles with the air conditioner for a few moments while we stop at a red light. The angry truck pulls up on my father's side. One of the men in the truck rolls down the passenger-side window and screams obscenities at us. My father stares at him for a few moments and turns to me.

"Look," he says calmly. "It's time we had a talk."

The light turns green and we move ahead slowly. The truck keeps pace with us, sometimes veering toward our car like it wants to hit us. Father doesn't budge or speed away. Now the truck and our car are rolling slowly down the road together. Cars behind us start to honk.

"See those guys?" Father points at the truck. "They're not like us. They're not educated. They're not ambitious. They're not intelligent. They work for people like us. That's our contact with them. We hire them or we buy from them. We sell to them sometimes. But we live different lives."

I have no idea why he is telling me this at this particular moment. "Can you take me to Lakeview, or give me some money for a taxi?"

The truck finally pulls ahead, and the cars behind it start to pass us, their drivers giving us dirty looks.

"Let me ask you this," Father says. "What does this friend of yours do? This boy you met at Lakeview?"

"His name is Gabriel Romero, and he works with his grandfather," I say.

"Doing what?"

"They have a landscaping business. What difference does it make? He's sick and I want to see him." I try not to sound irritated.

"Is he in school?"

"He's going to go to night school as soon as he can. He left regular school to support his grandparents. Dad, please."

"One final question. Why is this Gabriel Romero in Lakeview?"

"He was there for observation. It's possible he has a mental illness . . . just like me. All right?" I can't hide my anger any longer. We are now going up the ramp to the highway that will take us downtown, away from the hospital. Then I add, "And I need to pick up a prescription that Dr. Desai left for me, and schedule an appointment with her so I can see her next week."

My father is silent as our car zooms ahead and merges with the oncoming traffic. Once he's safely in the middle lane, he speaks again. "Maybe you're right," he says. There's a resigned acceptance in his voice. "Maybe there *is* something wrong with you. That's what Barbara says, that there has to be something wrong with you for you to take those pills. So we're willing to give you some leeway. You want to quit debate? Fine. You want to take a reduced load this semester? Okay. You're not going to get into an Ivy League. All right. We can live with that. We thought you had the brains to get good grades and it was a case of you not trying. But maybe you don't have the brains we thought you did, or maybe you do have a mental illness like you say, and this mental illness is keeping you from doing well. Okay, we'll give you some space and time to work things out.

"But there are limits to what we can allow you to do," he says. All throughout his speech, his voice has a tone of friendly authority. It's the voice of someone who knows he doesn't have to yell to be feared. "You are not going to hang out with kids with mental problems who mow lawns for a living. That's not going to happen." He glances over his shoulder and moves to the right lane. The exit to his office is a quarter mile ahead. Then he adds, "And if you are going to take medications, they are going to be prescribed by a good doctor, someone we can trust. So no. I will not take you to Lakeview."

I don't care what he says about my brains or lack of brains, or whether he thinks I'm a mule or even a jackass. None of this surprises me. What bothers me, what hurts me, is his attitude toward Gabriel and Dr. Desai. *Stand up to him. Don't be afraid of his anger,* Becca said.

"You're so wrong about Gabriel," I say. I don't say it with all the anger that I feel at that moment, because I can't. The sticky tarlike substance that likes to fill my head has been pouring in steadily all morning, and the little elves inside of me can barely move. "He's the kindest, most intelligent, most articulate, most mature boy I've ever met. He works so hard to support his family."

He takes the exit off the highway and stops at the light at the bottom of the ramp. "Jaime has been calling for you every day. Why don't you spend time with him? You're fortunate to have someone like him interested in you."

"You know what's sad?" I speak quietly, as best I can, trying to get my words out between my shallow breathing and racing heart. "What's sad is that I will never be able to convince you that Gabriel is a hundred times nicer and smarter and even more ambitious, in his own way, than Jaime. When your grandfather came from Mexico, was he rich and educated? When Mamá was alive, you'd tell us stories about him, how he came over from Oaxaca to make adobes in Laredo. *You* worked as a teenager delivering bricks to construction sites. You started at the bottom, like those guys in the truck. How did you become so different? What happened to you?"

At that moment in the car, I think my father comes the closest he's ever been to being speechless. When he finally speaks, his words have an edge of controlled anger, but the anger does not seem directed at me. "How did I become so different? Supporting you and your sister after your mother died. Making sure you didn't lack for anything."

"We didn't lack for anything when Mamá was alive. You were different then. Kinder. You looked at me differently. You spent time with me. You *cared*. You changed after Mamá died."

"Well, what about you?" He sounds flustered. "What happened to the Vicky who used to beat everyone when we had those swimming races with your sister and your mother? Why don't you answer that one first?"

I say calmly, "Dad, the last time you were in the pool with me was before Mamá died. I swim every day. You could have raced with me anytime you wanted."

He clenches his jaw and presses his foot on the accelerator, and all I can think is that I have touched my father in a place he has almost forgotten. Becca was right. He gets angry when he feels hurt.

chapter THIRTY-TWO

The headquarters for Cruz RC is a three-story modern build-ing in downtown Austin. Father rents the first floor to a Starbucks and a very exclusive gym where Barbara likes to go for her Pilates workout. The second floor is leased to a presti-gious law firm, and the third floor is occupied by Cruz RC. In back of the building, there is a small parking lot. My father's space next to the back door is marked with a white-and-red sign that says M. CRUZ. Barbara's space next to his is marked B. HENNEY. Barbara likes to use her maiden name at work.

My father zips from the street into the parking lot and then slams on the brakes. "What the . . ." he says.

Occupying his space is a huge, old-looking car that was probably yellow at one point but is now pale beige. It has a rust spot that looks like South America on the driver's door, and the back window consists of a clear plastic sheet. I can see a very-dark-brown elbow sticking out of the driver's window.

My father honks. The door to the beige car opens.

"E.M.!" I shout as he climbs out of the car.

"You know this guy?" my father asks.

"Yes, he's from Lakeview." I wave at E.M., but then I remember our car has tinted windows, so he can't see me. I open the door and get out.

"Hey, Huichi!" E.M. exclaims. He's wearing a white

T-shirt with the sleeves unevenly cut off. His baggy pants are kept up by a rope tied around his waist.

"How did you find me?" I ask. My father turns the car off and gets out to stand a few paces behind me.

"I remembered your father's company from one of our meetings. I went up to the office, but they didn't want to tell me where you lived. I asked to speak to your father and they told me he was on his way in. I saw the sign and thought I'd wait here to ask him how I could find you." He looks at Father and makes a move to shake his hand, but he stops when he sees the expression on my father's face.

"Dad, this is E.M.," I say. "Emilio Machado." E.M. nods. My father does not move. He's not even blinking. His fists are clenched.

E.M. takes a step forward, then relaxes and turns his attention back to me. He's comfortable with someone else's aggression. "I came to take you to Lakeview," he says. "Gabriel's in bad shape. He's talking some crazy stuff about leaving the hospital and finding Mona. I never seen him like that. I figured you were the only one that can help him. Convince him to stay. I wouldn't come get you like this if I didn't think it was bad."

I look at him and there in front of me are my fears. Fear of not being strong enough or brave enough or kind enough to help Gabriel. Fear of my father's anger, of letting him down once again if I leave. But I turn to face my father determined, without doubts or hesitation, just like I jumped in after E.M. when he was drowning. "Dad, I need to go," I say.

"You mind moving your car," he says to E.M. It's more a command than a request.

"Yeah. Sure. I'll move it," E.M. responds politely. He looks at me, waiting.

"I'll be back soon," I say to Father. I start toward E.M.'s car.

"Go upstairs, Vicky." My father's voice is stern but controlled.

I stop. "I need to go," I say. "It's important. My friend is very sick. Can you please understand that?"

"You're not going anyplace." Red blotches appear on my father's cheeks. "Go upstairs."

I stand there, my backpack dangling from my arm, staring at my father. I feel suddenly a tremendous sadness. It feels as if he is trapped in a world of pretend from which he can no longer escape. There's a kind, loving man somewhere inside of him, the man my mother fell in love with. But there's a sheet of ice blocking that kindness. How can I shatter that frozen surface?

I look at E.M. He smiles at me reassuringly. "It's up to you, Huichi," he says.

I walk slowly to E.M.'s car and open the passenger door. I glance at my father one last time as lovingly as I can. "Dad," I say softly, "I'm going to go see my friend. You have to trust that I can pick good friends, friends who are good for me. I need to do this to be who I am. I'm going to try real hard at Reynard and at home, and I'll even work on the website when I can, but there are some things that are up to me to decide.

Who my friends are is one of them. Who I see for medical help is another." Then I get in and shut the door.

"You drive off with my daughter and I'm calling the police," my father says to E.M.

"I'm cool with that," E.M. answers. "Meantime, I'll take good care of her."

He gets in the car, and it starts with a roar. I put my seat belt on as E.M. maneuvers back and forth to clear my father's car. Then he moves slowly and noisily to the parking lot's exit. I don't look back, but I feel my father's eyes follow us out.

"Sorry about that back there," I say when we are a block away. "He won't call the police . . . I don't think."

"So I go to jail." He shrugs. "Long as I get you to Lakeview before they catch me."

"How bad is Gabriel?" I ask.

"Bad. The voices are bad. I went to the hospital this morning to pick up some papers from Dr. Desai, and she let me see him."

"And how did he look?"

"You talk to him and he sounds normal one second and then poof. He wants to find Mona. He's got it into his head that her life's in danger and he needs to save her."

"And what did you say?"

"I just played along with him. Kinda like the way he played along with that lady in the purple robe, 'member?"

"Gwendolyn."

"Yeah. It doesn't do any good to argue with them when they're like that. I told him I was going down to the cafeteria to see if I could get Rudy's address from his boss. That's when I came to get you. Should I take the highway?"

"Yeah, take the highway."

"Why does he want to find Mona so bad?"

"The voice Gabriel hears told him he needed to give up his life so that another person may live."

"I don't get it."

"He thinks he has to die, and he thinks it's Mona's life he has to save."

"Man, that's so loco." E.M. shakes his head and grins. "You can't make this stuff up. I never met a group of people that was so full of doom and gloom as you Lakeview guys. If it wasn't so serious, it'd be, like, hilarious. What the hell's the matter with all of you anyway? Why is everyone so ready to die?"

I wonder if that is still true for me. Am I so ready to die?

"Hey!" E.M. elbows me. "You still thinking about it?"

"I haven't thought about it lately," I lie. Then, "That's not true. I thought of dying a couple of times the past two days . . . when I was home."

"Listen. Don't worry about those thoughts. You can't control them. What you can control is what you say to yourself when those thoughts come."

"Yes," I say, remembering Dr. Desai's words. *You are the sun.*

"I never understood all this crap about suicidal thoughts. I get tons of thoughts every day, doesn't mean I follow them. I'm walking down the street, I see a hot girl, *ping, ping, ping,* I get these thoughts to do this, do that. But I'm not like a dog who can't control himself, know what I'm saying? You're in control, not your thoughts. A bad thought comes, know what I do? I say something good. I push out the bad thought with good words. Something sad comes, *bang*, I talk to Huitzilopochtli. That's what you gotta do. Make up your mind and say, 'I ain't never gonna try to kill myself no matter what, no matter what thoughts I get, no matter how sad I feel.' You think Huitzilopochtli said, 'Oh, I can't fight the nighttime and shine another day 'cause I'm down in the dumps'?"

"All right, all right!" It's hard not to laugh. Who would have thought E.M. was so funny and smart?

"How long we keep on this road?"

"I'm going to give you directions back to where I live, and then from there I can get us to the hospital. It's not the fastest way, but —"

"How can you convince *Gabriel* to wanna live if you don't believe it?"

"Next stoplight, turn left," I say. "I live over on those hills. This road will take us to the hospital."

"Have you found your bamboo stick yet?"

"What?"

"Lady Charlie's bamboo stick. To hold on to. The picture of who you want to be."

"I might," I say. "Maybe I have." I think of that strange peace I felt when I was at the offices of *The Quill*, surrounded by books of poetry. It was a solid feeling. More a determination than a feeling, even — that I could spend my life learning the craft of writing. Can I hold on to that? And my mother's strength. My bamboo sticks.

We drive a few blocks in silence, and I say, "Do you really think he'll listen to me?"

"If he listens to anyone here on earth, it'll be you."

"Why do you say that?"

"Because he trusts you."

"He trusts you and Mona too. We all trust each other."

"But you have words to reach him that we don't have. Both of you like to mess with words."

"We do? How do you know?"

E.M. gives me a *Don't ask stupid questions* look. Then: "What about Princess Psycho?" he asks. "You heard from her?"

"I haven't been able to get in touch with her. All I have is the number of that phone she borrowed. I'm worried about her. I hope she's not doing something illegal."

"She's doing something illegal or insane, count on it. I know my people. She's weak."

"There's got to be a way to reach her."

"Rudy's boss was due in later this morning. Like I told Gabriel, I can find out from him where Rudy lives."

"What if he doesn't want to tell you?"

"I'll make him an offer he can't refuse."

We drive in silence, each lost in our own thoughts. I want to see Gabriel, but I am also anxious about it. Vicky Cruz versus God's voice. It doesn't seem like a fair contest. What can I say to Gabriel? E.M. is right. I have to believe with all my heart that life is worth living. Life is worth living at any cost. "There's the entrance to the hospital," I say.

"Like I can't read the sign." E.M. parks the car, turns off the engine, and fixes his eyes on me. "Okay, Huichi, let's get to work."

Help me be brave and strong like you, Mamá, I say again. I wonder if that counts as a prayer.

CHAPTER THIRTY-THREE

We take the elevator to the fifth floor. Margie, the nurse at the nurses' station, recognizes me.

"Vicky," she says, "so good to see you."

"Hi, Margie."

"Are you here for your prescription? Dr. Desai left it for you."

"And to see Gabriel."

She picks up a chart and reads. "I don't see you on the list of people who can see him."

"Am I on that list?" E.M. asks.

"Yes, you know you are. I let you in earlier this morning, didn't I?" Margie gives E.M. a look that is more flirtatious than severe.

"If I'm on there, then she should be there too. Dr. Desai just forgot to put her name down," E.M. says. "People in the group can talk to each other. That's the way it's always been."

Margie looks at E.M. and then at me. "Okay," she says, "but only for a few minutes." She comes out of the nurses' station, unlocks the door to the secured section, and holds it open for us.

"I'll come back in a little while. I'm going to find Rudy's boss," E.M. says to me. "Do your work." He turns and heads for the elevator.

Margie and I walk together to the third room down the hall. She stops by the open door. "There he is," she whispers.

"He's been in and out, you know" — she taps her forehead — "since he got here. His outs are getting longer, but I saw him a few minutes ago, so I know he's in. I'll come by to get you soon, okay?"

"Thank you," I say, and watch her go back to the nurses' station.

Gabriel is sitting by the window, staring out. He's dressed in regular clothes, and I notice the bag where he keeps his things by his side. I enter slowly. I'm afraid. I'm afraid of what his reaction will be after he told me he didn't want to see me, and also that I may not find the right words to convince him to stay here. I walk to the window and stand there in silence. He doesn't move. I can't tell whether he's ignoring me or whether he is totally lost in his thoughts. Finally, I say, "Gabriel."

His head jerks up like when you catch yourself falling asleep. "Vicky." A small worried frown appears on his face, but the sparkle in his eyes tells me he's glad to see me. "You shouldn't be here."

"I didn't want to come," I say, teasing. "E.M. forced me. He came to get me."

"E.M." There is a confused, scared look on his face, like a child who suddenly realizes he's lost.

"He's downstairs."

I bring a chair from the other side of the room and sit facing him. He wrings his hands anxiously for a few moments, and then he says with a sad laugh, "They locked me up with Gwendolyn."

"Until you get better," I say softly.

"I need to get out," he says, pleading.

"Soon."

"I have to find Mona."

"The voice is telling you to do that?" I ask.

A flash of terror crosses his face. This is a Gabriel I've never seen before. "I'm not crazy. The voice . . . it is real. God's voice. Lots of people could hear it if there was less noise."

"God told you it was Mona you needed to save?"

He wrinkles his forehead in thought. "I know she's in danger. I just know."

"So you must die so Mona lives. That's what you think God wants?"

"Yes."

"Gabriel." I pause to search for the right words, for any words really. How could E.M. have thought that I would find a way to reach Gabriel with my words? I go on haltingly, "Remember that first day when we met in the cafeteria? You said not wanting to live was an illness? It's no different with you now. Anything that asks you to die is not healthy. That voice you hear urging you to die cannot come from God. It has to come from an illness."

"He wants Mona to live."

"And not you? Gabriel, you're the one who told me I have things to live for, remember? The little things. And life. Green is for life that is all around us. You told me that too. What the voice is asking of you goes against who you are and all that you believe. You got me looking for the small pleasures, the bits of beauty that we run into every day."

He covers his ears with his hands. "The voice . . ."

"It scares you now, because how can something so painful come from God? But that's not the God you believe in. The God you believe in is a God who cares for the Gwendolyns of the world, just like I saw you care for her."

"Where does the voice come from, then? Why does it say it is from God?"

"I don't know. You need to find out. You need to stay here and let Dr. Desai do the tests she wants to do. You can't leave now, because when you hear the voice, you're not aware of where you are or what you are doing. You can hurt yourself or others. You need to stay. Take the medication Dr. Desai gives you."

"The voice is bad?"

"To ask someone to die is bad."

"It's bad to want to die?" I see him pulling away again, slowly. I reach over and hold his hands.

"Yes," I say. "It's bad. I believe that now, thanks to you." I laugh a short, quiet laugh, remembering the words E.M. wanted me to say on the drive to the hospital. "I ain't never gonna try to kill myself no matter what. There. That's my promise. Can you say that too — 'I'm gonna live no matter what'?"

Gabriel lowers his head. Then he lets go of my hands, covers his face, and sobs quietly. When the sobs subside, I reach out and touch his arm. I wait until he looks at me.

"Remember how you wanted me to remind you that you are just a regular kid? You're special but not better? I know it will hurt for you not to be the saint and the martyr and the hero who saves Mona. You're going to have to settle for being Gabriel. That's all you need to be. Just plain, regular, special-but-not-better Gabriel, who may be ill like Gwendolyn and your grandmother. Can you do that? Are you brave enough to be ordinary?"

For the longest time he doesn't answer. He just leans back in the chair, looking at me with an expression that resembles pride or love, or both. Finally, he says, "If I don't listen to the voice . . ."

"What? What will happen?"

"It may not come again."

"And then what? What will happen?"

"I'm scared not to hear it. I'll be depressed like before it came. I'm scared to hear it and to not hear it."

"Why? Is it because the voice gives meaning to your life, keeps you from feeling worthless, like you told me once?"

He bites his lip as if to keep himself from speaking.

"What about the little things that give life meaning? The green of life that is all around us will be there even if you don't hear the voice. Can't those little things and that green of life be the way God speaks to you from now on? How can you possibly believe that you are worthless without the voice? You give so much, you're needed so much by so many, you are so . . . so much more than someone who hears a voice, even if that voice is God himself speaking to you."

A faint smile, an almost-smile, appears on his face.

"Maybe you *will* be depressed when the voice goes away," I say after a few moments. "Then it will be the two of us struggling with depression. You and me, we'll be depressed together."

"You'll be there?" he asks quietly.

"Gabriel. You're my friend. My friend forever. I need you and you need me." I lean over and kiss his cheek.

"Mona," he says, drifting away.

"E.M. and I will find Mona. I promise you we will find her. But you need to stay here."

He is moving his lips, speaking to someone, his eyes closed. Then he opens them and whispers, "With Gwendolyn."

"Yes, with Gwendolyn. Remember how you made her laugh? You can make her laugh again today. The world is full of Gwendolyns that need you to make them laugh. I'm one of them," I tell him.

He nods. It is the slightest of nods, but that's all I need. Then he snaps his head to one side and freezes, listening. Fear crosses his face. He makes what looks like an immense effort to snap out of it and says to me, urgently, "Go." He shuts his eyes and covers his ears with his hands again.

"I'll be back soon," I tell him.

But I know he doesn't hear me.

chapter THIRTY-FOUR

E.M. is waiting for me by the nurses' station. He waves a small piece of paper when he sees me. "I got Rudy's address," he says. "I know where he lives. It's not far from here."

"Okay," I say. We start walking toward the elevator, then I remember. I turn to Margie. "Dr. Desai left a prescription for me."

"Yes." She opens a drawer and gives me a slip of paper. "See you soon, Vicky."

She means as a visitor and not as a patient . . . I think.

On the way to his car, E.M. says, "You convinced Gabriel to stay."

"Yeah, but it's not like he had a choice," I say, thinking of the locked doors to the upgrade side of the fifth floor.

"He had a choice," E.M. says.

We get on a highway heading in the direction of my house. I feel peaceful. I made a decision back there in Gabriel's room, one that I will always live by no matter how hard the days get. It's not happiness, exactly. It's more like a certainty, a determination, a quiet strength.

Twenty minutes later, we are driving past row after row of identical apartment buildings, the kind that resemble motels, with those small pools about the size of E.M.'s car.

"This is the street," he says. "Look for number 1475."

We slow down to peer at the numbers on the side of the buildings. "E.M.," I say, "Gabriel thought it might be dangerous . . . when we find Mona. Promise me you're not going to do anything to aggravate the situation?"

"Agra-what?"

"Promise me you won't get violent or anything."

"Me? Violent?" he says, pretending to be offended.

"I'm serious. Let's go over our plan. Wait. Do we have a plan?"

E.M. cranes his neck out the window, looking for house numbers. "Our plan is to find out what's going on with Mona. If she's with Rudy and in a bad place and can make decisions, then it's up to you to convince her to come back with us."

"Me?"

"You're the expert convincer," he says. "We'll know what to do once we find out what's going on. But . . . she's a big girl. She's got to make her choices, just like Gabriel did. Like you did." He looks at me briefly and winks. "That's it," he adds, pointing at a three-story brick building. Many of the windows have leaking air conditioners sticking out of them, but more of the windows are open, and in a few I can see people looking out at the street.

E.M. parks the car next to a row of aluminum cans overflowing with garbage. We get out of the car, E.M. not bothering to lock it. His is easily the worst car on the street. It is jarring to see glitzy, well-kept cars gleaming with chrome parked next to the oppressive apartment buildings and smelly garbage.

"Apartment 316," E.M. says.

We walk through a playground with a rusty swing set and a pair of plastic horses on springs. One of the horses has been decapitated. We find the stairs on the side of the building and climb up single file, E.M. leading the way. He stops when we get to the third floor and looks at me as if to make sure that I want to continue. I nod, and we enter the hallway that leads to the apartments.

Many of the doors to the apartments are open to create cross-ventilation with the open window at the other end of the hall. There are sounds of Mexican music and children crying and women yelling. From the doorway of one apartment, a man with a brown belly hanging over a pair of white boxer shorts leers at me as I walk by. He starts to say something, but then he sees E.M. glaring at him.

We keep walking, and a little devilish voice inside my head whispers, *So, Vicky, where would you rather live, all things considered? In your big, cold house with an alarm, a fence, a heated swimming pool in the backyard, and central air, or here?*

"Why are you smiling?" E.M. asks.

"I'll tell you someday," I say. *If we make it out of here alive.*

Rudy's apartment is the last on the hallway. E.M. puts his ear against the door before knocking. He shakes his head to tell me he can't hear any sounds and then he knocks. The knocks are polite, considerate. Inside we hear a man yell.

E.M. grabs the doorknob and begins to shake the door. I think he wants to kick it in, until the man's voice on the other side shouts, "Okay, okay, hold on to your shorts. I'm coming!" E.M. stops and looks at me, triumphant. "Lalo?" the man asks, or rather slurs.

"Yeah!" E.M. responds. He shrugs and lifts his eyebrows at me, then shakes the door again impatiently.

"Wait a second," the man pleads. There's a noise of someone fumbling clumsily with a door chain, then he opens the door. It's Rudy, but he seems to have aged twenty years since I last saw him in the cafeteria. He looks like he's having trouble keeping his eyes open.

E.M. steps into the apartment as if he owns the place and I follow behind him. "Hey, you're not Lalo," says Rudy, trying to focus. "Do I know you?"

"Where's Mona?" E.M. asks.

To the right as we enter the apartment is the kitchen and eating area. The sink overflows with dirty dishes, and the small wooden table has a box of Cheerios that has tipped over and emptied its contents. To the left is an old corduroy sofa, a La-Z-Boy with the stuffing coming out, and cans of beer scattered around. A reality show without any sound plays on a flat-screen TV propped up on a couple of chairs. I can see three doors down the hallway between the kitchen and the living room. Only one of them is open.

Suddenly, Mona staggers out of the open door. She looks like she's about to fall. E.M. rushes to grab her and hold her up. "Something's wrong with her," he says, laying her down gently in the hallway.

"Hey, I know you. You're one of those psychos from the hospital." Rudy stumbles back a few steps and grabs on to a kitchen chair.

"What you give her? She's not right," E.M. says. Mona is having trouble keeping her head up.

"She'll be fine," Rudy says.

I step over to Mona and hold her face so that her eyes can focus on mine. "Mona, it's Vicky. Can you hear me?"

Rudy stumbles toward the kitchen. "I'm just gonna get a glass of water," he says to E.M., who is watching him carefully.

"Vicky," Mona whispers, barely audible, "I didn't mean to."

"It's okay, Mona. We're here."

"I saw her, Vicky. I saw Lucy." Mona's eyes are fully open, her pupils the size of dimes. She's animated suddenly, a current of energy traveling through her. "She lives in San Antonio with a foster family. I waited for her to come out. I knew she would."

"Mona, you can tell me later. What did you take?"

"I waited for her to come out. I was going to take her. Then . . . she came out. With this lady. Lucy was skipping . . . pulling her hand, talking a mile a minute."

"I found out whereabouts the kid lived," Rudy says from the kitchen. "Cost me a thousand bucks. I drove her up there and back, and she was a mess. Needed to party a little, get her mind in a different groove, know what I mean? She'll be okay."

"I followed them." Mona makes an effort to lift herself up. Her head wobbles from side to side.

"Here, stay down. Do you want a glass of water?"

E.M. hears me. He grabs the glass of water that Rudy has been holding and gives it to me. I raise Mona and try to get her to drink, but she shakes her head.

"They went to this park." Her eyes begin to slowly shut and then she jolts herself up.

"Shhh. You can tell me later." I dig into my pocket and take out my cell phone.

"What you doing?" It's Rudy, alarmed.

"I'm calling an ambulance."

"Hey! No ambulances! No police!" he shouts. "She'll be fine."

"What you give her?" E.M. asks, moving closer to him.

"Some sweet stuff. Just enough to party. Chill."

I turn Mona's arm, and on the underside, there's a purple bruise from an injection. I don't know much about drugs, but I know this is bad.

I want to give the phone to E.M., but Mona lowers her arm. "In the park, first she got on the swings." Her lips are so swollen she has trouble getting the words out. "I watched her. She was so happy. Sooo happy."

Her eyes flutter and then she closes them. Her breathing gets heavier and then it stops. I drop the phone on the floor and push on her chest and she breathes again, but barely. "E.M., I think we're losing her. Call 9-1-1!"

"No! No 9-1-1!" shouts Rudy.

E.M. kneels down and picks up my phone. What happens next is like a bad dream you try to wake up from but can't. Rudy grabs a kitchen ax, the kind Juanita uses to dismember a chicken, and staggers toward E.M., who is concentrating on the phone. It takes me a moment to realize that is real, that the next thing I will see is an ax stuck in E.M.'s back.

"E.M.," I gasp. I mean to shout but there's not enough air in my lungs. But the sound I make is enough for E.M. to move. The ax misses him and comes crashing down on the back of the sofa.

E.M. stands there frozen, looking at Rudy in disbelief. Then he punches him on the jaw.

"Ow! Ow!" Rudy groans, rubbing the side of his face.

"E.M. 9-1-1," I say.

"You broke my tooth, man," Rudy mutters, spitting blood.

"Drop the ax," E.M. tells him. "Why you want to kill me for?"

His words seem to remind Rudy of what he was about to do. The ax goes up again, but E.M. grabs Rudy by the throat with one powerful grip and pushes him against the wall. The ax drops and Rudy's face goes from white to pink to red. I can't see E.M.'s face from where I am, but I can sense his power and his rage by the bulging muscles of his neck and the steel tension in his arm.

"E.M.," I whisper. Rudy's feet in their white socks are dangling off the floor. His face is turning purple. "E.M., no!" I shout.

E.M. lifts Rudy higher up the wall. Then he throws him to the floor, where Rudy immediately begins to cough and gasp and wriggle in pain like a worm cut in half. E.M. kicks the ax away and looks at me with the expression Gabriel had earlier, a look of not knowing where he is.

"9-1-1," I remind him. He nods. He looks around for the phone. "In your other hand." He looks at it, surprised, and then begins to call.

"Oh, oh, oh," Rudy moans, squirming on the floor.

"Shut up!" E.M. tells him. "My friend's hardly breathing. It looks like an overdose," he says into the phone and then gives them the address.

Mona's teeth begin to chatter as if she's cold. I get a *sarape* hanging over the sofa and use it to cover her. E.M. goes into the back room and then comes out again. "There's a whole drugstore back there," he says to me, and then to Rudy, "You stole all that from the hospital?"

"Mona, can you hear me?" I ask. "Hold on. You're going to be all right."

Rudy is crawling, going for the ax. E.M. sees him and steps on his outstretched hand. "Okay, okay," Rudy whimpers. "Let go. Let go."

"Is this what you gave her?" E.M. waves a small, empty vial in front of Rudy.

"Yeah, man, yeah. Let go my hand!"

"What is it?" I ask.

"What is it?" E.M. asks Rudy, stepping harder.

"Ow, ow. Ow. It's morphine, morphine sulfate. Let go."

E.M. moves his foot and Rudy crawls away from him. He leans back against the kitchen wall, sticks his fingers inside his mouth, and comes out with a molar. "I'm gonna sue you for ruining my face," he says.

"Your face got ruined when you were born," E.M. tells him.

At the exact moment the paramedics burst into the room, Mona stops breathing. One of them immediately performs CPR. E.M. and I stand in front of the kitchen table. When Mona begins to cough and gag, we both exhale, relieved. "You know what she took?" the second paramedic asks.

"She injected morphine. I don't know how much." I point to the vial on the kitchen table. Rudy wants the paramedics to look at his throat and hand and tooth. They ignore him.

Two police officers come through the open door. One of them scans the room and speaks directly to me. "Who called 9-1-1?"

"We did," I say, taking a step toward her and reading her badge. Her last name is Longoria, just like my teacher at Reynard. "Our friend overdosed or had a reaction. She injected morphine. The drugs are in the back bedroom."

Officer Longoria motions to her partner, who heads down the hall to the bedroom. "Who's he?" She gestures to Rudy.

"He's the one that stole the drugs from Lakeview," E.M. tells her.

"He busted my tooth. Tried to choke me." Rudy points a crooked finger at E.M.

"Self-defense," E.M. says.

"Oh, yeah?" Officer Longoria stares at E.M.'s tattoos suspiciously.

The paramedics have Mona on a stretcher and are wheeling her out. "Can I ride with her?" I ask one of them.

Officer Longoria says, "No, I need you to stay here and explain all this."

"Take her to Lakeview," I tell the paramedics. "She's a patient there. Her doctor is Dr. Desai. I need to go with my friend," I say to Officer Longoria.

"In a few minutes," she says. "Let's see if we can clear all this up."

The police hold all of us for an eternity while we explain what happened. There really is a drugstore of illegal pills in the bedroom. It is clear that many of them were stolen from patients at Lakeview. Finally, we are done and we can go. Officer Longoria gives Rudy a wet dish towel to wipe his nose and then handcuffs him.

I want E.M. to drive fast to Lakeview, but I'm also afraid to get there. I'm afraid of what is to become of Mona, and I am afraid for Gabriel, if the voice is angry at him for disobeying it. At one point E.M. stretches out his hand, the one he used to punch Rudy, and it is shaking. "I wanted to kill him," he says, opening and closing his fist. "It was so hard not to squeeze his life out."

"Good thing you didn't," I say.

I lean my head back and feel the air rushing through the open window. It is cloudy and the streets are wet. It rained at some point while we were in the apartment.

I close my eyes and speak to Gabriel's God.

Help Mona get well, please. And Gabriel — let him be. You don't need to talk to him. He'll find you on his own. I'll help him look for you. We'll search for you together. You need people like him. You need people like me.

CHAPTER THIRTY-FIVE

"We're here," E.M. says. He has pulled up in front of the emergency entrance. "I'll go park the car." I open the door and step out. "Hey, Huichi," he calls after me. I stop. "You did good . . . for a spoiled rich girl."

"Thanks," I say. "You did good too."

I check with the nurses in the emergency room to make sure Mona is there. The nurse tells me she was admitted and is being taken care of. Her condition is still critical. Then I take the elevator to the fifth floor to see Gabriel.

Antonio is sitting alone in the reception area in front of the nurses' station. He stands when he sees me. "He's sleeping," he tells me. "When I saw him, one moment he is here and the next his mind goes. But when he was here, he said yes to the medication."

"That's good," I say.

"Yes, it's good."

I tell him about Gabriel's voice, about what it was asking him to do, about the conversation I had with him before E.M. and I went searching for Mona.

"Thank you," he says.

We sit next to each other. Antonio says, "I saw Juanita last night. Did she tell you?"

"No," I say, surprised, delighted.

"I pick her up at her friend's and bring the two of them to my house. They like it. They like Chona, and Chona like Juanita. We decide to move her tomorrow. She comes to live with us, with me and Chona . . . and Gabriel."

"Yes." I try to say more, but I can't. There's a knot of tears in my throat that is keeping me from speaking.

After a while I go down to the ER and wait with E.M. for news on Mona. Another hour passes before Dr. Desai emerges. Her hug is long and strong. "Her condition is delicate but her vital signs are getting stronger. She's very lucky. If the para-medics hadn't gotten there to administer the overdose reversal medication . . . I don't know. You found her just in time. And you, Vicky? How are you?"

"I'm all right," I said. She keeps her eyes fixed on mine. "I'll be all right," I repeat. "And Gabriel?"

She frowns. Then, "He has a long hard road ahead of him. But he's willing to accept treatment. The antipsychotics will take a few days, but he took them. Did you have something to do with that? Margie said you came to see him this morning."

"Maybe," I say. Maybe I did. Maybe my words somehow reached Gabriel.

"I want you to come see me." She pauses. "No matter what happens here. I want to see you next week."

"All right," I say. I think of my father. What will he be like next week? If he says no, will I have the strength to insist on seeing Dr. Desai? If I'm as tired then as I am now, the answer is no, I won't have the strength to fight him. But maybe I can find it again.

"Did you pick up the prescription I left for you?"

"Yes. But I didn't seem to need any pills today," I say.

"Adrenaline will do that to you," she says. She hugs me again and I hold on to her, afraid to let her go. Or maybe she's afraid to let go of me.

E.M. and I wait, I don't know for how long. I go through the day and everything that happened. The drive with my father and all I said to him. Did my words hurt him? Was I truthful or just getting back at him? I decide the words were true and came from somewhere deep in darkness, and it was good for them to see the light of day.

"Vicky!"

I open my eyes and see Becca walking toward me. Behind her comes Father. "How did you know I was here?" I say.

I stand and we hug. "Miguel came to get me at the airport and told me about you taking off with some guy." She glances down at E.M., who grins at her. "Anyway, you told Miguel you needed to come to Lakeview to see a friend who was sick, so I asked him if we could come straight here." She leans close to me. "He and I had a little talk."

Father stands next to Becca. "Hello," I say to him.

He nods. In that small nod I see that he respects me for what I said in the car, and maybe even believes some of it to be true, but he's not happy with what I've done. And yet he's here with Becca to see me, to support me. For my father, that is huge.

E.M. stands and offers his hand. My father takes it, reluctantly. "How is your friend?" Father says. He seems to have difficulty with the word *friend*.

"The friend I came to see this morning is on the fifth floor. He's sleeping. We're waiting to hear about Mona, my other friend. She's in the ER."

"What's wrong with her?" Becca asks.

"She overdosed," I say, looking at my father. He shakes his head. "Some things happened this afternoon that I have to tell you about."

My father finds a chair and sits. Becca and I sit next to him. Becca says, "I like your new haircut." She giggles.

"I could get you one just like it," I say.

"So what happened?" my father asks before Becca can say anything more.

I'm about to answer when E.M. jumps in. "Your daughter, man, she's brave. She saved a life today, maybe two. When we got here, she convinced Gabriel — he's the one up in the psych ward — to stay in the hospital because he was ready to leave and go out and get himself killed maybe. Then we went looking for Mona and got there just as she was about to expire from an overdose, but first we had to subdue her junkie boyfriend."

"Expire? Subdue?" I ask, smiling. I'm not sure I've ever heard E.M. put so many big words together.

E.M. ignores me. "So that's two lives, right. Gabriel, because she got him to stay when he was ready to go out and die, and Mona, because we got there in time and the paramedics pulled her out of the overdose. Maybe three, 'cause she kept me from killing the worm that gave Mona the drugs." He stops then, remembering. "Not to mention that she jumped in the rapids and pulled me out of the river back at the ranch when I was drowned. So how many lives saved does that make?" E.M. counts with his fingers. "Four. Four lives are here today because of her. Not too bad, *verdad*?"

My father looks at me the way he is looking at my mother in one of their wedding pictures: like he can't believe that she is with him now and will be with him forever, that she has chosen to be with him out of all the men in the known world.

"I'm glad you're okay," he says.

I tell them about Lakeview and the ranch, and I can see in my father's face his struggle to understand how it all was good for me, was needed. About an hour after my father and Becca arrive, a man in light-green scrubs comes out of the swinging doors that lead to the ER.

"You all are here for Domonique Salas?"

"Yes," I answer, standing up. E.M. stands as well.

"She's not out of the woods yet. But we got her stable and awake. You can go in and talk to her for a few minutes."

"She going to be okay?" E.M. asks.

"Good as new," the doctor says. "After her body is clear of toxins, I'll hand her over to Dr. Desai."

"Thank you," I say. The doctor nods and walks back the way he came. He looks exhausted.

Thank you, I say silently to Gabriel's God. I turn to my father. "Is it okay if I go in and talk to Mona? E.M. can drive me home."

My father takes a long look at E.M. "We'll wait with you and drive home together. I'll call Barbara and let her know."

"You coming?" I say to E.M.

"You go," he says. "If she sees me, she'll want to take more of that morphine."

"No, she won't," I say. "Come with me."

We follow the nurse through the swinging doors, my heart racing. The nurse opens the curtain, and there is Mona, pale, tubes connected to her arm, monitors with fragile neon lines inching across dark screens. "One minute," the nurse says. She closes the curtain behind her.

Mona's eyes are closed, so E.M. and I stand in front of her, watching. I think of Mamá in those final days, with the oxygen mask. Mona's right hand is only partially covered by the light, white blanket. *Glorified sheets*, she called them. I place my hand on top of hers. She opens her eyes and makes a move to take the oxygen mask off, but the tubes on her arm restrict her.

"Shh," I say.

"Hey," E.M. says when her eyes fix on him.

She moves her free hand from under mine and lifts the oxygen mask. "I'm sorry," she whispers.

"Didn't I tell you the guy was bad news?" E.M. reminds her.

"It's okay," I say, elbowing E.M.

"What am I going to do now?" she asks, looking at me first and then at E.M. "Without Lucy?"

"First thing you gotta do is stay away from the garbage," E.M. says. "I don't mean just the drugs, I mean the people, like that Rudy."

"He turned out to be bad," Mona admits.

"But at least he found Lucy for you," I say. "And now you can be at peace knowing that she's well and happy. You can let go, move on."

"Move on? Where?"

"You'll find a way to keep going," I say, amazed that I am saying this and I believe it with all my heart. "There's lots of Lucys in the world that need you."

"Clean yourself up," E.M. adds. "Get a job. You can get permission to see her. Write the people where she's at or the State. I know a good lawyer. Or two."

"No," Mona says. "I start wanting to see her and then it's like a hunger. No more Lucy. Maybe someday, but right now, no more." She looks at me and then at E.M. "But how do you get rid of want?"

"You hold on tight as hell and do nothing," E.M. says. "Or you work, dig holes, anything until it goes away." The way he says this, both Mona and I know that he's been there and done that.

"Where will you go after this?" I ask Mona.

"Dr. Desai says I can go back to the ranch for a while until I find a job. Maybe in Fredericksburg. Home's probably not a good idea right now."

"You'll be lonely without the GTH," I say.

"Dr. Desai said that maybe Gabriel will need to spend some time at the ranch too. He's worse, isn't he?"

"He's worse than the last time you saw him, yes."

"Hey," E.M. says. "Pepe, you know the guy at the ranch. He said they were looking for an extra hand to work on an irrigation ditch that's all stopped up. It's only for two or three weeks. He said I could have the job. I don't have anything going on workwise at home right now."

"You threatening me with your presence?" Mona says, forcing a smile.

"Don't get any ideas. I'm doing it for the money."

"How about you, Vicky?" Mona whispers. "We can have the GTH back."

"Maybe I can come visit," I say.

"You're okay at home?"

I nod, and I'm surprised to realize it's maybe true.

She smiles a delicate, sad smile, squeezes my hand, and then places the oxygen mask over her mouth and nose.

"See you soon, Princess Psycho," E.M. says. Then he draws the curtains open and we walk out.

E.M. shakes his head when we are outside. "My people. You couldn't make this stuff up if you tried." The way he says this makes me laugh.

"I'm going to see if Gabriel is awake. You want to come?" I ask.

"No, I've had it with you crazies," he says, grinning. "I gotta go get me some normal."

I hug him and he hugs me back.

"Thank you," I say.

"For what?"

"For teaching me to be brave."

"Pshh." He waves his hand. "You were always brave."

On his way out, E.M. stops to say something to my father and Becca. I smile when I see him attempt some secret Chicano handshake on my father.

A new nurse I've never seen before leads me to Gabriel's room. "Two minutes," she says to me and means it.

Gabriel is in bed, with Antonio sitting in the chair next to him. Antonio stands when he sees me and leaves the room. He shakes his head sadly as I walk by.

I walk up and stand by Gabriel's bedside. He looks different somehow, calmer, as if a great storm has just gone through him.

"Gabriel?"

He speaks without looking at me. "A zero is nothing, but if the zero follows the one? Then it is something."

"Yes," I say, "that's true."

He licks his cracked lips. "Whenever the angel comes down, the first thing he says is 'Be not afraid.' Must be his beauty that makes people scared."

I nod. "Remember those little children your grandmother saw? When I went to your house for your birthday? They were angels, weren't they? She wasn't afraid of them."

"Little angels. Ask them for privacy when you need to do your business."

"Yeah, that's what you need to do now. Ask them for privacy." I wait until he finishes moving his lips and looks at me. "Mona's okay. She's safe."

"Mona's safe. I'm alive. I didn't die."

"Yes."

"Is God angry?"

"No."

"He told Abraham to sacrifice Isaac, but He never meant for Abraham to do it. It was to make Abraham strong."

The serious-looking nurse opens the door and waits for me.

"I have to go now," I tell him.

"Vicky."

"Yes?"

"Green is the color of life all around us."

Our eyes meet. There in the deepest part of his pupils, I see my Gabriel.

THIRTY-SIX

We stop at one of those twenty-four-hour pancake places. Becca and Father sit on one side of the booth and I sit on the other.

I know we're all thinking this, but I'm the one who says it. "Remember when we used to come here with Mamá?"

"Yeah," Becca says. "She liked the different syrups. Strawberry syrup was her favorite."

"Butter pecan," Father says. "That was her favorite."

"No," Becca says. "Strawberry."

"Boysenberry," I say.

They look at me and laugh. I am right. We are quiet, remembering. Then my father says, "What will happen to your friend?"

"Dr. Desai wants to do some tests to see if there are any physical causes for . . . the voice he hears. If there's nothing physically wrong with him, we'll wait and see. If the voice persists, he will need to be treated for schizophrenia."

"Is there a cure for that?"

"Maybe not a cure, but it can be managed. People can function and live their lives, with proper care."

Father stares at me, his jaws tight. It is killing him not to say something, I can tell, but he doesn't.

"Tell us about this new place you found for Juanita," Becca says.

"What's this?" my father asks, choking on his coffee. I give Becca a *Did you really have to bring that up?* look, and she gives me back a *Trust me on this one.*

I inhale. "Juanita is going to live with Gabriel's grandparents. They need someone to take care of Chona, Gabriel's grandmother. She doesn't want to go back to Mexico, Dad."

My father shakes his head. I expect anger, but when he speaks, he sounds exasperated. The day is taking a toll on him. "You don't know what you're taking on. Her arthritis is going to get worse. She doesn't have any health insurance. She'll need taking care of for the rest of her life. She's better off in Mexico with her family."

"Except she doesn't really want to go," I say. "We shouldn't abandon her just because it will be expensive to take care of her. Maybe you should have been paying for health insurance and Social Security while she worked for us."

His face turns red. *Here comes the anger.*

Becca says quickly, "It's a good solution, Dad. I don't think you can do anything about it. If you don't want to pay for future medical bills, you don't have to." She pauses and looks at me briefly. "Think about what Mamá would have done."

He shakes his head. "I'm not winning too many battles today, am I?"

The waitress comes with our plates. "Do you have any boysenberry syrup?" I ask.

"I'm sorry," says the waitress. "No more boysenberry since about a year ago. We discontinued it. Don't ask me why. There's people that stopped coming here because no boysenberry. I'll tell you what I tell them: Life goes on. Blueberry? Strawberry?"

"Thanks," I say. "I'll have the plain old maple." I begin to cut my pancakes into bite-size pieces. I wonder if in the silence that follows, we are all thinking of her. "You know what I'd like to do tomorrow?"

"Barbara wants to take us shopping," Becca says. "She texted me when we were coming out of the airport."

"I'd like for the three of us to go visit Mamá."

Becca looks at me and then at Father. He looks out the window.

"We haven't gone since . . ." Becca says. There's a strand of shame in her voice.

"We can take her some of her favorite roses, from the backyard," I say.

Becca and I both look at Father, waiting, waiting, and then he nods.

"So," he says abruptly, as if to move on to happier thoughts, "what are your plans, Vicky?"

I'm expecting the question. But the way he asks it is different than I expected. He really wants to know what *my* plans are. I study my plate. The three pancakes are now each in a dozen bite-size pieces. "I think I'd like to check out Westgate. Maybe transfer, like Mr. Robinson suggested."

"Public school?" Becca asks, her mouth full.

"I don't think so," Father says.

He and I stare at each other.

"I'll stay at Reynard," I say. "But I'm not going to the office on Saturdays. I need Saturday mornings to catch up on schoolwork and to work on stuff for *The Quill* and my own writing. I want to continue seeing Dr. Desai, and I'll need a new car to visit Juanita and Gabriel and see Mona and E.M., wherever they are." I look at my plate again and wait. I know Becca is smiling, so I don't dare to look at her.

"You can use Becca's car," my father finally says. "After you take driving lessons."

I look up just in time to see Becca wink.

EPILOGUE

Two weeks later, while I'm working on a poem, Galileo jumps through the open window.

AUTHOR'S NOTE

One December morning thirty-seven years ago, I found myself at Stillman Infirmary, the ten-bed facility of Harvard University Health Services. I was lying on a very tall bed, looking out the window at the first snowflakes of the season. The doctor who treated me when the Harvard police brought me in the night before had just finished telling me that I was "out of the woods." I was fortunate. My roommate's sister had unexpectedly returned home before the sixty or so assorted pills I swallowed could complete their intended task. I don't remember what I was thinking about as I watched the snowflakes float slowly down. It's possible that I was going over the implication of the doctor's words. I was *physically* out of the woods. Mentally, emotionally, spiritually, I was in the thick of them.

One key to the long, painful process of getting out of those other woods was the eventual realization that I was ill. The illness that sought to diminish (and extinguish) my life is called depression. Observing it, knowing when to fight it and when to surrender to it, functioning despite it, befriending it whenever possible, is part of my everyday existence.

Living with depression has taught me many valuable truths about myself, about others, about life and its purpose. One of the things I learned is that the act that brought me to Stillman when I was twenty-four was not caused by whatever circumstances I was finding unbearable at the time. Taking the pills was simply the ultimate symptom of a disease that I have been able to trace to my teenage years. I did not know I was depressed when I was fourteen. I'm not sure I even knew that something was wrong. I only knew that I hurt inside, and talking to someone about that hurt was not an option. I was too ashamed to admit to anyone (even to myself) that I felt constantly sad and lonely and unworthy. I know now that had I been able to share my feelings with someone who did not judge me weak or ungrateful (for I had many good things going for me), I might not have tried to end my life ten years later.

It is my hope that Vicky's story will make it easier for young people to recognize depression in themselves and others and to feel more comfortable talking about it. Listed here are some places where you can read more about depression, or talk to compassionate, nonjudgmental persons who will listen and understand.

National Suicide Prevention Lifeline
1-800-273-TALK (8255)
www.youmatter.suicidepreventionlifeline.org

The Trevor Project
(especially for LGBTQ young people)
1-866-488-7386
www.thetrevorproject.org

American Foundation for Suicide Prevention
www.afsp.org/preventing-suicide/find-help

A Teenager's Guide to Depression
www.helpguide.org/articles/depression
/teenagers-guide-to-depression.htm

Metanoia
www.metanoia.org/suicide

My Broken Palace
mybrokenpalace.com

This book was edited by Cheryl Klein and designed by Christopher Stengel. The production was supervised by Elizabeth Krych. The text was set in Sabon, with display type set in Neutra. This book was printed and bound by R. R. Donnelley in Crawfordsville, Indiana. The manufacturing was supervised by Shannon Rice.